The Matchmakers

A Match Made in Williamstown
by Jean C. Gordon

A Match Made in Sheffield
by Terri Weldon

A Match Made in Freedom
by Lisa Belcastro

UPSTATE NY ROMANCE

THE MATCHMAKERS

Trade Paperback
ISBN-10: 0-9967945-2-2
ISBN-13: 978-0-9967945-2-7

EBook
ISBN-10: 0-9967945-7-3
ISBN-13: 978-0-9967945-7-2

A Match Made in Williamstown

by

Jean C. Gordon

JEAN C. GORDON'S WRITING is a natural extension of her love of reading. From that day in first grade when she realized t-h-e was the word the, she's been reading everything she can put her hands on. Jean and her college-sweetheart husband tried the city life in Los Angeles for college, but soon returned to their native Upstate New York, where they share a 175-year-old farmhouse with their daughter and her family. Their son lives nearby. Connect with Jean on **Facebook**, as @JeanCGordon on **Twitter**, or on **JeanCGordon.com**. And sign up for her Readers Group on her website so you don't miss a single new release. You'll receive a free eBook.

Books by Jean C. Gordon

From Harlequin Love Inspired

Reuniting His Family (August 2017)
A Mom for His Daughter (January 2018)

The Donnelly Brothers

Winning the Teacher's Heart
Holiday Homecoming • *The Bachelor's Sweetheart*

Small-Town

Small-Town Sweethearts • *Small-Town Mom*
Small-Town Dad • *Small-Town Midwife*

Team Macachek

Mending the Motocross Champion • *Holiday Escape*

Upstate NY . . . where love is a little sweeter

Bachelor Father • *Love Undercover*
Mandy and the Mayor
Candy Kisses • *Mara's Move*

Chapter One

LIBBY SCHUYLER KNEW she shouldn't have answered her phone. There was a reason she'd assigned "Dangerous" as her sister's ringtone.

"You've got to do something about Grandmother," Stacey said without even a hello first.

Libby placed the mail on the table and leaned against the front door to her grandmother's duplex. Whatever Stacey had to say couldn't be good if she was calling their NeNe "Grandmother."

"Mom and I thought you moved back to Williamstown to keep an eye on NeNe," Stacey said. "She's eighty years old, after all."

Even at age eighty, Ellie Alexander could run rings around most people half her age. And Libby had moved back to Williamstown because Williamstown was home. She and Stacey had spent most of their childhood here. Libby had gone to college here.

"What's NeNe done?" Libby pushed away from the door and began pacing to counter the expected agitation her sister's latest rant would cause.

"She's got a boyfriend."

"What's wrong with that?"

"Aside from her age, she met him through a supposedly Christian online dating service and not one of the big ones."

Libby stifled the laugh that bubbled up inside her. NeNe could be doing—and had done—far more outrageous things.

"What's wrong with her dating? Before I left for my training presentations in California last week, NeNe was lamenting how her circle of close friends has gotten so much smaller the past few years." Libby shrugged. "So, she wanted to meet new people."

"This isn't something that developed since last week. Evidently, it's been going on for some time."

"She hasn't said anything to me." A dart of hurt pricked Libby that NeNe would have told Stacey and not her. Then, again, it was NeNe's business. It wasn't as if Libby discussed her dates with her grandmother on a regular basis. "How do you know?"

"The Newkirks are visiting Mom and Dad in Florida, and Judy said Betty Lindsay had mentioned it to her mother-in-law." Libby shook her head. The church's Senior Circle at work.

Libby heard a car slow down and speed up out front.

"He's not anyone that anyone we know knows," Stacey said. "I checked with my friends in Williamstown. He's from Pennsylvania." She voiced the last word as if she were saying Mars.

To Libby's way of thinking, NeNe needed more protection from Stacey and Mom trying to stifle her free spirit than from an online dating match. "I don't see the problem. She's a grown woman who's taken care of herself for the past twenty-five years and in a lot more exotic places than Pennsylvania. But I'll talk with her when she gets back."

"Gets back from where?" Stacey's voice rose.

"A medical conference." Libby swallowed. In Philadelphia. But Stacey didn't need to know that. "She texted me to feed her cats until she gets home Monday."

"She's probably seeing him," Stacey started in again.

And what if she were? Far worse things could happen to NeNe than a long-distance gentleman friend. Footsteps on the front porch closed Libby's mind to anything else her sister was saying. "I've got to go. Someone's at NeNe's door."

"But, but," Stacey sputtered.

Libby synchronized her end call with the knock on the door, smiled, and went to answer it. Anyone, even a vacuum cleaner salesperson, would be preferable to continuing her conversation with Stacey. She put her eye to the peep hole. Anyone except Jack Parker, the man standing on her grandmother's porch.

*

THE DOOR CRACKED open. Libby Schuyler, the woman Jack had once foolishly thought he'd marry, glared out at him. As always, the contrast between her long, naturally dark lashes and honey-brown hair drew and fixed his attention on her wide hazel eyes and the daggers they were throwing.

"What are you doing here?" he asked, surprise mixing with an anger he'd thought he'd released long ago.

"What am I doing here? What are you doing here?"

Jack was secretly very surprised that seeing him had left her as devoid of manners as his shock at seeing her had left him. "I was looking for 1235. Obviously, I have the wrong house."

But he'd been sure he had the right house, although it had no house number. To be certain, he'd driven by it once, then backtracked so he could check the house numbers on either side and across the street. He waited for her to invite him in. He shouldn't want her to, but he did. From what he could see, she looked good, possibly more beautiful than she had ten years ago when she'd ended their college romance. A couple of seconds ticked by, and he turned to leave.

"Wait."

He halted, his heart tempo rising.

"Why are you looking for 1235?"

Not, "it's been a long time, come in," or a friendly "what brings you to Williamstown, Jack," but a demand for the who, what, when, where, and how of the situation. That was the Libby he remembered. He'd often thought that if she hadn't been so dedicated to being a teacher, she would have made a crack journalist. Too bad her curiosity hadn't extended to wanting to know his reasons for taking the job with Stairway2Learning, instead of Teach for Tomorrow. He clenched his jaw. *No.* That was all old news.

"Invite me in and I'll tell you." He gave her a slow smile.

Libby opened the door for him. *Ah.* He still had it. Not that he had any plans to reconnect with Libby. She'd killed what they'd had for good with one fatal blow. But, if she was living in Williamstown again, she might be able to help him track down the person he was looking for.

She motioned him to the couch. "It's been a long time."

Had he caught a note of wistfulness in her voice? More like he was looking for a note of wistfulness. "So how have you been?" He sat on the couch, and she took the chair across from him. "Still with Teach for Tomorrow? I'm surprised they'd have a program here."

"They don't," she said, her tone so flat it was as if she'd steamrolled the words out. "I'm a program trainer now. How about you? Still with Stairway2Learning?" Libby puckered her lips as if trying to rid herself of a bad taste.

"No, I left when that big toy company bought it out. I teach math at Berkshire Community College. I started last semester." Jack rested his ankle across his knee. He shouldn't be enjoying putting Libby off guard so much.

"Oh. So you live in Pittsfield?"

"I have a place a little outside the city. And you live here?" *Of course, she lives here. She answered the door and let me in.*

"Actually, I'm here feeding the cats."

Two cats appeared as if summoned. One hopped on the arm of Lilly's chair, while the other prowled the floor around Jack's feet.

She petted the cat. "Now that we've caught up, what's your business at 1235? Who are you trying to get in contact with?"

The other cat jumped on his lap and nuzzled his hand until he petted it. "I'm looking for an elderly woman named Eleanor Alexander. She's swindling money from my grandfather."

*

LIBBY JUMPED TO her feet, shoved her hands onto her hips and leaned down toward Jack. "She is not."

"You do know her." His eyes narrowed.

Libby straightened. "Wait." Jack was originally from the Philadelphia area. "Your grandfather is NeNe's online boyfriend."

"Eleanor Alexander is your grandmother? The one who was a medical missionary?"

Libby dropped into the chair. "One and the same. She's the least money conscious person I've ever known."

"I was right. This is 1235." Jack's gaze moved around the simple, but tastefully, decorated room, and he had the decency to look chagrinned. He must have remembered her stories about NeNe and her work.

"Your outrage about your grandfather dating sounds just like my sister."

"I'm nothing like Stacey."

He remembered her sister, too. Libby's pulse quickened. But why wouldn't he? She still remembered everything about Jack—despite her gargantuan efforts to cut him from her mind, as he'd chosen to cut her from his life.

"And it's not about Grandpa dating."

"Then, what? Is it that they met online?"

"No. They didn't meet online, although Grandpa had used Christian Match. That's the dating service's name. They met at some pitch session about buying a local travel agency franchise offered by the corporation that owns Christian Match. Along with other travel, the agencies offer special deals on honeymoon vacations to couples who meet through Christian Match."

"When was this?"

"Late last year."

Libby's stomach dropped. What had NeNe done? A new travel agency, Honeymoon Travel, had opened in Williamstown on Valentine's Day. The business's motto, *Making every vacation a dream honeymoon from life*, had been well advertised. One of the members of the singles group at church met his fiancée through Christian Match, and they were using Honeymoon travel for their honeymoon.

Jack reached toward her as if to take her hand and then backed off. "Since then, my grandfather has put the family house in Philadelphia on the market. He has a pending offer that's supposed to close in a couple of weeks. And all he's told me about his plans for after the sale is that he'd like to live closer to me, that with the college and all, he thought Williamstown might suit him and he can stay with friends in Philadelphia until he finds a place."

Libby swallowed hard. Jack's grandfather might have found a place, but without confirmation, she wasn't going to say anything to Jack. NeNe had decided not to rent out the other half of the duplex to students this semester, as she usually did. Libby hadn't really understood the reasons NeNe had given her, but figured it was her grandmother's house, and she could do whatever she wanted with it. Maybe she should have pursued it more, but she'd been doing more travelling than usual.

Jack pushed his hands through his hair, resting them, fingers-folded, at the base of his neck. The familiar action and the way it made his sandy brown hair stand on end made her smile. She doused it before he looked up.

"It's not about him dating, using an online dating service, or even selling his house. That's all his business. What has me concerned is that he's emptied his bank accounts and his individual retirement account. As part of his estate planning, he made me joint owner on the accounts, and he's arranged for me to receive copies of his IRA statements. That's where he gets his income. I doubt a little start-up franchise can match his investments . . . former investments. I'd hate to think he's getting senile or that someone is taking advantage of him."

"If someone is, it's not my grandmother." Libby re-raised her defenses.

"I didn't say it was.

"Yes, you did."

"All right, I did. But I need to find out what's going on, whether Grandpa isn't able to manage his money anymore. He's being secretive, which isn't like him, and I don't want to question his abilities if there's a good explanation."

Her heart softened. "I'll talk to NeNe when she gets home on Monday."

"She's away? Where?"

"At a medical conference."

Jack frowned, as if he'd expected more details.

She frowned back. What business was it of his? Contrary to what her sister thought, she wasn't her grandmother's keeper. But as much as she wanted to paint Jack as jumping to conclusions, Libby couldn't stop the concern that seeped through her.

"I'm sure I'll be able to clear this up for you in no time," Libby said.

"I hope so, and I appreciate it."

They exchanged phone numbers.

"I'll call you Tuesday," she said. "What's your schedule?"

"My last class ends at eleven."

"Okay, talk with you then."

Through the window in the door, she watched Jack walk to his car. In the years since she'd seen him, he'd lost the hint of gangliness he'd had as a college senior and added an assurance to his stride he hadn't possessed back when he broke her twenty-two-year-old heart.

Her knees weakened. How could she still be susceptible to him after the way he'd betrayed her and their dreams? Libby steeled herself. She'd better be able to get to the bottom of things quickly and get Jack Parker back out of her life. Because, if this encounter was any indication, too much exposure to him wasn't in her best interest.

Chapter Two

LIBBY SQUATTED AND picked up the cat that had been rubbing against her legs. "Aren't you the friendly one today? You're missing NeNe, aren't you?" Her phone rang in her pocket and the cat leapt from her arms, not bothering to sheath his claws. "Ouch." She wiped the dot of blood off her forearm before grabbing her phone.

"Hey," Libby said, recognizing her cousin and close friend Stephanie's number.

"Hi, you back from California?"

"Yep, I'm at NeNe's feeding the cats." Libby tapped her little finger against the side of her cell phone. Should she tell Steph about her and Jack's concerns about NeNe?

"Right, she's in Philadelphia. She told me about the conference at lunch when we got together in Boston last week."

"She gets to as many places as I do, with my work travel."

"You've got that right." Steph laughed.

Libby bit and released her lower lip. "Did NeNe seem off at all when you saw her?"

"No, why?"

"Stacey called. She and Mom are concerned—"

"When aren't they?" Stephanie interrupted her.

"True. So did you just call to talk or do you need something?"

Steph was right. It was probably nothing. She should hold off saying anything about NeNe until she knew more. Yeah, the surprise of seeing Jack had clouded her thinking.

"A little of both," Stephanie said. "I want to invite you and

NeNe to come down to the Vineyard for Memorial Day weekend."

"I'd love to. It would be nice to travel for fun for a change. But I'm filling in for the organist at church on Sunday, and NeNe volunteered us to help with the kids who'll be riding on the Sunday School float in the Memorial Day Parade."

"Maybe, Fourth of July," Steph said.

Libby heard the catch in Stephanie's voice. She knew all too well how it felt to have the man you love break your heart. They'd had many late-night phone calls over the last three weeks after Tim had crushed her cousin's heart.

"I'll get it on the calendar. We'll be there." Libby's phone hummed in her hand and she checked the screen and didn't recognize the number. "I've got another call. It may be work."

"Okay, I'll be talking to you."

"Bye." Libby disconnected and took the other call. "Hello," she said tentatively.

"Hi," NeNe said. "I didn't know if you'd answer, since I'm calling from my room phone. I forgot to charge my cell. Have you gone over to my house yet?"

"I'm here now."

"How are my boys?"

"Rocky is fine. Chester is on my list. Stephanie just called me, and when the phone rang he clawed me to get out of my arms."

"Chester is the more skittish one. What's up with Steph?"

Libby reached down and scratched Chester behind the ear. *The bigger question is what's up with you.* "She invited us for Fourth of July."

"Good, would you put it on my calendar?" NeNe didn't wait for an answer. "What I'm calling about is my geraniums. My weather app says there may be frost tonight. Can you bring them in?"

"Sure." Libby hesitated. "Do you have a minute now? There's something I want to talk with you about." She twirled a strand of hair around her index finger, hoping that rousing her grandmother's curiosity would work. The sooner Libby helped

Jack resolve his situation with his grandfather, the better.

"Yeah, I have time. We're on a break."

"Do you remember Jack Parker? I dated him in college." The call went silent, and she strained to hear her grandmother breathing, anything.

"Yes and no. I didn't remember the boy's name, only how upset you were when you broke up."

Libby's chest tightened. She remembered, too. "Jack showed up here about an hour ago. He was trying to track down a woman he thought was taking financial advantage of his grandfather."

"Busted," NeNe said.

"You're not." Was NeNe going senile? Was that how she'd gotten talked into buying the franchise? And who'd done that talking? Jack accusing her grandmother flashed in her mind, and Libby's hand tightened on the phone. Maybe it was NeNe who was being taken.

"Of course I'm not taking financial advantage of Blake. He's my partner."

"In Honeymoon Travel?"

"You guys are good."

"And he's the gentleman friend Stacey and Mom are all concerned about."

"Yes, gentleman friend, that's a good way to describe Blake. How did Stacey and your mother find out?"

Libby could almost hear the smile in her grandmother's voice and see the laugh lines at the corners of her eyes crinkle.

"Somehow, Betty Lindsay knew about you and Jack's grandfather."

NeNe laughed. "That woman never ceases to amaze and irritate me. I'm sorry I didn't tell you about Blake. I've been so busy and you've been traveling." NeNe's voice lowered. "And I wanted to be sure we had something real before I told many people. But I guess Betty has taken care of that."

"And you two have something?"

"Something very special."

Libby's heart filled with joy for her grandmother.

"As for the business, I wanted to see our first quarter earnings before I went public, even with the family. You know how your mother and sister think I'm an eccentric old woman who needs a keeper. For that matter, your mother thought I was an eccentric younger woman, too."

"But the travel agency is open, and obviously you're not working there. You had to have hired people."

"Blake did the hiring."

"Oh." Libby pushed her hair behind her ear. Even though she understood, she was uncomfortable with her grandmother's uncharacteristic secrecy. Jack's grandfather's influence? "Since the agency opened in February, you must be about ready to wow everyone with your success?"

"I'm afraid not. Some of the franchise expenses, the cost of the computer equipment and setup, have been higher than we estimated, and we've had to hire some office help from a temp agency that we hadn't expected to need."

Jack's concern about the parent company might be right on. NeNe was the type of person who went into things eyes wide open. She would have planned everything carefully. Unexpected franchise expenses raised a red flag about the parent company.

"Maybe I could help," Libby said. "I have vacation time accrued and no real vacation plans. Use me instead of hiring temps." As an employee, maybe she could poke into things without making NeNe suspicious.

"I'll consider your offer. But you deserve to use your vacation time for fun."

"One more thing," Libby said.

"Ye-es."

Did NeNe already suspect something or was she reading too much into her grandmother's inflection? "When do I get to meet Blake?"

"Tuesday. He's picking me up from the conference hotel Monday, and we're following the moving van from his house to Williamstown. Blake is going to rent the other side of the duplex."

As she'd speculated. *Won't Mom and Stacey just love that?* Her amusement disappeared in a poof. Now that she thought about it, Jack's grandfather living next to NeNe wouldn't exactly further her plan to get Jack back out of her life.

*

"THAT'S IT," BLAKE Parker said closing the car trunk. He looked over his shoulder at the stately Tudor home where he'd lived for his entire life and Ellie caught a flash of sadness in his expression.

"You okay?" she asked.

"I'm fine. It was way too large for me alone. But the clincher was you weren't there."

For the hundredth time, Ellie thanked the Lord for leading her, after all the years she'd spent alone, to a man—this man— who could make her feel as loved and cherished as she had when she was a twenty-three-year-old bride.

He opened the door for her, and they settled in for the five-hour drive to Williamstown.

"Did you talk with your grandson and reassure him about your finances?"

"I called him back last night after I finished packing and explained that I'm only keeping the money uninvested until we reconcile the first quarter numbers and have a better idea what we'll need for the next six months. I'm not certain that reassured him. He's reminded me twice that I'll have to pay income tax on the IRA money if I don't get it rolled over to another IRA within sixty days. And I told him you're kicking in your share to get that 'taking advantage of me' nonsense out of his head."

He gave her a crooked smile that sent a tingle up her spine and a thrill that a smile could still make her tingle. "I left out the specifics about my relocating to Williamstown and the house closing being moved up to this morning. Better that Jack finds out after the move is a done deal. I didn't want to give him anything more to bother your granddaughter about before we get there."

"I'm not sure Jack bothered Libby in a bad way. Did he say anything about Libby?"

"Not really."

For a split second, Ellie weighed whether she was crossing the line into interfering with Libby's life and decided it was a good interference. "The two of them dated in college."

"I didn't know that. We were semi-estranged for a few years over his choosing Williams College rather than the University of Pennsylvania. We Parkers had all gone to the University of Pennsylvania. He had an academic scholarship offer. It seems so silly now."

Ellie patted his arm. "Libby and Jack were pretty serious. I remember my daughter telling me she expected Libby to get an engagement ring for her birthday the May before graduation. My daughter was all psyched about Jack's Main Line family connections."

"How would she have known that?"

"You haven't met my daughter yet. She probably Googled him."

Blake raised an eyebrow.

"Don't worry. She lives in Florida and doesn't visit often. Anyway, it all blew up, and Libby was heartbroken, although she tried to deny it to me, to everyone. Even to herself, I think."

"Hmm."

"Watch out," Ellie said.

Blake slowed the car for a squirrel darting across the road.

"Anyway," she continued, "remember how I told you Libby offered to take some time off her job and work in the office without pay to help out?"

"Yeah. I don't think that's a good idea."

"I don't either. But I have another idea that I think would benefit us all."

Chapter Three

11:10. JACK TRIED to ignore the clock clicking on his office wall and concentrate on the student quiz he was supposed to be grading. Just because he'd told Libby his class was over at eleven, didn't mean she'd call him exactly then, although if it was him, he would have. Not that he wanted to be involved with Libby again. *No.* Grandpa had been too vague for him when they'd talked. Jack wanted to find out what his grandfather had really gotten himself into businesswise and personally and then get Libby back out of his life and mind.

Jack looked at the same equation on the same student's test for the third time and dropped his pen. Who did he think he was fooling? Libby Schuyler was a beautiful woman, on the outside, at least. A guy would have to be dead to not find her attractive. He picked up the pen and twirled it in his fingers. He wasn't being fair. She'd been beautiful on the inside, too. Or so he'd thought until she'd refused to listen to reason and hear him out about why he'd taken the Stairways2Learning job. She'd judged him unworthy and that was that.

He gripped the pen, took up the exam again and tried to follow the student's mathematical logic to give him any points he might deserve for his incorrect answer. It wasn't fair to take his frustration with Libby and his grandfather out on the kid.

His cell phone rang, and his heart pounded. He breathed deeply and released the breath and his tension when he recognized his grandfather's phone number. "Grandpa, I've been trying to get ahold of you."

"I got that idea from the three messages you left me since we talked Saturday night."

Jack winced. It wasn't as if they normally talked every day. He rubbed the back of his neck. He couldn't tell his grandfather he was worried about him. Not if he wanted to get any information.

"Something important to tell me?" Grandpa asked.

"Not really. After we talked, I realized you hadn't told me about your living arrangements after you sell the house. Isn't the closing next week?"

"No, I closed yesterday morning. Since it was a cash deal, everything came together more quickly than expected, and the buyer asked to close sooner."

The seconds crawled by while Jack waited for more.

"That's what kept me too busy to call you back. I had to have everything out by yesterday."

Jack drummed the desk. "So where are you? Renting your former colleague's carriage house like you talked about until you find something permanent? You said you were thinking about Williamstown. I know you wanted to take your time and find the right place."

"I've found the right place. We moved my things in yesterday."

The word "we" sent a chill through Jack. Grandpa and Libby's grandmother? He mentally contrasted a picture of the home his grandfather had sold with Libby's grandmother's comfortable, but decidedly more downscale, duplex. His concern escalated at the note of chagrin that entered his grandfather's voice.

"But the real reason I didn't call before now . . ."

Jack waited, teeth clenched so he could control his response to what his grandfather might say. Maybe he'd realized Libby's grandmother *was* preying on him. Sympathy flowed through him. Admitting a mistake to his grandson wouldn't be easy for the old guy,

"Is that I misplaced my cell phone charger and was too tired to go out and buy a new one last night."

That was it? Jack laughed his relief. "We all do that. You didn't tell me where your new place is."

"Williamstown, as I said before." Grandpa addressed him as if he were one of his theology students who wasn't paying attention. "I know it's short notice, but I'd like you to come over this evening for dinner and see the place. Tuesdays are one of the few nights you don't teach." Grandpa paused. "And there's someone special I'd like you to meet."

Someone special. Libby's grandmother. Jack checked his office clock. 11:35, and no call from Libby. Maybe he was going to have to get to the bottom of things himself.

"Sounds great. What time do you want me?"

"Dinner is at five thirty."

"I'll come early so you can show me around."

"I suppose that would be all right. But my friend and the food aren't arriving until five thirty, and there's not a lot to show you."

Jack swallowed to wet his throat. Did the woman have that much of a hold on his poor grandfather that the man couldn't act without her? All the more reason to visit with him alone before she arrived. "I'll see you around five."

"Wait. I didn't give you directions. It's a nice two bedroom duplex near the college."

Jack listened as his grandfather gave him the directions he already knew too well.

"Got that?" his grandfather asked.

"Yep, I'm familiar with the area. See you then." Jack placed his phone on the desk and stared at the time display clicking off another minute. He was in no frame of mind to correct quizzes. *Might as well get some lunch*, he thought quashing a fleeting idea he'd had earlier of suggesting to Libby that they meet in person over lunch to talk. He pushed away from the desk, stood, and strode out of his office, locking the door behind him.

His phone pinged with a text as he left the diner near the college where he'd gone for lunch.

"Sorry, I'm tied up with unexpected conference calls to put

out a minor fire at one of the TFT programs. Can we talk tomorrow?"

Jack started to text back an "okay," but his fingers seemed to have a mind of their own, cancelling the text and punching contacts to call her instead.

"Hey."

The friendly timbre of her casual greeting summoned a memory of the closeness they'd once shared. Jack grit his teeth and told himself he hadn't called because he wanted to hear her voice, but because talking was easier than texting.

"Hi. I . . ." A beep interrupted him.

"Sorry." Libby rushed her words. "I can't talk. I've got to take that. It's important."

Those words and tone resurrected another, less pleasant memory. He rubbed his chest. The Chimichanga Blaze he'd had for lunch had never bothered him before. Jack pounded the unlock button on his key fob with his thumb and yanked open the car door. Why, after their short talk Saturday, would he think Libby had changed, that anything, including their grandparents, was more important to her than her blind ambition to save the world one student at a time?

*

"YOU'RE JUST IN time," NeNe said, swinging the front door open and hustling Libby in before she could even say hello. NeNe glanced behind Libby before she snapped the door shut. "Did you park on the street as I asked?"

"Yes." Even though there was plenty of room in the shared driveway behind NeNe's and, Libby assumed, Blake's cars.

"Good. Come on into the kitchen and help me get the rest of the food over to Blake's. I have the roast and vegetables cooking over there already."

Libby trailed behind her grandmother, who looked past her and out the front window at the street again before entering the kitchen.

"I thought you said dinner was at five thirty, that you wanted me to come early and decorate the cake for you." Libby checked the clock on the stove. "It's not quite five yet."

"Well, everything went more quickly than I thought it would, and I had time to make the salad and decorate the cake myself." With an exaggerated flourish, NeNe motioned toward a chocolate-frosted two-layer cake with "Welcome Blake" scripted on top in yellow icing. Something was up. Was NeNe nervous about her meeting Blake?

"I'm sure I'll like him," Libby said.

"Hmm?" NeNe handed her the cake and picked up the salad.

"Blake. I'm sure I'll like him."

"Of course, you will. But not if I don't get you over there to meet him. Let's go the back way. We can put the food right in his kitchen, and I can check on the roast." NeNe held the door open for her.

"Have you thought about my offer to help out at Honeymoon Travel?" Libby asked. Maybe changing the conversation to business would make her grandmother less edgy.

NeNe bit her bottom lip.

Or maybe not.

"I talked with Blake. We appreciate the offer, but this is our baby."

Libby's stomach rumbled and not from the delicious chocolate smell rising from the cake she was carrying, nor from the fact that she'd skipped lunch and was starved.

"And, as I said, you should use your vacation time for vacation." Her grandmother's face lit up. "I know. You and Steph could take a cruise. You both need a break, and I can give you a great deal."

Libby didn't know whether to smile at NeNe for looking after them or be concerned that business was so bad she was trying to sell her a vacation. She needed to compare notes with Jack and soon.

"Come in, ladies. You're right on time." A distinguished silver-haired man who had to be Blake met them at the kitchen door, interrupting her thoughts. He held the door wide open.

What was so important about the time? Libby's nose twitched

as she followed NeNe up the steps and into Blake's kitchen, where the aroma of roasting beef and onions enveloped her.

Blake gave NeNe a peck on the cheek as she passed him, and Libby's face warmed.

"You must be Libby. You look just like Ellie did when she was your age." His blue eyes, so much like Jack's, twinkled, as Jack's always had when he was up to something. "We've been looking at family albums."

"Nice to meet you, and I'll take looking like NeNe as a compliment. Where would you like me to put the cake?"

"On the counter," NeNe answered, placing the salad on the kitchen table that she or Blake already had set—for four.

The doorbell buzzed before Libby could form words to ask who was joining them. As if she didn't have a good idea

"I'll get that," Blake said, disappearing through the kitchen doorway."

Libby faced her grandmother, hands on hips. "Jack?"

"Yes," NeNe said, lifting the roast from the oven. "Blake invited him, too. We thought we might as well get all the introductions over at once."

"And you forgot to tell me this?" Libby shook her head slowly side to side.

"No, I thought I'd surprise you." Her grandmother gave her a broad smile. "Why don't you go in the other room and say hello while I make the gravy. Then everything will be done."

Libby headed in the direction Blake had taken. At least she knew now why NeNe had been nervous. She'd wanted to get her here before Jack arrived. Not that the knowledge that Jack was part of their get-to-know-each-other dinner calmed *her* nerves. In fact, the way her heart was thumping. Exactly the opposite.

*

"LIBBY." HER NAME burst from Jack's lips when he spotted her in the doorway. "I didn't realize you were coming for dinner."

She shot him a look he could read only as *not my idea.* He pressed his lips together. Grilling her grandmother to satisfy his concerns about her taking advantage of his grandfather was going to be hard enough as it was with his grandfather there. Libby being at the table would triple the difficulty.

"I didn't know you'd be here either, until now." She inclined her head toward his grandfather and then toward the kitchen.

Their grandparents had set them up? More likely her grandmother. *Safety in numbers.* Easier to hide her scheming from him with her granddaughter there to support her. He eyed his grandfather's smiling face. Libby had probably been as much of a dinner-guest surprise to Grandpa as she'd been to him.

"I'm going to go mash the potatoes for Ellie," Blake said. "You two sit and get reacquainted. We'll call you in a few minutes when everything is ready."

Jack frowned. He and his grandfather had been estranged during his college years, so Grandpa wouldn't have known anything about Libby. And he hadn't mentioned her when they'd talked earlier. It had to be Libby's grandmother again.

"That happy to see me?" Libby sat on the end of the couch nearest him, her expression challenging him. "Was it my putting you off earlier?"

He *was not* going to let on that that was part of it. Nor that his returning suspicions about her grandmother was the other. Jack lowered himself into the chair across from Libby and feigned a smile. "No, just surprised."

She cocked her head.

"I mean, yes, I'm glad to see you. Maybe we can talk today after all and not have to get together tomorrow."

She lowered her eyelids and studied her hands in her lap. "Yeah, sure, we can try. What did you find out?"

"Not much more than I knew after talking with you Friday. Grandpa only confirmed the basics you and I had already figured out. And I was too tied up with classes and student office hours yesterday to check out the local or state business license filings."

Libby leaned forward. "I thought about getting ahold of the franchise contract, if we could."

"Good idea. I have a friend from my church softball team who's a lawyer and owes me a favor. If we get a copy of the contract our grandparents signed with the Christian Match corporation, I could ask him to look it over."

"Yes, see if there's a reason the quarterly numbers for the franchise aren't coming in at what NeNe expected."

Jack moved to the edge of his chair. "She told you that?"

"She did." Libby crossed her arms. "And my cousin Natalie is a legal secretary, one course short of her law degree. She can handle any legal legwork we need. Keep it in the family."

"Your family." He placed his elbows on his knees and drilled his gaze into hers. "You can't think that my grandfather is skimming money, or that I would have my friend cover up anything he might find."

"You thought my grandmother was. . ."

"Dinner's ready," NeNe called into the room.

Jack unfolded fists he hadn't realized he'd clenched and looked over Libby's head at her grandmother. He pasted a smile on his face. "I'm ready. I haven't had a good home-cooked meal in months, not since the last time I visited my parents."

"Stick around here, and I'll take care of that," Ellie said before turning back toward the kitchen.

Jack dropped his gaze to Libby. Her usually rosy complexion was white.

"You don't think she heard us, what you said about your grandfather, What I was thinking?"

He had no idea. "No, I'm sure she didn't."

"I hope not. I'd hate to hurt her feelings."

The uncertainty on Libby's face threw cold water on his plan to put Ellie on the spot to ferret out information. But, to act in his grandfather's best interests, he needed to know what was going on. And Ellie having any hint of his suspicions would make it more difficult for him to trip her up and get information out of her over dinner.

Libby rose and Jack escorted her to the kitchen.

"Jack, you can sit next to me," his grandfather said "and Libby on your other side."

Ellie placed a gravy boat on the table and joined them.

"Blake, will you say grace?"

His grandfather took his and Ellie's hands, so he reached for Libby's and enclosed it in his. He'd forgotten how much smaller and softer it was than his. Clearing his mind, he closed his eyes and concentrated on his grandfather's words.

"Dear Lord, thank you for bringing us together today for the enjoyment of this wonderful food given to us through Your bounty and for the fellowship of family to share it. And thank you for enriching my life by bringing Ellie into it. Amen."

"Amen." Jack released his grandfather's hand, Grandpa's words dissolving any remaining thoughts Jack had of questioning Ellie about Honeymoon Travel today in front of his grandfather. He wanted to help, not hurt Grandpa.

Libby pulled her hand from his still-firm grip, and his chest hollowed with an inexplicable let-down.

*

"I THINK THAT went well," Blake said as he and Ellie settled onto the couch in her living room to watch a movie after Jack and Libby had left.

Ellie lifted the remote and started the DVD, smiling at the generous man beside her. "Only if you excuse my granddaughter's rude insinuations."

Blake patted her hand. "She's looking out for you, as Jack is for me."

She squeezed his hand. "I've spent a good portion of my life successfully avoiding my family's 'good' intentions to look out for me, with Libby on my side."

"There's nothing wrong with letting someone take care of you sometimes."

Ellie warmed at what she read as Blake's underlying meaning of him taking care of her, but still couldn't let it go. "So you wouldn't mind Jack questioning me the way Libby harassed you?"

Blake's snort made her smile.

"I'd hate it, like I hate Jack's concern about my finances. My fault for making him my financial back-up."

"No, that's a smart move for people our age, as much as I hate to say that. I should do the same." Ellie bit her lip. "What I shouldn't have done was share my disappointment in the Honeymoon Travel's first quarter profits with Libby."

He wrapped his arm around her and she placed her head on his shoulder.

"It's perfectly all right," Blake assured her. "Jack will be tracking my replacement of the rest of the money I took out of my IRA, if not directly asking me about the agency's earnings."

Ellie straightened and faced Blake. "Do it. Show Jack our balance sheet."

He looked at her as if she'd gone mad. "He's fussing at me enough already, as if I didn't know what I was doing. Those numbers aren't going to do anything to help."

"Maybe not with his fussing." She patted his arm. "Did you know that he thinks I lured you into the partnership, that I'm after your money?"

"He what?"

"Calm down." She rubbed the spot she'd patted. "How is that any different from Libby thinking you're siphoning money out of the business without my knowing?"

"That's what her questions were about?"

"Yes, although she didn't say that exactly."

His brow creased in thought. "I can see her wanting to protect you." Blake drew her back to his side.

Ellie resisted. "On pain of sounding like I'm repeating myself, how is that any different from Jack being protective of you?"

"Well, I'm the. . ."

She placed her finger on his lips. "Don't even say it. It's as much of an insult to me as it is to you. I've taken care of myself in all kinds of situations all over the world."

Blake favored her with a smile she might have thought of as patronizing if the man was anyone but him. "I concede. You think it's wise to give him our balance sheet?"

"Definitely. He'll take it right to Libby."

"Ah, I see where you're going."

"That'll keep them busy together for a while. And while they are, we can figure out some way for one of them to get ahold of our franchise agreement and they can widen their investigation."

"Did your granddaughter say something about the agreement?"

"No, but that's where I'd go next once I'd proven to myself that neither of us was taking advantage of the other."

Blake's eyes shown in understanding and something more. "Have I told you that you're as brilliant as you are beautiful?"

Ellie's cheeks warmed. "Not today."

Chapter Four

JACK FINISHED READING the bank statements for Holiday Travel and tapped the bottom edge of the pages on his desk. *This was too easy.* How he'd received them was a mystery. His grandfather had said the statements must have been sent to him accidently. *Come on.* Banks, as a rule, didn't accidently send statements to people not on an account at a different address. Unless an account owner requested them to. His grandfather had to have requested it, maybe added the business account to the other accounts Jack regularly received statements for. He thought again. His grandfather wouldn't lie to him.

Maybe Libby's grandmother had asked the bank to send them. Taking a preemptive strike before he started asking the questions of her that Libby had asked of his grandfather at dinner the other night. He had to admit that the strike had been successful. Jack knew how much his grandfather had invested in the travel agency. From the statements, apparently Libby's grandmother had invested even more. A picture flashed in his mind—Libby all fiery eyed at his insinuation, no accusation, that her grandmother was taking advantage of his grandfather.

He scrubbed his hand over his face. But his grandfather certainly wasn't siphoning money out of the business for himself as Libby had seemed to think. Jack didn't need the business's quarterly financial statement to know his grandfather wasn't doing anything wrong, but Libby did. She didn't trust his grandfather as she hadn't trusted him back in college, at least not enough to hear him out on his career choice change. Jack slapped his palm to his desk. Until he proved his grandfather's innocence, she wouldn't give up on her suspicions and be out of his life again

Do you really want her out of your life? a nagging voice asked, probably from the same inner source that had flashed the picture of Libby in all her beautiful, outraged glory. He did want her out. He needed her out of his mind and his life. He was where he wanted to be with his life, and he didn't need Libby pulling him out of the comfort zone he'd found. It had taken too long to get there.

Jack pushed away from his desk and paced the floor. Libby wasn't the question. The question was how to get ahold of the business's financials to compare those figures to the bank statements. Grandpa had already refused him once. Jack stood and paced his home office. He could take a different tact. Rather than concern for him, as Jack had expressed before, he could couch it as concern for Ellie. That's it. He'd tell his grandfather that by going over the bank statements and the business financial statement with Libby, he should be able to get her to lay off on badgering his grandfather and upsetting Ellie. That might be laying it on a little thick, but he'd do it.

Although he wasn't one hundred percent comfortable with the situation, dinner with Ellie, Libby, and his grandfather had shown him that Grandpa cared for Ellie and wouldn't want her upset, and that the elderly woman cared for Grandpa. Unless she was a very good actress. It could run in the family. After all, he'd once believed Libby had loved him.

Jack dropped back into his chair. Everything kept coming back to Libby. He picked up his phone. "Hey, Grandpa."

"Jack. What's up."

"I want to thank you again for dinner."

"It's Ellie you should thank."

"You can do that for me. I called to run something by you."

"Okay, shoot.

"You know how Libby was questioning you at dinner. It seemed to me like that was upsetting Ellie." Jack didn't wait for a confirmation. He rushed ahead. "I have an idea for putting a stop to future interrogations."

"I wouldn't say the girl was interrogating me. I rather enjoyed the sparring."

He would. "But think of Ellie. How would you like it if I had questioned her the same way?" As he'd planned to until Libby had put a halt to it with her comment about not wanting to hurt her grandmother's feelings. He hadn't wanted, didn't want, to hurt Grandpa's feelings either.

"Don't even think of it," his grandfather warned.

"I'm not. My idea is to go over Honeymoon Travel's quarterly financial statement with Libby, comparing it to the bank statements I received to show her everything is on the up and up with you. So, Libby will stop upsetting her grandmother."

"Your plan may have merit. I don't like seeing Ellie upset."

Another warning? "By the way," Jack said, "it struck me that possibly Ellie had the bank statements sent to me. I didn't check with Libby to see if she got a set, too."

His grandfather cleared his throat, confirming Jack's suspicion. "Did she send you the business statement, too?" his grandfather asked.

"No, that's why I'm calling. To ask you for a copy. You could scan and email it to me."

His grandfather hemmed and hawed. "I guess that would be all right. I already scanned it to have an electronic copy."

"Thanks, I'll be on the lookout for it."

Jack said goodbye and cradled the now-silent phone in his palm, debating whether to call Libby with the news. A *ping* interrupted his contemplation. The email from his grandfather. He rolled his shoulders as if the action would stop the unease creeping up his spine. His grandfather was up to something. Asking for the financial report had gone too smoothly. But since he had the report, he should call Libby.

Not because she'd been haunting his thoughts day and night. Not because he wanted to hear her voice, see her face in person. *Not because going over the numbers with her would exonerate Grandpa and take care of all of the above so he could get his life back to normal.*

*

ALL THAT ENTHUSIASM. Libby watched the last of the new Teach for Tomorrow teachers leave the hotel meeting room where she'd conducted their final training session. She and Jack had been like them. Brimming with hope and expectations for their future students and teaching careers. Until he'd abandoned that plan. She walked behind the podium and picked up her leather business bag. Sometimes, she missed being in the classroom with children. Was that why Jack had left Stairway2Learning and gone back to teaching? For the one-on-one with students? She'd never understood why he'd taken the software design job in the first place, except for the money and showing his family he didn't need theirs. *Maybe I should ask him*, she thought, searching her memory for whatever explanation he'd given her at college and coming up blank. *No*. It didn't matter. Any reason for knowing was in the past.

Packing her training materials into her bag, she saw the sea of eager faces that had filled the room minutes ago. She was, or had been, as excited about training new teachers as she'd been about teaching children. But lately, the heavy travel schedule had taken some of the glow off her work. This session had been only two days and in Springfield, an hour-and-a-half drive from Williamstown. She'd be home in her own place tonight.

Libby's cell phone buzzed, and she pulled it from her bag. A text from NeNe, wondering when she would be headed home. NeNe liked to know Libby's itinerary when she was out of town. Her grandmother's small tokens of love never failed to warm Libby. That love was why Libby needed to get to the bottom of whatever was going on with NeNe, Blake, and Honeymoon Travel.

Leaving now. Libby typed. I'll text when I'm home

Okay, drive safely, NeNe came right back.

Closing her message app brought up a missed call alert. She tapped the phone icon. *Jack*. Her heart rate picked up and, then, slowed down. *Get a grip on yourself. Stay in the present.* The only thing he could be calling her about was their grandparents and Honeymoon Travel. He'd left right after dinner the other night, claiming a pile of tests he had to grade for a class the next morning. So, they'd made no definite plan to move forward with their investigation of Christian Match and its travel franchise. She wasn't about to drop her concerns and doubted Jack was either.

But he hadn't left a message. Had he found out something? Something he didn't want to leave in a message. She caught her breath before touching the screen to call him back. This wasn't high intrigue. More likely, he'd turned into one of those people who didn't leave messages. When they'd dated, he'd always left her a message. Her thoughts meandered to some of the sweeter ones she still vividly remembered. But they weren't dating. They were working on opposite sides to protect their respective grandparent.

"Hey." The old familiarity of Jack's voice sent a shiver through Libby.

"Hi, I'm returning your call." *There, that sounded nice and businesslike.*

"You won't believe what I've gotten my hands on." he said.

Triggered by the excited pitch of his voice, Libby's mind went back in time to another call from Jack, when he'd been offered the job with Stairway2Learning. That call had been the beginning of their end. She shook off the memory. What was with her that she kept going back to the past? She had a perfectly good present.

"You're not going to guess?" he asked. "Want me to give you a hint?"

"No. Just tell me please." Her business tone had taken on shades of peevish.

"Right here in front of me, I have . . ." Jack paused. "Copies of both the Holiday Travel bank and first quarter financial statements."

A smile tugged at the corners of her mouth as she pictured the expression on his face. The goofy math-nerd-that-he-was grin he got on his face whenever she'd gotten a calculus problem right when he'd tutored her their sophomore year in college. She couldn't remember now how her roommate had talked her into taking the advanced math class she hadn't needed. But Libby remembered the grin. It was how Jack had convinced her to go on their first date.

"Your grandfather gave them to you?"

"Grandpa sent me the financial statement. The bank statements came in the mail from the bank."

Was Jack splitting hairs to keep her on the phone. But why? "Your grandfather had the bank send the statements?"

"No, he didn't. We suspect your grandmother had them sent to me."

Libby blew a breath out her nose. "She might have. She wasn't happy with me questioning your grandfather."

Jack mumbled something that sounded like, "She wasn't the only one."

Libby's fuse shortened. She'd only been looking out for NeNe—not that her grandmother had appreciated that any more than Jack seemed to.

"My having the bank statements is how I got Grandpa to send me the financial statement," Jack said.

"And what do they show? NeNe taking advantage of your grandfather?" An innate instinct for self-protection against past memories took hold, putting her on the offensive.

"No, and they don't show my grandfather siphoning off money from the business, either," Jack lobbed back. "That's why I called. All I found are what may or may not be excessive payments to Christian Match, depending on whether they are one-time startup costs or recurring expenses."

"Oh. They aren't described?"

"Not clearly. I can ask Grandpa, but I've already gotten more from him than I expected. Do you know who their accountant is? I might want to suggest he and your grandmother look into someone else."

"I don't think they have an accountant. I got the idea from NeNe that they are using an online accounting program."

"What we really need is a copy of their Honeymoon Travel contract with Christian Match. Think you could get a copy from your grandmother? I got the other documents."

Just like the old Jack. He was making this a contest. "Didn't you say the bank statements came from NeNe?"

"Grandpa and I think she may have asked the bank to send them," he conceded.

Being right didn't give her the satisfaction she expected. "I don't think NeNe will give me their contract with Christian Match, but I have another way we might be able to get hold of one."

Chapter Five

WHY HAVE YOU chosen Christian Match?

Jack stared at the question on his laptop screen, his fingers itching to type *because of a hair-brained scheme a woman I can't get off my mind came up with.* He didn't want to lie.

Because I'm looking for a woman who shares my faith and values. A pat answer, but the truth. That was one of the most important things, something that had drawn him to Libby, along with her desire to help others and her smile, sense of humor, the way she tilted her head and wrinkled her brow when she was thinking. . .

Snap out of it, Parker. Eyes on the future, not the past.

When Libby had suggested he sign up for Christian Match, go on a date or two and see if he received an invitation to a Honeymoon Travel franchise seminar, he'd reluctantly agreed. She'd figured that since Williamstown already had a franchise, her signing up for the service wouldn't work. He wasn't sure that Pittsfield was far enough away from Williamstown that he would either. Then, the idea of signing up had grown on him. He'd dated, had a couple of semi-serious relationships since college, but nothing as serious as him and Libby. He had his house, a job he liked. He wouldn't mind finding someone to love and settle down with.

Jack hit return to go to the next question and checked the time. He had only forty-five minutes until 8 o'clock to finish his profile and send it if he wanted to be included in the local Christian Match's twice a month Saturday night Meet Your

Match at Flavours Restaurant in Pittsfield tomorrow. The meets were part of the company's personal touch service. Although members signed up online, Christian Match tried to introduce members to their matches in person through local offices.

He answered another question and watched the spinning arrow on the screen, waiting for the next one to pop up. He'd been fine waiting the couple of weeks for the next meet. But Libby had insisted they attend tomorrow's meet, and he'd complied as he'd always done. Except when he'd taken the position with Stairway2Learning. He'd prayed hard for guidance on his decision, and the answer he'd gotten was that he could make a positive difference for more students by developing the learning software than as a math teacher. If only Libby had been willing to listen to that or anything he'd had to say on the subject.

Jack completed the rest of the questions and clicked to his photo file folder to add his professional Berkshire Community College headshot to his profile. He reviewed his profile, returning to the top and his photo. He looked so stiff, so math instructor. If he was going to use Christian Match as the dating service it was in addition to finagling an invitation to a Honeymoon travel seminar, he wanted to attract someone fun, like Libby or like Libby had been. He deleted the professional photo and replaced it with one someone had snapped of him barbequing at his church softball team's annual end-of-season picnic. Satisfied with his profile, Jack shot it off.

The next evening, he walked into Flavours with a bounce in his step, fueled by unexpected anticipation of a good time.

"Good evening," the hostess greeted him.

"Hi, I'm here for the Christian Match event."

"Yes, the group is meeting in our banquet room upstairs, the doorway to the left in the back."

"Thanks." Jack strode by the diners and up the stairs. He took in the nearly empty room. Ten—he counted them—tables for two were set up. Soft Christian rock played in the background.

"Hello, welcome," a fortyish-looking woman said. "I'm

Maggie Hensen. My husband Dave and I are your Christian Match hosts for tonight."

Jack glanced at the other man in the room. *Right. The managers of the local office.* He recognized them now from the website. "Jack Parker." He glanced at his watch. "Did I have the time wrong?" He didn't want to appear over eager, not that it mattered.

"No, you're right on time. We have hors d'ovevres, and you have your pick of a table."

The laugh that followed Maggie's invitation made Jack feel all the more conspicuous. He walked down the line of what should have been tempting foods and absently placed a few choices on his plate before slinking over to a far-corner table and sitting. Had it been so long since he'd attended a party that he'd forgotten that most people didn't arrive on time? A couple more people walked in, and he relaxed, until their host Dave walked a petite blond arrival toward his table. He straightened in his seat. Although, he'd indicated no preference for hair color in the physical attribute section of the member application, somehow he'd expected someone with more honey brown hair, like Libby's. Dave and the woman walked by him to a nearby table. Jack shook his head. He had to get Libby off his mind.

He bit into a bacon-wrapped scallop he speared and almost choked at the sound of a familiar voice. His gaze shot to the doorway. What was Libby doing here? And why was Maggie walking her toward his table? Jack looked at the two closest tables. One was empty, and the blonde sat alone at the other. She smiled at him and he forced a smile back.

"Jack," Maggie said when they reached the table. "This is Libby Schuyler, your match for the evening. Libby, this is Jack Parker.

Jack stood and swallowed the scallop that had lodged in the back of his throat.

"Nice to meet you, Jack."

They may have been apart ten years, but Jack had no trouble reading the flash in Libby's eyes. He'd play along—for now.

"The same here." He pulled out a chair and seated her.

Maggie gave them a broad smile. "I have to tell you. You two had the highest compatibility ratio of any two members we've had in the six months we've been here with Christian Match. Higher than Dave's and mine."

He and Libby were the most compatible match they'd ever had. That statement had Jack wondering about the success of the service. But using the service for himself was secondary to protecting their grandparents.

"You and your husband met through Christian Match?" Libby asked.

"We most certainly did." Dave came up behind his wife and placed his arm around her shoulders. "A year ago, February. The membership fee was the best money I ever spent."

Maggie blushed. "We'll let you two get to know each other. Everyone should be here in a minute or two and we'll start dinner."

"What are you doing here?" Jack asked as soon as the Hensons were out of hearing range. "We agreed I'd be the one to sign up with Christian Match, since your work takes you out of town so much. I could be more active, more likely to be invited to a travel franchise seminar."

Libby shrugged. "I *was* skeptical. That's another reason I asked you to sign up. But one of the members of the singles group at church met his fiancée through Christian Match and can't say enough good about it. I read through the website and his experience seems to back up everything it says. I thought, why not?"

"For yourself. Dates." Jack stretched his legs under the table, careful not to touch Libby. *That sounded brilliant.*

"As you said, I travel a lot. My job doesn't leave much time for a social life. It's a way to meet people, and doubles our chance of getting hold of a Honeymoon Travel contract."

Libby's reasoning sounded a lot like his. But somehow hers didn't sound nearly as reasonable to him.

*

LIBBY FINGERED THE fancy folded napkin on the table in front of her. She knew Jack would be here. She knew he'd be surprised to see her. Not in her wildest dreams did she imagine they'd be matched. This put a damper on any efforts to double their information gathering and her meeting a match. While she wasn't as onboard with Christian Match as she'd sounded talking with Jack, the prospect of meeting someone new had attracted her—if only to distract her from the irritating memories of her and Jack that kept invading her thoughts.

"Good evening," Maggie said into a microphone to be heard over the couples' chatter. "As the wonderful aromas say, Flavours has our buffet ready. Dave will lead us in grace. Then, feel free to start through the line."

Seconds after the "amen," Jack rose. "I'm ready to eat."

Libby wasn't surprised. Jack was always hungry, or he had been as a college student. *Those confounded memories.*

He stepped behind her chair, rested his hands on the back to pull it out, and leaned toward her. "Libby, it's dinner, not a firing squad you're facing."

His words and nearness tickled her ear. "Sorry, I was thinking about something else."

Jack placed his hand on the small of her back with more familiarity than she'd accept from someone she'd just met. But it wasn't as if there was anyone here to pass judgment. He guided her to the buffet and headed right for the pasta and carving tables.

"Whoa!" Libby slowed him down. "I want to check out the soups, salads, and veggies first."

"Works for me. I'll see you at the table."

Libby nodded, her attention already on the feast before her. She dropped a heaping spoonful of broccoli coleslaw on her plate. Although she wouldn't admit it, she was as hungry as Jack appeared to be. Nerves about meeting her date, questions about what he'd look like, if they'd hit it off or not had killed her appetite earlier in the day. Moving down the serving table, she made up for that and carried her overloaded plate to the table. Everything had looked so good, and she didn't need to be concerned about making an impression on Jack. He knew her. Libby misstepped at the warmth that thought shot through her. A strong hand gripped her elbow.

"Having trouble carrying all that?" Jack eyed her plate.

"No more than you are," she shot back. He had at least double the amount of food piled on his plate. Then again, he had to be at least half-again her size. She allowed her gaze to run over him. His slightly too long hair, sports jacket, open-collared shirt, jeans, and Doc Martens. Libby suppressed a giggle.

"What?" He looked at the gravy on his plate and inspected the front of his shirt.

She checked out the elbows of his jacket for leather patches. "You look like a math professor."

"I am a math professor." The corners of his mouth turned down. "But I was trying not to look like one. I've found it's a profession that's not exactly a chick magnet."

Chick magnet? Libby sputtered.

That got her another "What?"

"Never mind," she said.

Jack tried to hide it. But despite his polished good looks, impeccable manners, and ease dealing with students, he was more adept at number situations than social situations, especially social situations involving women. Or he had been.

Hand remaining on her elbow, he guided Libby to their table, placed his plate at his setting, and seated her.

"Jack. Jack Parker. It is you."

Libby turned to see an attractive woman with long, nearly black hair making her way to their table. She couldn't place what, but there was something familiar about the woman.

"Constance," Jack greeted the woman when she reached them.

Libby could be wrong, but the smile on his face seemed pasted on and didn't meet his eyes.

"I never would have expected to see you here." Constance motioned around the room.

Libby felt Jack tapping the floor under the table with his foot.

"It is a small world," he said. "Constance, this is my match date, Libby Schuyler. I work with Constance in a program at the college for promising high school math students." She's a teacher at Pittsfield High School.

From the way Constance was leaning into every word Jack said, Libby was pretty sure the woman wanted to be more than a colleague. "Nice to meet you," Libby said.

Constance dragged her gaze from Jack and stared at Libby. "Sorry to be rude. You look so familiar. "You're with Teach for Tomorrow, right?"

"I am." Libby searched her memory, which had worked so well for remembrances of Jack and her, but came up blank for Constance. She tended to remember people who'd gone through her full training sessions.

"I started my teaching career as a Teach for Tomorrow teacher. At my training, you were assisting the instructor."

"Yes! I was in training, too. To be an instructor."

Constance nodded. "Do you guys want to join me and my match? The tables are large enough for four."

Libby held back her answer. They couldn't talk about their grandparents or their investigation with Constance and her match with them. But if Jack was interested in Constance, Constance certainly seemed interested in him.

"No," Jack said. "We should get to know our chosen matches. That's what we signed up for." He pulled out the paste-on smile again.

"You're right," Constance said with a sigh. "I thought we'd be given several possible dates to choose from, like other services do."

And Libby knew what Constance's choice would be. "I don't know," she said. "Christian Match may be on to something. Did you see their success rate on the website?"

"I supposed you're right. My guy seems nice enough." Constance focused on Jack. "Catch you later and, remember, you still owe me that coffee."

"A work challenge," Jack clarified after Constance left.

"What you do with your personal life is none of my business," Libby said in what could only be called a school-teacher tone.

"Right, our only business together is protecting our grandparents." He sliced his knife through a thick slab of roast beef.

Libby lifted her fork and swirled the gravy into her mashed potatoes. That was the plain truth. So how did she explain the empty void that opened inside her?

Chapter Six

"KICKBOXING WAS SUCH a better idea than dinner," Libby said as she folded her workout clothes into her gym bag Monday evening.

"Kickboxing *and* dinner," her adopted cousin Natalie corrected her. "I had the free pass, and you sounded frustrated when you called and said you needed to talk."

"I am less frustrated and more hungry now. What do you want to do? This is your territory."

"Why don't we pick up some Mexican takeout and head to my house. I didn't have to work overtime this weekend and am caught up in my class, so I cleaned, and need to show off to someone. Who knows when I'll have time to do it again."

"Certainly something to celebrate," Libby said. "Lead on. I'll follow in my car."

A half hour later, Libby pulled her car into a parking space on the street up from Natalie's historic home. She joined Natalie inside. "I like what you've done with the living room. Blue and yellow. Very period."

"Thanks," Natalie said. "I usually eat in the kitchen."

"Fine with me." Libby trailed after Natalie and the spicy scent of the food into the kitchen.

Natalie placed the takeout bag on the yellow and red laminated top of the classic 1950s chrome table that had come with the house and pulled out one of the red and chrome padded chairs. After a short grace, they dug in.

"Spill it," Natalie said.

Where to start? "Have you talked with NeNe, Gran"—unlike Libby and her sister and other cousins, Natalie called their grandmother Gran—"since she got back from Philadelphia?"

Natalie nodded.

"You know about her new tenant?"

"Yep. Gran ran the lease agreement by me before she went to her conference."

Libby pressed her lips together. "So you knew about Blake before he moved into the duplex?"

"Only from the lease."

"Not about their partnership in Holiday Travel?"

"I found out about that yesterday."

"And their relationship?"

"I read between the lines." Natalie placed her burrito on the wrapper on the table and frowned. "You have a problem with Gran dating?"

"No, not at all. The problem is that Blake is Jack's grandfather."

Natalie tilted her head and looked thoughtful. She was younger than her. She might not remember Jack, and Libby hadn't made him a topic of conversation since she'd moved back to Williamstown and become close friends with Natalie. Hadn't, until now.

Her cousin's jaw dropped. "Your ex-boyfriend."

"Bingo. He teaches at Berkshire Community College now."

"You've seen him?"

"We all had dinner together last week. But Jack's not the problem." At least not the problem she wanted to talk about right now.

Natalie raised an eyebrow.

Libby ignored her. "The problem is that Jack and I are concerned about NeNe's and his grandfather's investment in Holiday Travel. Let me start at the beginning." Libby went back to her sister's phone call and filled Natalie in on all of the details from her and Jack's original, seemingly unfounded suspicions to now, down to their "date" on Saturday. "We've gone over the business's' bank statements and the first quarter financial statements, which show a loss NeNe and Blake didn't anticipate. Our concern now is that Christian Match may be taking advantage of them. We're going to stay active in Christian Match until we, hopefully, receive an invitation to a Honeymoon Travel seminar and get our hands on a copy of the franchise contract. When we do, I'd like you to look at it with me."

"I don't think that's necessary," Natalie said.

Libby swallowed her mouthful of food and drilled her gaze into her cousin's. Natalie wasn't concerned after all she'd said?

Natalie's face split into a wide grin. "Gran sent me the Honeymoon Travel contract to review last Saturday."

*

"IT WAS NICE of Maggie and Dave to share what a perfect match Libby and Jack turned out to be." Ellie placed her teacup on the matching saucer on the coffee table in front of the loveseat where she and Blake sat in her living room. "And you were concerned they might end up with different dates for Saturday's dinner meet."

"I'm still uncomfortable with your asking Maggie." Blake fidgeted next to her, as much as a man of Blake's demeanor could fidget. "Jack and Libby's friendship with each other or with anyone else is their business."

Ellie waived him off and reached for a cookie from the plate next to their teacups. "If Libby didn't want me knowing her business, she wouldn't have given me her power of attorney when she started traveling so much. She wanted someone to represent her in any legal or other decisions that might have to be made while she's on extended work travel. My questions to Maggie fall in the other category."

"Eleanor. At the moment, your granddaughter is right here in Williamstown. Further, I'm sure she didn't give you power of attorney to enable you to check up on her status at a dating service. And I don't know that you've reciprocated and given her your POA."

"Don't Eleanor me. I've set up an appointment with my

lawyer to draw up a POA that will take affect if I'm incapacitated. It was her idea, not mine, to make her POA live, rather than taking affect only if she was incapacitated. Besides, left to their own devices, Libby and Jack might go their separate ways and take another ten years to reconnect and see they belong together. We're not getting any younger, you know. With all my grandchildren grown, I wouldn't mind a great grandchild or two."

Blake choked on his tea. "You are incorrigible."

"Thank you. I take that as a compliment."

He kissed her temple. "More seriously, do you think the kids have the Honeymoon Travel contract?"

"If not yet, soon. Libby and Natalie talk often."

Uncertainly clouded Blake's face.

"What? It's not as if I can call Natalie and ask."

Blake threw his head back and laughed, a deep, from-the-belly laugh that had Ellie weighing whether to pinch him or hug him. She went with the hug.

"Do I dare ask what's next?" Blake asked.

Ellie lifted her head and peered up at him. "We wait."

Chapter Seven

JACK STOPPED IN front of the gilded mirror as he passed through his living room. It had come with the house. Removing his baseball cap, he studied his reflection. Community Chapel softball jersey that had shrunk some in the wash to stretch across his chest, faded jeans, contacts, yesterday's haircut. Satisfied he projected the picture of an athlete, not a math nerd, he replaced the cap, grabbed his mitt, and headed out the back door to his car.

Libby hadn't taken his insistence that his lawyer teammate, Grady, review the Honeymoon Travel contract that she'd gotten through her cousin Natalie any better than he'd expected her to. While he was willing to take Libby's word that Natalie was a competent paralegal, she wasn't an attorney, and she was Natalie's cousin. He wanted an impartial review. Jack pulled into the lot next to the park playing fields. Libby had challenged him on Grady's impartiality and he'd gotten the last word with "two reviews are better than one." Or, at least he thought he'd gotten the last word. Libby had insisted on meeting Grady. He had no idea what that would accomplish, but he'd agreed. The only time the three of them all had free was tonight after the game.

Not that he really minded Libby coming to the game, if she did. He was the current church league home run leader. He scanned the bleachers and caught sight of his grandfather and Ellie, sitting front and center near his team bench. But no Libby. Jack dragged his feet. He'd given her the choice to meet them after the game.

"Your lady's not here?"

"Huh?" Jack responded to Grady's question.

"Point proven," Grady said. "The woman who has you so distracted. The one I'm supposed to meet tonight. Better not let it affect your game."

"Lay off. It, she won't. I don't think she's coming until after the game." Jack tossed his glove on the bench, laced his fingers and stretched his arms overhead, ending with a glance toward his grandfather and Ellie—and Libby. His gaze snagged hers and she dropped hers to study the ground in front of her. Jack raised his chin. Because she'd liked what she'd seen? He rolled his shoulders. What was with him? He needed to get his mind out of the quagmire of his feelings toward Libby and onto the game.

"Jack." Grady grinned at him. "We're taking the field."

He grabbed his glove and jogged out to shortstop.

Bottom of the ninth, Jack and the rest of the team hustled in from the field behind five-two. This had to be the worst game he'd ever played. He'd struck out his first time at bat. Weak ground out his second time up. And made it to first his third, only to have the next batter be the third out of the inning. He was surprised coach hadn't benched him. Forcing himself not to glance at Libby right behind him in the stands, Jack watched his three teammates ahead of him bat and walk the bases loaded. Stepping up to home plate with no outs took off some of the pressure.

"Strike one."

"Strike two."

Jack flexed his fingers on the bat and got a piece of the third pitch. First. One run in. He saw his hit bounce off the fence as he rounded second. Two runs in. He barreled for third. Three runs in.

Tie game.

The next batter stepped up and, out of the corner of his eye, he caught Libby raise her fist to him. Jack grinned and danced on and off third.

Crack. The batter connected with the first pitch. A line drive to the shortstop, out at first, with a throw to third that almost caught Jack off base. He winked at Libby. Then, a lazy fly to short right field. Jack made a split-second decision, tagged up, and beelined for home, sliding head first in a race with the ball for the winning run.

"Safe," the umpire called.

Grady offered him a hand up. "Idiot move."

"Yeah, but it worked." Jack dusted himself off.

"I suppose you calculated your odds," Grady said.

Jack's head involuntarily turned toward Libby and the grandparents. "I saw the right fielder step back so I figured I could make it."

Grady shook his head. "That guy has a cannon for an arm. So, next on, I get to meet your Libby."

Jack refrained from any immediate response. Libby wasn't his. He didn't want to think in that direction, didn't need his friend thinking in that direction. "After we shake hands with our opponents," he reminded Grady with a frown. The guy was that anxious to get their meeting over? Or that anxious to meet Libby?

Jack and Grady joined their teammates to congratulate the other team on a good game.

"I'll get Libby," Jack said when they finished.

"You do that. I'll come along and say hi to Ellie."

Jack halted. "You know Ellie?" He eyed his friend. "Don't tell me you already know Libby, too."

"No, only Ellie. One of her rescue kids got himself in some trouble and I represented him, got him back on the right path."

Jack's throat tightened. A jumble of stories that Libby had told him about her grandmother and her mission work tumbled through his mind. This was the woman he'd thought was cheating his grandfather? He strode to the bleachers where Libby and their grandparents were rising from the bench.

"Nice way to take things into your own hands," his grandfather said.

Jack smirked at Grady over his shoulder. "Grady, this is my

grandfather, Blake Parker. You know Ellie."

Ellie and Blake greeted Grady. He nodded.

"And this is Libby Schuyler."

"Libby," Grady said. "I've heard a lot about you." His voice rose suggestively.

He had to have done it on purpose. *Grady better not be like this all evening.* Anything he'd told him about Libby was pertinent to their investigation of Berkshire Christian Match and protecting their grandparents.

"Nice to meet you, Grady" she said before turning her attention to Jack. "As for you, hot shot, you're bleeding all over your shirt."

Jack raised his elbow and looked at it. He hadn't noticed.

Libby pulled a tissue from her bag and wiped his arm.

A twinge that had nothing to do with her gentle ministration shot up his arm and down his tensed frame to his toes.

She tossed the tissue in the trash can on her other side and handed him another tissue. "Press this against your arm," she said, with no indication that her touching him had had any effect on her.

Jack did as she instructed until he felt real pain. "Do you want to ride with me or follow us to the diner?"

"Parker, Hunter, get over here," Coach called. "I'm only going to give the practice info once."

"I'll meet you by the cars and follow you over," Libby answered.

"Guess she shot you down," Grady said. "And after all the effort you put into impressing her."

Grady's adolescent comment didn't merit a reply. Jack had played for the team tonight, not to impress Libby. He lifted his cap, scraped his hand over his hair, and replaced the cap. Who did he think he was kidding? He'd done it to impress Libby, and hadn't made any impact that he could tell. His saving grace now had to be Grady finding nothing wrong with the Berkshire Christian Match contract, that his grandfather and Ellie were simply not managing the business as well as they could be. Then, he and Libby could, what, part ways and leave their elders to flounder into bankruptcy? Jack kicked a stone in his path. He'd never do that. At the moment, the only thing he had straight in his mind was that he wasn't going to let himself be ruled by feelings for a woman who didn't return them.

*

LIBBY WALKED TO the cars with NeNe and Blake, half-listening to her grandmother's explanation of how she and Grady knew each other.

"…you won't find a finer attorney in Berkshire. He's dedicated to his work as a public defender." NeNe stopped. "It's good to see you getting out with some people your age," she said.

Libby opened her mouth to protest, but there was nothing to protest. Except for kickboxing and Mexican with Natalie and her Christian Match "date" with Jack, she couldn't remember the last time she'd socialized, other than coffee hour after church and the singles group. And with her work travel, she hadn't made it to any of the group's meetings lately.

"Are you going for pizza?" NeNe asked. "I hear that's what the guys and their wives and girlfriends usually do."

"No." Was NeNe implying she and Jack were a couple? The only place that was true was in the Christian Match database.

NeNe looked at her expectantly.

"Jack, Grady and I are going to the diner," Libby said.

"That's nice. Is Grady bringing a friend?"

"I don't think so."

NeNe shook her head. "That boy spends all his time working, just like you."

Was NeNe matchmaking her with Grady now? Libby cleared her head of the thought. While it was no secret NeNe would like to have her and her two cousins in loving relationships on the path to marriage, she didn't actively matchmake. Or she hadn't in the past.

"Would you like us to wait with you?" Blake asked when they reached their cars.

Libby glanced over her shoulder at the playing field and saw Jack and Grady walking toward them deep in discussion. She couldn't help comparing the two men. Grady was taller, with broader shoulders and more classic tall, dark, and handsome features. Despite that, she wasn't drawn to Grady's looks. Of course, she'd always preferred lighter haired men with compact builds and less perfect features, someone who didn't tower over her five-foot four frame and seemed more approachable. Men like... She stilled. Men like Jack. It struck her. Sadly, since college she'd judged any man she dated against Jack. And none of them had quite passed muster.

"Libby, are you all right?" NeNe asked.

"I'm fine. Here come the guys. You can go ahead."

"Okay," her grandmother said.

Blake put his arm around NeNe's waist and guided her to the car, leaning down to say something in her ear, followed by what sounded like a giggle from her grandmother. NeNe never giggled. A deep longing filled Libby. She blinked with disbelief. She was jealous of her grandmother.

"Didn't Grandpa and Ellie wait with you? It's almost dusk," Jack said, a frown creasing his handsome face.

Libby bristled. She wasn't in any danger, surrounded by Jack's teammates walking to their cars. Besides she traveled enough on her own to know how to take care of herself. Before she could say anything, she caught a soft flash in his eyes. *Concern.* Warmth flowed through her. "I saw you guys coming, so I told them to go ahead."

Jack nodded while Libby worked at discounting her reaction to Jack's thoughtfulness. Whatever else she might feel about Jack from their breakup, he was a gentleman. He'd have had the same concern for any woman.

"I'll give you the directions to the diner, and you can follow me," Jack said.

"That's not necessary."

He raised an eyebrow.

"The following you." She needed a break in contact with Jack to get herself in check before sitting next to or across from him for who knew how long at the diner. "Give me the directions and the address, and I'll use my travel app."

"Okay, whatever suits you." He rattled off the address and the directions. "You've got my number if you have any problem."

Thank you, Lord. Jack's insinuation that she might not be able to find the diner on her own was enough to get her feelings in line. She opened her car door and slid in. It wasn't really an insinuation. More like what he'd say to anyone. But she needed any lifeline, no matter how thin, to keep from falling for Jack again.

Libby smiled as she pulled into the diner parking lot ahead of him. Her app must have sent her a slightly different route. She hadn't seen him behind her on the way, even though he'd left the parking lot after her.

"So, Speedy," he greeted her in front of his car. "How did you get here first?"

"Following my app." She gave him the route.

He pulled his mouth into a straight line as he always had when he was thinking. Libby had to stop herself from chuckling. He was probably doing a mathematical comparison of their drives.

"Your route was longer, but given the traffic from the ballgame and the pool closing at the same time, it was the faster one."

Libby burst out laughing.

"What?" he said.

"Nothing, except I was thinking you were calculating the reason I was able to get here first."

"You know me too well."

Her stomach flip-flopped.

"I probably shouldn't do that with other people. Dates. Christian Match. Right?" He fumbled over his words.

Her mirth fled. Jack needed to meet someone who understood him, like her. She raised her head. His gaze focused on her, dropping to her lips. She couldn't help looking at his. He closed the distance between them and lowered his head.

"I'm not interrupting anything, am I?" Grady said, coming up behind her. "I thought we were going to talk inside."

"No," Jack said, jumping back from her.

A cool breeze filled the space he opened between them.

"Really? Out here?" Grady said.

"He meant you aren't interrupting anything," she said. *Men.* Grady was acting as adolescent as Jack, although there had been nothing adolescent-like in Jack's expression a moment ago. And she wasn't any better. Her heart was still thumping from the anticipation that Jack had been going to kiss her.

"Then, lead the way," Grady said.

Jack stomped up the restaurant steps.

Libby fell into step with Grady. "I don't know what's with him."

"I do," Grady said as they reached the top of the stairs, but he didn't elaborate.

Jack held the door for her. Then he stepped behind her and in front of Grady and let his friend catch the closing door.

The hostess seated them and they ordered coffee, Jack and Grady supplementing their drinks with a piece of pie.

"Gotta replace the carbs I used up in that final play," Jack said.

"You know I was up next and would have batted you in," Grady said.

"With your RBI stats, I couldn't be sure," Jack came back.

"Guys, you can replay the game later. I have to be up and ready for an eight o'clock conference call with my director in the morning." She placed the folder she'd carried in from her car on the table between her and Grady and fingered the edge closest to her. Libby hoped the call wasn't because Elaine had picked up on her recent loss of enthusiasm for her job, that it had been affecting her work. She buried the thought. "My grandmother gave you such a stellar chat-up, that I'm comfortable having you review her and Blake's Honeymoon Travel contract." *Much more comfortable than I am sitting a hair's breath away from Jack in this booth for any length of time.*

"Jack said you already had someone look at it."

"My cousin. She's with Montgomery, Haynes, and Preston." Libby felt no need to fill in Natalie's position there. "She didn't see anything out of line."

Grady's cell phone rang. "Sorry, I have to take this. A client." He stepped from the booth.

"You didn't tell me your cousin had finished reviewing the contract," Jack said.

"Yes, I did. Just now." She grinned at him.

Grady returned with a glum look and picked up the folder. "Okay, if I take this and run? I have a situation."

"Sure. Give it back to Jack with your comments when you finish," she said. "He'll share them with me."

"Will do."

Libby finished the rest of her coffee in two gulps. "I'd better get going, too."

Jack was out of the booth in a snap. As anxious to escape the weird vibes between them tonight as she was? They walked outside to their cars in awkward silence.

"Goodnight." Libby stepped toward hers.

"Wait." He grabbed her hand. "I forgot something."

"What?" She turned toward him.

Jack tugged her to him, laced his arms firmly around her waist, and pressed his lips to hers. After the initial jolt and instinct to pull away, Libby melted into him as if the years since college hadn't existed.

A catcall from the street broke them apart.

"That's what I forgot," Jack whispered. He tapped his forefinger to the tip of her nose. "Goodnight."

He strode to his car and waited until her wobbly legs got her the few steps to her car and safely inside. Jack tooted his horn and drove away. Libby finished catching her breath. Did he know what he was doing to her? Or, maybe, the better question was, why was she letting him?

Chapter Eight

LIBBY SCRUBBED LAST night's memories of the parade of dreams about Jack and her that had robbed her of most of her sleep. She made a decision. The only way she was going to get any peace in her life was to explore the feelings she still had for Jack with him. That was what his kiss last night was about, right? She dressed, energized herself with her morning devotion, and turned on her laptop. Then she logged into the conference software and twirled a pen in her fingers while she waited for Elaine to join her.

"Good morning," she said when Elaine appeared on her screen.

"Hi," Elaine answered. "I have a meeting at eight thirty, so I'm going to get right to business. Stop me if I'm wrong, but I've picked up on some restlessness on your work approach recently, as if your work isn't giving you what you need.

That was one way to put it. Libby gripped the pen she'd been twirling until her fingers hurt. *Here it comes.*

"I think you're ready to move on," Elaine continued.

Libby swallowed, deciphering the HR-ease in her head. "You're letting me go?"

"Heavens, no," Elaine answered. "I'm offering you a promotion to instruction manager for the east coast here at our DC headquarters."

All of the air in her lungs whooshed out. "I…" She gulped air back in and swallowed. "I don't know what to say."

"Say you'll take it."

Excitement bubbled through her. "I'll take it."

"Great. I'll email a confirmation letter today with the job details and have HR send you the employment contract. That may take a few days. You know how backed up they usually are."

"I'll be looking for them. Thanks so much for this opportunity."

"You're welcome, but we wouldn't have offered you the position if we didn't think you were the person for it." Elaine ended the call.

"Yes!" She did a fist pump. *East coast instruction manager.* She'd planned on applying for a manager position with Teach for Tomorrow, but not until she had a few more years under her belt as an instructor. This had to be the answer to her prayers about her and Jack.

Libby rose, refilled her coffee cup, and paced the kitchen with it. DC wasn't too far away to maintain a relationship with Jack, and the move would give her some distance to figure out exactly what her current feelings for Jack were versus the vestiges of her old feelings. If things with Jack worked out to be serious, the DC area would give him countless opportunities to work with underprivileged high school or college students. Whichever he wanted.

Libby reached for her phone and went to her contacts to call Jack. *No. Something this big needed to be shared in person.* She called her grandmother instead.

"Hi, honey," she answered. "Did you and Jack have a nice time after the game?"

Libby touched her lips before she answered. "It was okay." Maybe if she downplayed the evening to NeNe, she could get things in perspective and Jack's kiss would stop haunting her. "Then, Grady got a call and had to leave."

"That boy. Always working. You and Jack stayed?" NeNe prompted.

Maybe she'd been wrong about NeNe pushing her and Jack together. If that was the case, NeNe may have succeeded. "Only until we finished our coffee," Libby answered, impatient to get to her news. "I had an early conference call this morning with my Teach for Tomorrow director."

"Oh," NeNe said.

"That's why I'm calling. Guess what?"

"I don't know. A curriculum change you think will benefit the students?"

"Better than that. I've been offered a position as instruction manager for the whole east coast."

The line went dead on NeNe's end. "Are you there?" Libby asked.

"I'm here. You're thinking about taking the job?"

"I already accepted it. NeNe, I'll get to formulate programs, policy."

"You'd have to move," NeNe stated.

Libby twisted a strand of hair around her finger. In her excitement, she hadn't thought about leaving her grandmother. "Only to DC, a place you go often."

"Three or four times a year," NeNe muttered. "I'm sorry. I'm being selfish." Her voice came stronger. "If this is what you want, I'm thrilled for you. Congratulations."

"Thanks."

"Have you told Jack yet?"

"If he's free this afternoon, I thought I'd invite him on a picnic and tell him." Libby filled her grandmother in on how she thought the distance could be good for their budding relationship. "I should get to work now if I want to have time to spend with Jack later. Be happy for me."

"I am. It's just so sudden."

Libby said goodbye and hung up. NeNe's lukewarm reaction had dimmed some of the glow of the job offer. Her phone grew heavy in hand. Things would go better with Jack. In person. Feeding Jack had always been a good approach. Her thoughts drifted to the Christian Match dinner. Besides, despite their differences, he'd...they'd always supported each other's core career goals for putting students first, using their abilities to the fullest to help bring quality education to the kids who needed it most.

*

ELLIE PULLED ON a cotton sweater and marched next door to Blake's. "We have a problem," she announced when he opened the door.

"Good morning to you, too." He chuckled.

She brushed by him and into the living room, dropping onto the couch. "Good morning, and this is no laughing matter. Do you know what my granddaughter has gone and done?"

"No, I don't." Blake took his time joining her on the couch. "Would you like some coffee or tea?"

She waved him off. "No, no thank you. This is more important."

He sat beside her. "What has Libby done?"

"She's gone and taken a promotion at Teach for Tomorrow."

"And this is a bad thing?"

"The job is at the headquarters in Washington, DC. She'll have to move. Just when we're on the cusp of getting them back together." Ellie shared Libby's intention to explore a relationship with Jack.

"I see." He patted her hand.

Blake's complacent tone and action riled her. "Don't patronize me. It is a big deal. From what I remember, Libby and Jack's college breakup was caused by Jack taking the Stairway2Learning position without talking with her first, although I think there must have been more."

"I'll give Jack a call this morning and feel him out."

"Don't tell him what Libby said to me about having feelings for him. That should come from her."

"Yes, dear. Give me some credit. I have more finesse than that."

"Of course, you do. But I so want the two of them to be happy together. They're made for each other. Even the Berkshire Christian Match computer agrees."

"I haven't talked with Jack yet about his review of the travel agency's financial statement. I'll call him about that and whether he got hold of our franchise contract."

"We're not supposed to know about that," Ellie warned.

"He'll tell me. I'll razz him about introducing his lady to his friends. Your Natalie must have given the contract to Libby. Why else would she and Jack have been meeting with Grady after the game?"

"My thoughts exactly."

"I expect I'll get a feel for what's going on between him and Libby from that conversation."

Ellie pursed her lips. "If you say so. You know him better than I do."

"And if I don't succeed, I have another plan to encourage them to admit their feelings to each other." He leaned close, treating Ellie to the crisp scent of the aftershave he favored.

*

JACK EXPLAINED THE problem's solution to his student in a third way and still got the blank look he'd gotten the other two times. Generally, he enjoyed the challenge of figuring out how to present problems in a way that clicked with a student who was having difficulty. Today, he selfishly wanted the guy gone, since it was almost time to leave to meet Libby at the park for their picnic. He glanced outside at the darkening sky.

"Wait," the student said. "I subtract the nine from both sides of the equation before I divide by the six."

"Yes," Jack said, raising his hand for a fist bump while thinking *Wasn't that what I said three times?* "Should we do another one?" As much as he'd like to be dashing out of the door, he would *not* let Libby take over his life that much. He wouldn't shortchange his students for the uncertainty that was him and Libby. But this afternoon he'd cut through that uncertainty.

"Jack?" his student said.

"Hmmm?"

"I said I'm good. I'm going." The student stood.

"Sorry, I was thinking of something else."

A short rap on his office door sounded, followed by the door opening and Libby walking in.

"Right," his student said, giving Libby a once-over that alternately made Jack fist his hands and throw his shoulders back.

"Oh." Libby stopped, her hand still on the door knob. "I didn't realize you were with someone. I'll wait in the hall."

"No need," his student said. "I'm out of here. Practice."

"Baseball," Jack said, taking in how cute Libby looked in her cut-off jeans, tank top, and glitter flipflops, her natural lip color enhanced by something shiny. In some ways, she looked more beautiful than she had all dressed up for their Match dinner.

Thunder cracked outside. "I don't think so. Not with the thunderstorms that followed me. That's why I'm here and not at the park. Did you get my text?"

"No." He couldn't seem to form more than one-word sentences.

"Can we picnic here, or do you have a better suggestion?" Libby rested the picnic basket she'd brought against her leg.

His mind raced for ideas. They wouldn't have any privacy in the instructors' lounge and his place…well he hadn't cleaned in a while. "Here is good." There, he'd gotten out three words. "I'll clear off my desk." He brushed the books and papers and pencils into a pile that he placed on the file cabinet behind his seat to sort out later and took the basket from Libby.

She placed the basket on his cleared desk, opened it, and started removing the food while he walked around the desk and grabbed the chair his student had been sitting in. Libby smiled at him. He caught his foot on the chair leg and had to brace himself not to stumble. *Get a grip, Parker or you're going to kill yourself one way or another before you tell her—if you can get the words out.*

He sucked in a deep breath and placed the chair next to his. His equilibrium somewhat restored, Jack motioned at the desk and his stomach growled. "Excuse me." He closed his eyes. *Kill me now.*

"Sounds like I got here with the food just in time."

"You know me when it comes to eating. Anytime is a good time." He eyed the thick pastrami sandwiches. "You went all out."

"We aim to please," Libby said. "The diner and me."

"I'm wounded." He placed his hand over his heart and was startled by the thumping against his palm. "You didn't slave over a hot stove to prepare my lunch."

"In your dreams. Are you going to sit and eat or shall I pack it all back in the basket?"

"I'm sitting. I'm sitting." He pulled Libby's chair out for her and sat in his.

He dug in and they ate in relative silence. By the time he got to his pie, an edginess triggered by the lack of conversation had overshadowed his enjoyment of the lunch. Something was off with Libby. In the past, she'd always been the more social one, the one who kept the conversation going whether they were out with others or alone. Had his kiss been too much, too soon? He'd thought it perfect at the time, and afterwards.

"You didn't ask me if Grady had looked at the contract," he said when he couldn't take the quiet any longer.

Libby stopped eating mid-bite and stared at him wide-eyed, as if she'd just noticed he was there.

"Sorry. My mind was else…focused on this yummy sandwich." She covered herself with a crooked smile that pierced Jack with both uncertainty and longing. "Did he find anything?"

Jack shook his head. "The same as your cousin found— nothing out of order, a recommendation that Grandpa and Ellie sit down with a good business accountant."

"I guess that's good. It takes away the worry." A shadow clouded Libby's eyes. "Then, we're done." She placed what was left of her sandwich on her place and brushed her palms.

"Done?" Ridding herself of crumbs *and* him? Good thing he hadn't gone through with his thoughts about sharing his growing feelings with her.

Libby's hand covered his. "Done with investigating our grandparents and Honeymoon Travel."

The relief that flowed through him left him boneless.

She squeezed his hand, igniting whatever of his nerves that

weren't already flaming. "I think I'm re-falling in love with you," she said. "I want to try again…us."

Robbed of speech, Jack pivoted his chair toward her and responded the only way he could manage. He kissed her sweet and slow.

Blinking at him after he'd pulled away, she said, "I'll take that as a yes."

"A definite *yes*," he said thickly.

"Great, and wait until I tell you my other news." The sparkle in her eyes rained on him like glitter.

"Shoot."

The glitter dimmed as Libby told him about her promotion and plans for them. "You've done it again." He interrupted her.

She drew back in her chair. "What?" she asked, her bewilderment obvious in her expression.

She had no clue.

"You've gone and put conditions on our relationship, on our *love*. It's all dependent on your plan for *our* life, *my* career."

"I…no…" She touched his forearm, and he shook off her hand.

Old hurt blinded him. "You never let me explain why I took the Stairway2Learning position after college."

"Jack, that was then."

"And this is now. I'm going to have my say. I prayed long and hard about the Stairway2Learning offer and the answer I received was that I could do more for more students by developing the software. I thought our love was strong enough to withstand a temporary long-distance relationship. You didn't give me the chance to say that. You shut me out. Case closed. Relationship done."

"We're strong enough now," she protested.

"But only if I'll eventually join you in DC. I believe that I did do more to help students at Stairway2Learning than I would have with Teach for Tomorrow, and that God led me from there to Berkshire Community College. It's where I'm supposed to be now. I would have told you that, if you'd asked me before taking the promotion. We might have worked something out."

Jack's cell phone pinged a reminder. Three fifteen. He'd lost track of time. The faculty meeting was in fifteen minutes. He stood. "I have a meeting. Push the button on the doorknob when you leave so the office is locked."

Libby blanched, and he strode out before looking at her caused him to pull her into his arms and never let go. Taking the stairs two at a time, he wondered if, after Libby had broken up with him at college, she'd felt one tenth of the red-hot pain shooting through him now. How was he going to survive getting over her a second time?

Chapter Nine

*L*ORD, *WHAT HAVE I done?* Jack prayed for the millionth time as he left his meeting with no retention of anything that had been said. *And forgive me for my vengeful words and actions.* Unable to face his office, he walked straight to his car. He needed to talk with someone, get help unjumbling his feelings so he could try to fix things with Libby. He loved her and, with God's help, they could work something out. But right now, the message he was getting was that he needed mortal help to hear His real answer.

Settling into the driver's seat, Jack pressed Grady's contact button on his phone.

"You've reached the office of Grady Hunter. I'm either away from my desk or on the phone. Please leave your name, number, and a short message, and I'll get back to you as soon as I can."

Jack ended the call with no message. What was he thinking? He jammed his key into the ignition and drove the short distance out of the city to his house. He and Grady were softball and Bible study buddies. They didn't discuss their personal relationships. Jack rubbed the back of his neck. He didn't discuss his personal feeling with anyone. Except Libby, and look how well he'd done with that. *Grandpa.* Grandpa had talked to Jack about Ellie. Sort of. Anyway, Grandpa had some idea of the relationship between him and Libby. Ellie must have told him.

Walking toward the house, Jack pressed his grandfather's number.

"Jack," he answered his phone. "You must have read my mind. I was about to call you."

"What's up?" Jack unlocked the side door and stepped into his kitchen. Letting Grandpa talk first would be a good way to ease into his problem. He leaned his shoulder against the wall. Besides, he didn't know how to broach his situation without looking like the idiot he was. Not that Grandpa would care, but Jack did.

"I thought I'd check to see if your friend Grady had finished looking over our Honeymoon Travel contract."

"Yeah, he got back to me this morning. Wait!" Jack pushed away from the wall. "How did you know?"

"A simple deduction. Ellie gave the contract to her granddaughter, Natalie, ostensibly to review, knowing she and Libby were getting together. I figured Libby would tell you she had the contract, and you'd insist on your own legal review. You and Libby went off with Grady after the ballgame." Grandpa harrumphed. "What I don't get is why you and Libby were so skeptical of my and Ellie's relationship that you had to go behind our backs and investigate."

"Sorry, Grandpa. Chalk it up to what I don't know about women and relationships."

"Things not going well with Libby?"

"You know about Libby and me? I mean now, not before." Of course, Grandpa knew. Wasn't that why he'd been about to call him? Because he figured Grandpa knew the situation. Loving Libby seemed to have robbed him of most of his brain cells.

"Anyone who looks at you two would know."

"Well, I blew it. Big time. Libby's taking a job in Washington, DC, and probably won't ever talk to me again."

"It can't be that bad."

"It's that bad." Jack told his grandfather about Libby's announcement and his reaction.

"I see," his grandfather said. "Do you love Libby?"

All the pain of his hasty words rushed over Jack. "I love her. I've always loved her."

"Have you told her?"

Jack's mind raced back over the past couple of days. "Not in so many words." But their kiss outside the diner should have said something. "Not since before we broke up in college."

"Hmmm."

His grandfather was judging him and finding him wanting. He'd thought they'd gotten past that when they'd reconnected after Jack had graduated college. He jerked his hand through his hair in reaction to the spark of anger, followed by resignation, that had come with his hasty jump to conclusions.

"Did Libby demand you leave your job and follow her to DC?"

"No, she wanted us to reconnect, see where things went before I considered moving to DC. But I believe what I'm doing here is what God wants me to be doing."

"I'm sure it is, for now," his grandfather agreed. "But situations change. We can't know what His future path for us may be."

"I know." Jack tapped his foot.

"Hear me out. I fell in love with Ellie almost at first sight and made plans for fitting her into my so-called life in Philadelphia."

Like Libby had done with him, twice. He wasn't exactly following his grandfather's thread. Was he saying he needed to understand where Libby was coming from? Hadn't he already admitted his inability to do that?

"Ellie wouldn't hear of my plan."

"So," Jack interrupted, "to cut to the chase, you're saying I should give up my life here and follow Libby to DC, like you did with Ellie." Although Jack had mulled that idea over and over since he'd shut his office door behind him, Grandpa putting it into spoken words set him on edge.

"Not at all. Ellie, wise woman that she is, said we had to pray for the path we should take together. That freed me to see that I was only going through the motions of living in Philadelphia and holding onto my house there out of some familial obligation that didn't exist. Your parents didn't want it. You didn't want it. And your grandmother wouldn't have wanted me kicking around there when I could be happier elsewhere. Ready for my advice?"

Jack laughed, a weight lifted from his shoulders. "I think I have it already. If Libby and I are going to have a chance together, we have to stop thinking mine-yours and start thinking ours."

"You always were a bright boy, even if you didn't go to the University of Pennsylvania."

"But not bright enough to come up with a way to get Libby to talk with me again. I don't think a simple apology will do it."

"If Libby is anything like her grandmother—and I think she is—a sincere apology would be a start, but not the *piece de resistance*. I can't tell you how to do it, but you need to bare your soul. Give her your heart."

"And let her trample it again?"

"Unfortunately, that's always a possibility. Are you willing?"

Jack reached deep inside himself. *Libby was his heart.* "More than willing, but how can I if I can't get her to meet with me, talk."

"That's where I can help," his grandfather answered with a hint of smugness in his voice.

*

LIBBY THREW THE lunch things, trash and all, into the picnic basket and made sure Jack's office door was locked as tightly as he'd locked out her love. She held her tears until she was in her car and, then, let them come in torrents. A few minutes later, she regained her control enough to drive home and to see her part in firing Jack's actions. She'd been selfish in college and selfish now, letting her excitement, herself, take front and center stage and relegating Jack to a supporting role. No wonder he'd walked out on her—as she'd walked out on him at college.

Libby didn't know where to turn. She needed to do something fast, or she'd lose Jack for good—if she hadn't already. Her cousin Steph had enough heartache of her own. She didn't need Libby dumping more on her. Libby checked the dashboard clock. Natalie would be at work, and she had her law class tonight.

Her cellphone rang. "Hello."

"Hi." NeNe's voice came over her hands-off Bluetooth car speaker. "Got a minute?"

She had the rest of her life—alone.

"Are you there?" NeNe asked.

Snap out of it. "I'm here. I'm driving. On speaker. You know how that breaks up sometimes." She was babbling.

"I need a favor. Are you doing anything tonight?"

"Nothing special." *Other than a few more crying jags and a lot of self-examination.*

"Betty Lindsay offered me two tickets to *A Midsummer's Night's Dream* at the college. She and her sister were going to go, but they came down with the summer bug that's been going around."

Libby wasn't exactly in the mood for a play about romantic love. "I don't know. Wouldn't you rather see it with Blake?"

"I plan to," NeNe said. "Oh, you thought I was inviting you? No, I'm checking to see if you could cover Honeymoon Travel tonight. Our evening person called in sick. If you can't, one of us will have to or we'll have to close for the evening. Business has started to pick up. I'd hate to lose any potential travelers. You did volunteer to give me a hand with the office work."

She had, and NeNe had been quick to give her a *no thanks.* Libby couldn't help thinking her grandmother was up to something. But what?

"It won't be difficult, and it's possible no one will call or come in. You could catch up on our prospect email campaign for me or bring a book and read. Either is fine."

"Sure, I can help." It would give her something to do other than sit in her empty apartment and think about Jack. "When do you need me?"

"Five to eight. Come around four, so I can familiarize you with everything."

"See you then." Libby ended the call.

She showed up at exactly four, changed from the shorts and tank top she'd worn for her picnic with Jack into a blue and white stripped boat-neck T-shirt and navy canvas slacks, her hair pulled back in a high ponytail.

"Perfect," NeNe said. "You look like you're all ready for vacation."

Libby struck a pose. "I thought it would get me in the mood for travel." *And out of my funk about Jack.* "If I have some down time and it's okay with you, I might search around for a trip Steph and I could take, like you suggested."

"Do that. Maybe a nice ro—" NeNe coughed. "A nice Caribbean cruise."

Her grandmother explained what Libby needed to know to get by for the couple of hours she'd be running the agency.

"Any questions?" NeNe asked when she finished.

"No, it seems simple enough."

"Good, because I have to run. I'll talk to you tomorrow."

After NeNe had left, Libby noticed that her grandmother hadn't flipped the sign on the door from "closed" to "open."

"Don't," a deep voice from behind her said as she touched the sign to change it.

"Jack!" Libby could almost feel the color drain from her face. "What? Where…?

"I've been in the service closet." He stretched. "Your grandmother went a little overboard on explaining the job. I was getting claustrophobic in there. By the way, the agency isn't open tonight."

"Since when?" Libby narrowed her eyes. NeNe wouldn't have lied to her, even if she were trying to push her and Jack together. Besides, Libby hadn't told her about what happened with Jack. Had Jack's grandfather snuck him in without NeNe knowing? Her heart skipped a beat.

Jack held up his phone showing Honeymoon Travel's Facebook page with a *Sorry, we're closed tonight* message. "Since about five minutes ago." He grinned.

A grin that erased the fears and doubts that had plagued Libby all afternoon. "I didn't think I'd see you again."

"I'm not twenty-two anymore. You can't get rid of me that easily."

She tilted her head. "I seem to remember you were the one who walked out this afternoon."

"But my anger lasted only until about the time I hit the sidewalk outside the math building."

Libby closed the distance between them and took his hands. "For what it's worth, in college, I wasn't so much angry as hurt. I felt you betrayed me by not following the dreams for the future we'd planned."

"It's history, but if you had let me explain, I was following those dreams. My changing my career direction didn't have to crush our love. But it did." He rubbed a warm thumb across her knuckled. "Because we let it."

She squeezed his hand for the joyful rush of having him squeeze hers back. "Hey, I was only twenty-two, too."

"We weren't ready to fight for our love then. I am now."

Jack's gaze drilled into hers, his pupils widening until his eyes were nearly black. "I am, too." A whisper was all she could manage.

He dropped her hands and pulled her so close their hearts beat as one before he kissed her so lovingly, so thoroughly, she never wanted it to end.

The ring of the travel agency's phone broke them apart. Her face grew warmer. They were standing in front of the picture window. Anyone walking by could have seen them.

She reached for the phone for something to do while she collected herself.

"Let it go," Jack said, his expression soft from their kiss, radiating his love.

The pieces of her life that he'd shattered this afternoon and again this evening in a different way, fell back together. "I can let the promotion go, too."

Jack pulled her back into the security of his arms, and she didn't care who saw them. "No, you can't." He spoke into her hair. "Not any more than I could have given up the offer I had from Stairway2Learning."

"What are we going to do?"

"Be adults. You go to DC. I stay here. We build our relationship long-distance. It worked for our grandparents. And we ask God for guidance for us. Not you for you, and me for me. But for us. See where He takes us."

Libby's throat constricted. "I love you with all my heart, Jack Parker."

"And I love you with all of mine, Libby Schuyler." He took her hand in his and pulled her to the office in the back of the travel agency, kicking the door shut with his foot. "Now, I'm going to really kiss you," he said.

His words blew any concerns about the future from her mind. She might not survive the present.

A Match Made in Sheffield

by

Terri Weldon

Terri Weldon is a lead analyst by day and an award winning author by night. Her novella The Christmas Bride Wore Boots won the best novella category in the 2016 Lyra Awards. She enjoys traveling, gardening, reading, spending time with her family, and shopping for shoes. One of her favorite pastimes is volunteering as the librarian at her church. It allows her to shop for books and spend someone else's money! Plus, she has the great joy of introducing people to Christian fiction. She lives with her family in the Heartland of the United States. Terri has two adorable Westies—Crosby and Nolly Grace. Terri is a member of ACFW and RWA. She is a member of the Seriously Write Team (www.seriouslywrite.blogspot.com). Readers can connect with Terri at www.terriweldon.com

Books by Terri Weldon

The Matchmakers
The Christmas Bride Wore Boots
Mistletoe Magic

Chapter One

Natalie Benton leaned back in the plush cream dining chair. She'd never dined in a five-star restaurant before. She took in every detail from the luxurious eggplant paint on the walls to the elegantly dressed tables and crystal chandeliers. When the waiter placed the dessert plate in front of her, the La Galette Perougienne served with fresh pears and crème fraiche nearly made her drool.

Never, in a million years, would she have dreamed she would meet a man who could afford to dine at Revolutionary Cuisine. The urge to pinch herself just about overwhelmed her. Instead she focused on her date—Jason Whitney. Impeccably cut, sun-streaked hair, tan skin, sparkling green eyes, and a mischievous grin rolled into one handsome package. And to think they had met when she ran into him—literally—at the country club.

Mr. Montgomery, the senior partner at the law firm where she worked as a law clerk, had requested a stack of depositions be delivered to him at the exclusive country club. He often spent Friday's golfing with the other partners in the law firm.

Her penchant for volunteering to run errands had paid off in spades today. She smiled at the man seated across from her and sent up a silent prayer of thanks for their accidental meeting.

The waiter placed the Pear Brandy Tart in front of Jason and then lifted a bottle of wine and filled his glass. Jason lifted the goblet and toasted her glass of water.

"To the first of many wonderful evenings together."

While the words were over the top and she'd have laughed at

any other man, her heart still thrilled at them. Warmth crept up her cheeks. She took a sip of the cool water and placed the goblet on the table. Natalie lifted her dessert fork, but before she could cut into the scrumptious concoction, two men stopped at their table.

"Jimmy White, I'm Detective Henderson of the Pittsfield Police Department. I have a warrant for your arrest." The detective motioned for Jason to stand up.

She tried to get his attention, but Jason avoided her eyes. Instead he pushed back his chair and stood. "You're making a mistake."

"Tell it to the judge." The detective turned him around and cuffed his hands behind his back. "Mirandize him," he said as he passed him off to the officer beside him.

Every eye in the room watched her date being escorted out—Natalie's included.

Next, he turned to face her. "Natasha Brent."

Her jaw dropped and she started to speak.

"I also have a warrant for your arrest."

The fork in her hand clattered as it fell against the plate and splashed the crème fraiche across her black cocktail dress. "I'm not Natasha Brent." Her voice shook as the words tumbled from her mouth. "I'm Na—"

"Save it sister." The detective reached for her wrist and pulled her to her feet.

"Detective, stop." The waiter appeared at the table.

Natalie wilted in relief. Thank heavens the waiter planned to tell the detective he was making a horrible mistake.

"The bill hasn't been paid."

Both men looked at Natalie. She shook her head from side to side. "Oh no, if you think I'm paying for this overpriced dinner, you're wrong." Her words came out loud and reverberated through the dining room. Now every eye in the place stared at her. Twin crimson circles of heat stained her cheeks a brighter red than any blusher could have.

"If you refuse to pay, then the manager will go to the police department and file charges," the waiter said.

"Fine." Natalie reached for her black evening bag.

Detective Henderson grabbed the small bag from her hands. "Not until I look inside. For all I know, you've got a weapon in that bag.

A weapon? Natalie wanted to laugh. There hadn't even been room to slide her oversized wallet inside. Oh, no! In her haste to leave the house, she'd forgotten to remove her driver's license from her wallet and slip it inside the small evening bag.

He unhooked the rhinestone clasp and searched the purse before handing it to her.

"How much?" she asked.

"Three hundred and twenty-two dollars and fifty-eight cents." The waiter handed her the leather ticket holder.

Natalie choked when she looked at the ticket. Tonight's dinner had cost as much as her monthly grocery bill. She looked in her purse and the money from the sale of the chest she had found at a garage sale in Albany stared back at her. The second she'd spotted the old hope chest covered in layers of paint, she'd known the piece was an antique. The seller had let it go for a song. Gran had taken it to a friend who ran an antique store in Williamstown and sold it for her. After work Natalie had run by Gran's and picked up the money. Money she'd intended to use to pay the tuition for the last class she needed to complete her law degree. Now she would be forced to wait another semester. She counted out the money and placed three hundred and twenty-three dollars inside the holder and handed it back to the waiter.

"Place your hands behind your back." Detective Henderson slapped the handcuffs around her wrists. "You have the right to remain silent. Anything you say can and will be used against you in a court of law. You have the right to talk to a lawyer and have him present with you while you are being questioned. If you cannot afford to hire a lawyer, one will be appointed to represent you before any questioning if you wish. You can decide at any time to exercise these rights and not answer any questions or make any statements. Do you understand each of these rights I have explained to you?"

Before she could respond, the waiter piped up. "Excuse me, but a twenty percent gratuity is standard."

"You've got to be kidding!" Natalie turned to Detective Henderson. "Please, get me out of here." She kept her head down as he escorted her from the restaurant. Warm air assaulted her the minute she stepped outside. At least the dark night sky helped hide her shame. She prayed no one would recognize her. Considering none of her friends could afford to dine at Revolutionary Cuisine, she should be safe. Now Taco Bell, well that would have been a different story.

They reached the unmarked police car, and he opened the back door. "Watch your head." Detective Henderson placed a hand on her head. She assumed he meant to ensure she didn't whack her head. Instead it felt like he shortened her neck by an inch.

He slammed the back door and walked to the driver's side of the vehicle. Natalie felt a sense of relief when she saw Jason. "Thank goodness you're here. Do you have any idea what's going on?"

He ignored her and stared straight ahead. Panic swelled up in her chest and her heart sped up. She waited until the detective climbed inside and started the engine to speak. "Do you mind telling me what I'm being arrested for?"

"Insurance fraud, internet fraud, forgery, and romance scams." He turned his head and looked behind him, then merged into the lane of traffic. "Same with your boyfriend."

She glanced out of the corner of her eye to see Jason turn his head away and stare out the window. The look on his face warned her that this wasn't his first arrest. "He's not my boyfriend."

At the police station she was fingerprinted, photographed, and— horror of all horrors—strip searched. An experience she hoped to never repeat again in her life.

"You're allowed one phone call," the female officer said.

"When can I post bail?" Natalie asked.

"I don't have a clue. Detective Henderson will need to call a clerk magistrate on your behalf. Meanwhile you're being held as a guest of the citizens of Pittsfield tonight." The officer laughed like she'd made a joke.

She thought about calling Gran. The idea of waking the eighty-year-old woman and having her make the drive into Pittsfield seemed wrong, but if she just had her identification she could prove she wasn't Natasha Brent. Of course that would mean Gran would have to drive from Williamstown to Sheffield to pick up her driver's license. No way would she have her driving from one end of the state to the other to pick up her identification and then trek halfway back so she could deliver it to her in Pittsfield.

But if Gran tried to call her later and couldn't find her, she'd worry. Natalie desperately tried to think of another solution, but none came. She looked around the stark room with the dingy paint. The black telephone her only link to the outside world. Natalie's fingers shook as she punched in the number. "Gran, it's me," she wailed, "and I'm in jail." So much for playing it cool.

"Jail! Are you all right? Natalie Benton what did that horrible man do to land you in jail?"

"Oh, Gran, he's a con man. I can't explain now. I wanted you to know where I was so you wouldn't try and call me later and worry when I didn't answer."

"Tell me exactly where you are and I'll be there in less than an hour," Gran said.

Natalie's eyes took in her surroundings. An hour might seem fast to Gran, but it seemed an eternity to her. "Please Gran, I shouldn't have called. The magistrate will be here before you could drive down. I'll be out of here in no time. I'll call you in the morning and we can talk then. Really, I'll be fine." She whispered a silent prayer of forgiveness for the lie.

"The least I can do is make a few telephone calls to ensure they don't slow roll you."

The phone clicked in her ear when Gran pushed the end button.

"Detective Henderson wants to see you." The female guard led her to an interrogation room.

Hope welled in Natalie's heart. Maybe he'd discovered the mistake and planned to release her. There was no one in the room. The guard left her in the chilly interrogation area in an uncomfortable metal chair for what felt like hours. Without a clock, it was impossible to tell how long she'd waited. The dull paint in here looked even worse than the area where the phones were located. And it seemed so dark. She looked at the ceiling. Probably a third of the bulbs were burned out. When the door opened, Detective Henderson walked in. One look at his drawn face knocked the idea of being released right out of her mind.

"Your *"Gran"* called me on my cell phone—FaceTime. I've got to hand it to you, Natasha, the old lady is a nice touch. For her sake, not yours, I reassured her you'd be fine. I even convinced her not to rush down here. Elderly people don't need this kind of stress. But thank her for insisting I look up your driver's license." He held up a photocopy of her Massachusetts driver's license complete with her picture. "We've been trying to find out your true identity for months."

"You've made a horrible mistake." She looked him straight in the eye. "Natalie Benton is my true identity. It's my only identity. I don't have a clue who Natasha Brent is. Please, check my statement out. You'll realize I'm telling the truth."

"Such sincerity. Any minute now, you'll turn on the tears."

"I know my rights. It may be after hours, and the start of the weekend, and I realize I can't be arraigned until next week, but I want you to call a clerk magistrate for bail." Natalie could tell the skeptical detective had already made up his mind. Nothing she said would convince him of her innocence. "And I want a lawyer, a public defender."

Detective Henderson chuckled. "Well that didn't take long. The guilty ones always lawyer up fast." He stood, opened the door, and left the room.

Natalie wanted to cry more than she had since the day she turned eight and realized her mom wasn't coming back to get her. How had this happened to her? "Why God?" She looked at the ceiling, as if she expected to see the answer written out on the stained ceiling tiles.

The female guard came back in the room. "The detective is trying to locate a magistrate. Meanwhile, we're moving you to a cell. You probably won't get a lawyer until morning unless one falls out of the sky." The woman guffawed. Seemed she thought her jokes were funny. Maybe she'd just been doing the job too long.

Ten feet down the stark hall, she heard Detective Henderson yell, "McBride, take the prisoner to a visiting room. Tonight's her lucky night, Hunter's here and he's agreed to act as counsel."

*

GRADY HUNTER GLANCED at his watch. Ten forty-five on a Friday night and instead of going home, he had agreed to see another client. Man, he needed a life. Ever since his fiancé dumped him two years ago, he'd filled all his spare time with work and coaching basketball. Oh, he'd had his fair share of dates the first six months. After one last boring date with a friend of a friend's second cousin or something like that, he realized he'd been dating a stream of women he didn't care about simply to prove the opposite sex found him attractive. Just one more way he'd allowed his ex-girlfriend to continue to control his life.

His stomach rumbled reminding him he hadn't eaten since the bag of chips he'd wolfed down on his way to court at noon. But it had been worth it. His client had been proven innocent, and the fifteen-year-old's uncle had made arrangements for the teen to live with him in Virginia. Away from the bad influence of his so-called friends.

Exhaustion beat against Grady's back and he shoved a hand through his disheveled hair, then felt the stubble on his jaw. He hoped he wouldn't scare his client. When he reached the visitation room, he shoved the door open and went inside. The woman sitting at the table stopped him in his tracks. Clichéd or not, it was the God's honest truth.

Mesmerized by the beautiful woman in front of him with the

light smattering of freckles, warm brown eyes, and ginger hair, he dropped the file on the table. He stared until she offered a nervous smile, obviously confused by the crazy man in front of her. His whole being warmed with her smile.

He tried to think of something, anything, to say. After a minute, the obvious words rushed from his mouth. "I'm Grady Hunter, your public defender."

He pulled the chair out from the table and sat across from her, reminding himself she was a client, very likely a criminal. Somehow he couldn't believe this woman belonged here. There had to have been a mistake.

He opened the folder the detective had given him and flipped through it. Natasha Brent arrested for insurance fraud, internet fraud, elder fraud, forgery, and romance scams. Romance scams—he had to admit that she would be a natural.

"So Natasha, do you understand the charges that have been filed against you?"

"I'm not Natasha. I'm Natalie and I don't understand any of this." She dropped her head into her hands. "All I'm guilty of is going out to dinner with a man I met this afternoon at the country club."

"What did he say his name was?" he asked.

"Jason, Jason Whitfield." She straightened her shoulders and looked him in the eye. "Shouldn't a man at the country club be safe? It's not like I met him in a nightclub."

Grady's stomach clenched and he felt like he'd been sucker punched. Her words reminded him of something his ex-fiancé would say. If a man had money and prestige, that must mean he was a stand-up guy. Look where that had landed Natalie. "A country club is a common place to find a con man. He's looking for a woman with money."

"I don't have any money."

"But did he know that?" She wilted like a day-old lily as the truth of his words sank in. "Now I'm your attorney, so anything you tell me is confidential. Are you Natasha Brent?"

"Absolutely not." She leaned across the table toward him. "I told you, I'm Natalie Benton."

He might be crazy to trust her, but something about her words rang sincere. "Then Natalie, we've got to find a way to prove your true identity, because you're a doppelganger for the woman in the warrant, right down to your initials and the freckles on your nose."

Chapter Two

NATALIE SURGED TO her feet. "That's probably why Jason Whitfield asked me out, to protect Natasha. There has to be a way to prove it. Just tell me what to do." She paced back and forth across the small room.

"How long have you lived in Pittsfield?" Grady asked.

"I don't live in Pittsfield, I work here. My home's in Sheffield." Grady's face didn't give a thing away. She couldn't tell if he believed her or not. "I've been there for seven years." She thought of the cozy two-bedroom home with the enormous gardens she'd inherited. The home had been an inheritance from an aunt she'd never even known existed. To this day, she wondered why the woman had cared enough to leave her a house, but not enough to pull her out of the foster care system.

"How long have you worked in Pittsfield?"

"A year and a half."

Grady flipped through the file in front of him. Natalie could tell he had a goal in mind and she found herself biting the corner of her lip while she waited.

"I found it!" He stabbed his index finger into one of the pages. When he looked up, the twinkle in his blue eyes sent her hear racing faster than Perry Mason could file a corpus delicti. "Have you been to Chicago lately?"

"Chicago? Never." She took a deep breath and decided to go for total honesty. "Between my schedule, my salary, and my tuition I can't afford to travel."

"Consider that a plus. Six months ago, Natasha and Jimmy

ran one of their scams in Chicago. There is a wealthy widower who says over the course of four months, Natasha swindled him out of a substantial sum."

"So this scam…" The word left a foul taste in her mouth and she swallowed before continuing. "It proves I'm not Natasha Brent?"

"You bet it does. All we have to do is obtain a notarized statement from your employer stating you were at work during the time the crimes in Chicago were being committed." He shot her a grin that would have melted a block of ice in the middle of winter. "This whole mess can be cleared up in a couple of hours. Where do you work?"

"Montgomery, Haynes, and Preston." She whirled around to face him. "But you can't contact them. I work there as a law clerk." She pushed a strand of hair behind her ear. "I'm one class short of my law degree. As soon as I pass the bar, I hope to work there as an attorney. They're a very conservative firm and there has never been the slightest hint of a scandal associated with them. If they find out about this mess, they'll never hire me to work for them. In fact, they'll fire me!"

"I went to Harvard with Montgomery's son Corey. Let me talk to him, before you make that decision."

"No. There has to be another way." She pulled the chair back out and plopped into it like a rag doll. "What about my identification? Doesn't it prove I'm not Natasha Brent?"

"Your identification muddies the water. All of Natasha Brent's aliases have the initials NB. Just like your name. I don't think they'd fire you over a false arrest and a statement from them would clear your name."

"That's not a risk I'm willing to take. You're my attorney. Can't you call a magistrate and arrange for bail?" She clenched her hands in her lap to hide the trembling in her fingers. "I have to be at work on Monday."

"I still think you're making a mistake." He stood and walked to the door before he turned back to her. Natalie could feel the frustration radiating from his body all the way across the room.

He blinked and she noticed the dark circles beneath his eyes.

"I'm going to call a magistrate. When he arrives, I'll request you be released on your own recognizance. If he refuses, then he will set a bail amount. It shouldn't be too high," he said. "No more than five thousand which means the max you'll need to pay is five hundred. Plus a small fee for the magistrate. Cash or a check will work."

He pulled the door open and walked out before she could tell him she only had a hundred and eighty dollars in cash with her and her checkbook was at home on her dinette table. The room seemed empty without his presence to brighten it. She glanced around the small, sterile room and fought back tears. Why had she paid the bill at the restaurant? If she hadn't, she'd have enough money to pay a magistrate fast and she would be out of here within the hour. Then a quick trip on the BRTA bus and she could pick her car up from the office. Instead she'd blown her chance to escape this nightmare tonight. She laid her head on the hard table, closed her eyes, and prayed.

The door squeaked as it opened and snapped her out of a light sleep.

"Natalie." Grady walked into the room. "The magistrate should be here soon."

She jerked her head off the table and wiped her bleary eyes. "I don't have five hundred dollars with me and my checkbook is at home in Sheffield. Please." Natalie swallowed around the lump in her throat and forced the hardest words she had ever spoken out. "Call the magistrate back and tell them not to come."

"Surely there's someone you can call to bring you the money."

"Tomorrow morning, I'll ask Gran." She held up a hand. "There's no way I'm asking a woman of her age to drive down tonight."

"That means you'll spend the night in jail."

"I understand." Natalie held his gaze. She refused to let him see the fear his words invoked.

"Give me your Grandmother's name and phone number. I'll

call her in the morning."

Natalie rattled off the information. "But don't call her until eight."

"Wait a minute, I know Ellie Alexander. She has three grandchildren." Palms flat on the table, he leaned forward. "None of them have the last name Benton."

Pulling up every shred of self-worth she could muster Natalie said, "You're right, Gran has three biological grandchildren— Libby, her sister Stacey, and their cousin Stephanie. I'm not a biological grandchild. Gran and I adopted each other." The words sounded silly and heat burned the back of her neck. "How do you know Gran?" She worked hard to keep a defensive tone from her voice. Judging from the look on his face, she hadn't succeeded.

"Jack, Libby's fiancé, and I go to church together. We play on the same softball team. I've had dinner with Ellie, Blake, Jack, and Libby a couple of times." A quizzical expression flashed across his handsome face. "Why don't you call Libby or her sister? One of them could bail you out."

Oh, she wished she could. "Libby's out of town. And there is no way I'd ever call Stacey. She's convinced I'm out to swindle Ellie out of every dime she has. And Stephanie, well, all I can say is she's going through a tough time right now. She doesn't need my problems piled on top of hers."

"There's no reason for you to spend the night in jail." Grady crossed his arms in front of his chest. "Let me post your bail. You can pay me back tomorrow."

The thought of getting out of here tonight nearly had her accepting his more than gracious offer. She could taste freedom, but she refused to use his friendship with Jack as her means of escape. "Absolutely not."

"Fine, I'll call Ellie in the morning."

When he left the room, Natalie felt like the foster kid who had fallen through the cracks in the system yet again. Maybe if she was quiet, the officer would forget she was in the room. Then she could spend the night here instead of in one of those horrid cells. It was Friday night. What if the jail was crowded and she had to share with someone else? Someone mean and intimidating. Her and Big Bertha, the scene played in her mind and she shuddered.

The door slammed open and Officer McBride walked in. "Your room's all ready." The officer laughed and this time the sound grated on Natalie's nerves. She bit the inside of her cheek to keep from saying something she shouldn't and followed the woman down the hall. Relief assaulted her when the guard stopped in front of an empty cell and unlocked the door. At least she'd be alone. She stepped inside. Before she could turn around, the door to the cell slammed shut. It sent a jolt through her body and she lurched forward.

*

THE ALARM JARRED Grady awake. With one hand, he swatted at where it normally sat on his nightstand. When he knocked a picture frame over and the obnoxious sound continued, he remembered that his sister had moved the alarm to prevent him from oversleeping. Bleary eyed, he stumbled across the room and turned the clock off. Two feet away, the door to the master bathroom and a hot shower beckoned. He had to hand it to good old sis, she knew how to arrange a room. Probably came from being the mother of two teenagers.

Twenty minutes later, he strode out of the house with a steaming mug of coffee and his briefcase, hopped in his classic 1965 Mustang, and drove to the courthouse. He requested to see Natalie and within moments, she was led into the room. Her red hair stood on end and black smudges of mascara framed her red-rimmed eyes. Hand cuffs bracketed her wrists. Definitely not the look they wanted to make in front of the magistrate.

"We need to get you cleaned up."

Her head snapped up and the fire in her brown eyes made him want to chuckle. Somehow he knew she wouldn't appreciate the sound. He slid his mug of coffee across the table to her. "Here, drink this."

While Natalie gulped the steaming java, he opened the door

to find Lori Wade standing guard. "Hey, Lori, when my client's grandmother, Ellie Alexander, arrives please let me know."

"Sure thing."

When he turned back around, Natalie looked a little less bleary eyed. "I guess the coffee helped." He spoke casually trying to put her at ease.

"It did." She slid the empty mug across the table to him. A faint stain of red that resembled an early summer sunburn worked its way up her neck into her cheeks. "But I'm afraid I drank all your coffee."

"No problem." Grady pulled out the chair across from her and slid into it. He picked up his briefcase and placed it on the small table, then flipped it open. "Okay, I've got a mirror, facial wipes, a brush, and breath mints." He removed a couple of files and turned the briefcase to face her. "Clean up while I go over the facts and our plea with you."

"I'm planning on entering a plea of not guilty. Are you in agreement?" He looked up to meet her angry gaze, head on.

"I'm not guilty. Why would I plead anything else?"

The distress in her voice, coupled with the exhaustion marring her face, tugged at his heart strings. Grady reached across the table and covered her soft hand with his much larger one. "I believe you. But I'll tell you the same thing I say to the kids on the basketball team I coach on Thursday evenings—you have to have a game plan. Same thing applies here. So, we still need to go over this paperwork together. Make sure I'm doing things the way you want before we meet with the magistrate."

He knew he should move his hand away, but he liked the way hers felt beneath his. Liked it more than he should. He pulled his hand back. "Now, I'm going to ask the magistrate to release you on your own recognizance. You've lived in the area for seven years and this is a simple case of mistaken identity."

A flicker of joy lit her eyes. He hated to be the one to extinguish it, but he didn't want to give her false hope. "I don't think he will, but I do believe he will set your bail at a reasonable sum."

A rap sounded at the door and a minute later Ellie Alexander walked into the room. Her black slacks and green and black printed tunic showcased her gray bob and sparkling green eyes. "Gran!" Natalie jumped from her seat and embraced the attractive elderly woman.

Grady stood and held his hand out. "Ms. Alexander, it's always great to see you. I just wish it were under better circumstances." He gestured for both women to sit down before he continued. "Natalie needs your help to post bail."

"Grady, call me Ellie. Are you still coaching basketball for those underprivileged kids?" she asked.

"You bet. It's the highlight of my week. I love working with those kids."

"Now explain to me why you let my granddaughter spend a night in jail?" The mischief in her green eyes took the sting out of her words.

Ellie turned to face Natalie "And you should have told me you needed money last night. To think you spent the night in jail, just to keep me from driving in the dark. Good grief girl, don't start treating me like a doddering old woman."

Grady bit his lip to keep from smiling. Before Natalie could respond, Officer Lori Wade stuck her head inside the room. "The magistrate is here."

"Show him in." Grady looked into Natalie's chocolate brown eyes. "Stay calm and this will all be over before you know it."

A surge of relief hit Grady when Patrick Ames walked into the room. The man was one of his favorites. "Patrick, glad you're here."

"I understand you need me to set bail for your client Natasha Brent."

"My client is not Natasha Brent. Her name is Natalie Benton and she's lived in Sheffield Massachusetts for the past seven years. This is a case of mistaken identity and I request she be released on her own recognizance."

"Considering the man she was with pleaded guilty this morning and failed to either acknowledge or deny your client's identity, I'm afraid I can't do that."

"She's not a flight risk. Natalie Benton has lived in Sheffield for seven years, she owns her own home. She has close ties with her grandmother and is employed in Pittsfield."

Patrick pulled out his tablet, opened a search engine, and typed. "I do see where a Ms. Natalie Benton owns a house in Sheffield. So, I'll set bail at the sum of five thousand dollars."

Grady felt a grin tug at the corner of his lips. "So, we need to pay you five hundred for bail and then your fee. Is that correct?"

"That'll cover it," Patrick said.

Gran wrote out the check and handed it to Patrick who gave her a receipt before standing. "Good luck, ma'am." He nodded to Natalie before turning to face Grady. "See you around, Counselor."

"Ladies, I suggest we blow this joint." Ellie seemed thrilled at Grady's suggestion, but Natalie looked ready to cry. "What's wrong?" He scrunched his brows. "I thought you'd be relieved to get out of here."

Chapter Three

NATALIE'S TEARS EMBARRASSED her, but she couldn't stop them. She felt like the ten-year-old foster child who had to get the free lunch tickets at school. They were always a different color from the other children's tickets. Back in fifth grade, she'd been playing with Tessa Murphy. They became fast friends, but once Tessa saw her orange lunch ticket, she looked at her like she smelled worse than a week-old boiled egg. Humiliated beyond belief, Natalie would've crawled in a hole if there had been one nearby. She vowed that someday she wouldn't have to worry about money. And here she was fifteen years later, taking a handout from Gran. *God, I promise you this isn't the same as a love of money. I just want enough to have some security.* She ignored the quiet voice that told her security was in God, not money.

"Gran, as soon as I get home I'll write a check and bring it to you." With Grady's blue eyes drilling a hole through her, she had to fight to keep from squirming.

"You are the granddaughter of my heart." Gran took both of Natalie's hands in hers. "I would have done this, even if you could never pay me back." She leaned down and kissed Natalie on the forehead. "I love you, Natalie Benton, nothing is going to change that."

Natalie tightened her arms around the older woman's shoulders "I know you do; sometimes I just need to be reminded."

"Consider yourself reminded." Gran made a pretext of checking her watch. "My, will you look at the time. I'm meeting

Blake for brunch. I'll catch up with you later Nat, but you two kids go and celebrate."

She left the room before Natalie could ask for a ride to her car. Looked like she would be catching a ride on the BRTA. Or she could walk. Who knew if it was sunny or pouring rain? She'd been trapped in windowless rooms since the arrest the night before. At that moment, Natalie wanted nothing more than to run out of the police department and dance in the sun. Instead she kept pace beside Grady Hunter as they walked toward the exit.

The second they stepped into the Massachusetts sunshine, Natalie said a prayer of thanks for the blue skies. Immediately her stomach growled louder than a lion on that channel with all the animals. Why, oh why did she have to keep embarrassing herself in front of Grady? And why did she care? Even if he did have iridescent blue eyes that changed colors depending on his mood and a laugh that made her smile in response. After all, he was her attorney, not her date.

"I could pretend I didn't hear that," he said.

Natalie rubbed her stomach. "Everyone in Pittsfield heard that."

He laughed and she smiled as if on cue. But a little fun at her own expense wasn't bad if it elicited that beautiful sound.

"Well, I'm not going to pretend, because I'm starved. What do you say we go to that all-you-can-eat place down the street and have a late breakfast?"

Temptation and hunger tugged at Natalie's heart, but was sharing a meal with him a good idea? Grady Hunter didn't fit anywhere in the five-year plan she'd mapped out for her life.

"Come on, we can call it a working breakfast. We'll discuss your defense and the best way to clear your name."

"When you put it that way, I can't refuse." Natalie opened her small purse on the pretext of looking for her lipstick. She applied a quick swipe while she did a visual on the money left in her bag. "But only if you let me buy." Before he could protest, she held up a hand in a stop motion. "You're a public defender.

My breakfast won't go on an expense account or get billed into the hours you spend on the case, so I insist."

"You're on." Grady started up the street then stopped. She saw him look down at her high heels. "Would you prefer driving to walking?"

Natalie mentally calculated the distance. The heels were pretty comfy and she'd walked that far in them before. "No way. After being cooped up inside for so many hours, I'm ready to stretch my legs."

"You know, Natalie," Grady said as they walked side by side, "you were only there for twelve hours, not twelve years."

"Make fun all you want, but it felt like forever." She sidestepped a crack in the cement. "The Good Lord made me an outside girl. I can't handle being cooped up for hours on end."

"Then you don't want to be an attorney." Grady shrugged out of his suit jacket. "There are days I'm in the office for twelve hours straight."

She shuddered at the thought. "Not me. I volunteer to run every errand that needs to be done at the office."

"Before I make a major decision in my life, I always pray." He looked straight ahead and continued walking. "Just pray about your decision to be a lawyer. Think about your motivation and be sure you're doing what God has planned for your life."

"I lack one class before I apply to take the bar exam." Natalie yanked open the door of the restaurant before Grady could reach it. "It's a little late to rethink my career path now. You're my lawyer not my life coach so please, keep your comments to yourself." She refused to admit she hadn't prayed about her decision to go to law school.

*

GRADY HELD HIS tongue while they went through the line and Natalie paid for their buffets. She marched straight for a table in a back corner, and he knew it wasn't because she wanted to be alone with him. More than likely, she planned to chew him up one side and down the other. For some reason a tongue lashing from Ms. Benton seemed like something to look forward to. The thought made him want to chuckle, but he didn't want to anger her.

He followed her through the buffet line and piled his plate. Having grown up with two sisters, he knew better than to mention it, but being mad didn't seem to affect Natalie's appetite. Her plate was piled high.

When they sat down, he bowed his head and said a quiet prayer. He noticed Natalie did the same and the action warmed his heart. In this day and age, and in his profession, it was hard to meet Christian women.

She dug into her food and he followed suit. "They make a really good breakfast here." Grady offered the words as a peace offering.

Before she could reply, her phone chirped. "Excuse me, that's Mr. Montgomery. I recognize the ring tone."

She reached in her purse and pulled out her phone. Grady noticed a slip of paper fall out and float to the floor. He leaned down to retrieve it while she talked.

"Good morning sir, what can I do for you?"

He admired the way she kept her words bright and cheerful as she talked with her boss. The man would never guess she'd spent the night in jail. He bent sideways and nabbed the slip of paper. The words *five-year plan* were written across the top. He scanned the list: *Finish my law degree, pass the bar exam, meet the perfect, successful man with a six-figure income, get married, produce one child, become a partner in a law firm.* Unreal! She had her entire life mapped out, and she'd have to be a super hero to achieve her goals.

Her voice trailed off mid-sentence and her eyes narrowed into two small slits. "You'll have it this afternoon. Goodbye."

Busted. She'd seen him reading the list. He held the paper out for her. "You dropped this when you pulled your phone out of your purse."

"You knew it was mine and you still read it?" The anger in her voice resonated across the table.

He handed the folded scrap of paper to her. "You're right. I knew it was your list and I read it anyway." He lowered his head, ashamed of his behavior. "I'm sorry." Yet a part of him was glad he'd learned the kind of woman she was before he fell for her.

"You had no right." Her voice shook with fury.

"Tell me that list is a joke. Tell me you don't have your life mapped out for the next five years."

"Haven't you ever heard of long-range planning?" Anger laced her voice and scalded his skin. "I want a secure future. A successful future, for me and for my family. Unless I plan for it, that won't happen. I mapped my goals out and I carry that list everywhere to keep me focused. So yeah, sit over there in your chair, Mr. Public Defender, and make fun of me."

Mr. Public Defender—big words for someone who needed his services. He was about to retort, but she wasn't finished.

"My child will never know what it's like to be alone or wonder where her next meal is coming from."

Compassion welled in his heart and Grady felt horrible for pushing her. What had happened in her past to make her so fearful? He longed to ask the question, but now wasn't the time. The thought of her being scared, alone, and hungry hurt his soul.

Still, the thought that she looked at his career, at him as a man, and found him lacking angered Grady. "Money isn't the only measure of success. I like being a public defender and the work I do makes a difference."

"Plenty of successful attorneys do pro-bono work. You don't have to choose between security and helping others." She yanked the paper out of his hand then took a long pull of coffee.

"If I were you, I wouldn't knock a public defender as long as I was dependent on him to help me clear my name."

Her face turned bright red with anger and he swore he could see lasers shooting from her eyes. When Natalie's hand slapped the top of the table, he thought he might have pushed her too far.

"How dare you! I may be availing myself of your free services, but at least I'm trying to move forward and better myself. And that's more than I can say for you." Natalie tossed her napkin onto her plate, pushed back her chair, and turned to leave.

"Natalie, wait. You don't have a car."

She ignored him and stormed out of the restaurant. Grady leaned back in his chair and took a drink of orange juice. Yeah, well that could have gone a little better. They hadn't even discussed her defense. A slow smile spread across his face. But then again, there was always tomorrow.

Chapter Four

ANGER FUELED NATALIE'S steps as she raced to the BRTA. Just as she drew close enough to flag down the driver, the bus pulled away. She stopped and leaned forward with her hands on her knees, trying to catch her breath. The black heels she had deemed comfortable last night rubbed the back of her left foot and the side of her right baby toe.

She hobbled onward, tempted to flag down a taxi, but her budget couldn't stand another hit. Pride kept her from calling a friend for a ride. Praying the blister on her foot wouldn't get too miserable Natalie forced one foot in front of the other. Three blocks later, her perseverance paid off. As she dragged herself up the steps of the bus, she dug through her purse and came up with the required fare. *Thank You, Lord.* She offered up the silent prayer as she collapsed into an empty seat.

The events of last night had caught up with her. Her fingers shook as she opened and closed the clasp on her small evening bag repeatedly. Exhaustion caused her eyelids to droop, but she forced them to stay open.

Fear she'd miss her stop kept her from resting her head against the seat or closing her eyes. As the bus neared the building that housed the law firm where she worked, Natalie pulled the cord above her window. The driver went through the intersection and eased the bus to a stop. She hurried forward and hobbled down the steps. As she waited for it to pull away from the curb, she fished her key fob from her purse. The second the road cleared she ran across the street to the employee parking lot. Only two vehicles were parked in the lot—hers and Grady Hunter's.

What was he doing here? She couldn't believe he had the gall to lean indolently against the side of his classic Mustang. She ignored him and eased into her tiny economy car. Then she slid the black heels off and tossed them onto the passenger seat. No doubt about it, tomorrow she'd have a raw blister the size of Rhode Island on the back of her foot. Right now, all she wanted was to go home and hide in her cottage until Monday.

The tap, tap, tap against the car window set her teeth on edge. The urge to ignore him, throw the car in drive, and peel out of the parking lot almost consumed her. Two things stopped her. One—he was her attorney, and two—she didn't want him to drop her case in the lap of a new public defender. Grady was smart and savvy. Last night when he showed up at the jail and agreed to take her case, she'd been blessed. No doubt about it, God had been watching over her just as he had Joseph when he'd been thrown in Pharaoh's prison. She didn't expect to become ruler of the land, but she did hope to have her name cleared.

She pushed the power button and the window rolled down.

"Jimmy White made bail." Grady squatted down and rested his forearm on her door. "On my way over, I made a few calls. He isn't a member at the country club. Ruby Languard sponsored him. Seems old Jimmy claimed to be her late friend Gloria Payne's grandson."

"That's despicable." Her eyes narrowed and she knew the freckles across the bridge of her nose stood out. They always looked more prominent when she became angry. "Taking advantage of an elderly woman's failing memory."

"Ruby told me he's staying at The Benedict Arnold Bed and Breakfast here in Pittsfield."

"Sounds appropriate. Can we go see him?"

"Now you're reading my mind." Grady flashed her a smile and the dimples in his cheeks made him look like a young Cary Grant. Coupled with her tiredness, the image nearly made her swoon.

"You mean, we can talk to him?" Her voice rose in excitement. "Maybe I can convince him to clear my name. If he'd admit I'm not Natasha Brent then the charges against me could be dropped today." For the first time since her arrest, Natalie felt a glimmer of hope.

"I think we should go see him and make an appeal," Grady said. "And while I don't know how cooperative he'll be, it's definitely worth a try."

Her hand squeezed his arm resting on the door. "Then what are we waiting for?" she asked. Surprise filled her at the solidness she felt. Who would have guessed the muscles his shirt hid? "Hop in and I'll drive." The blisters on her feet throbbed. This time if something went wrong, Grady would have to hobble across town to his car, not her.

Grady sat back and watched as she weaved the little car in and out of traffic. Natalie bit back a smile when he gripped the arm rest until his knuckles turned white.

"We don't have to set a speed record in getting there."

"I'll have you know I'm driving exactly the speed limit. Thank you very much."

"Okay." Grady held his hands up in mock surrender. "Just remember if you crash and die, everyone will think you're guilty of elder fraud. Stacey will be convinced she was right and you had plans to swindle your Gran next."

"That's low." She took her foot off the accelerator and the car slowed down. "Now I'll be scared to drive anywhere until my name is cleared."

"Lucky for you, we're here and there is a parking spot right out front." The second the car stopped Grady opened the door and unfolded his long legs.

She bit back a giggle. His knees had practically been under his chin. Once Natalie locked the car, they walked inside the bed and breakfast and stopped at the front desk.

"I'm an old friend of Jason Whitfield's. Can you tell me what room he's in?" Grady asked the middle-aged woman standing behind the counter.

"Sorry sir, I can't give you that information," the woman winked, "but I can tell you he's sitting outside on the verandah."

"Thanks."

They walked through the oversized living room where various guests sat reading or working on their laptops, then exited outside via the garden doors. The large verandah ran the length of the house and looked out over the wooded grounds. The view was breathtaking.

Natalie spotted Jimmy, aka Jason, and marched straight to his table, pulled out a chair, and sat down. "Much nicer accommodations than what we were treated to by the citizens of Pittsfield last night."

"Darling, I've been so worried." Jimmy squeezed her hand tight then released it. "They refused to let me see you."

"Funny," Grady flipped a chair around and straddled it. "When your attorney and I spoke, he failed to mention that."

"Attorney-client privilege. I hope neither of you were violating such a sacred oath." Jimmy turned and smiled at Natalie.

Yesterday afternoon, she had found his smile disarming. Had almost pinched herself over the notion that he could possibly be shining it on her. Now that same smile made her think of what a cobra would look like if it smiled before striking its prey. Sitting beside Grady, it was apparent Jimmy was a man without substance. How could she have been so blind? Had she let the lure of the money she thought he had blind her to his true nature?

"I believe you." She forced herself to rest her hand on his arm and look at him earnestly. "No doubt last night was a mistake. Detective Henderson made hash of the entire situation and arrested us when he shouldn't have." Memories of last night flooded her mind and tears filled her eyes. "I'd never spent the night in jail. It was, well, devastating. Something I never want to repeat."

He patted her hand and she could read the condescension in

his eyes. "And I hope you never have to."

"Will you help me?" Natalie felt like a beggar and she didn't like the feeling one bit. "You can clear everything up in a matter of minutes."

Jimmy arched one eyebrow in question.

"Tell them I'm not Natasha Brent. Explain to them we had never met before yesterday afternoon. If you do, they'll drop the charges against me."

"I can't perjure myself just to save you." He reached over and moved her hand off his arm. "Really, darling, I'm shocked you would ask me to do such a thing." He laughed and the sound felt evil as it danced to her ears. "You are Natasha Brent. I've already explained that to Detective Henderson and my attorney."

"You and I both know that's a lie. Why are you doing this to me?" Natalie jumped to her feet. "Why did you single me out to send to prison for a crime I didn't commit. A horrible act I'd never contemplate doing." Her voice had risen and numerous other guests stared at her in shock. Some even had their cell phones out, taking photos. Humiliated, tears spilled down her cheeks and she covered her face in shame. Inside she still felt like the eight-year-old little girl no one cared about. As a child, she'd often prayed she could just disappear—just cease to exist. Meeting Gran had changed all that. Or so she'd thought. The feelings hadn't gone away. She'd suppressed them. Meeting Jimmy White brought those painful emotions back with a vengeance. A strong, comforting weight settled around her shoulders and pulled her close. Grady. The bunched muscles in her neck and back relaxed. She rested her head against his chest as he led her through the bed and breakfast and outside to her car, every eye in the place on them.

*

ANGER FILLED GRADY at Jimmy's words. Natalie looked broken and ready to retreat into herself. He refused to let that happen. *I believe you sent me to her for a reason, Lord. I vow to do whatever it takes to clear her name. Only You can restore her spirit, but let me be Your instrument. Use me as You deem fit. But I've got to warn You, I may be in trouble here, because I think I'm beginning to care too much about this woman.*

He opened the car door and helped her inside. Eyes squeezed tight, she faced straight ahead. "Why is he doing this to me? Why won't he admit I'm not Natasha?" she asked.

"Jimmy and Natasha have been partners in these scams for years. My guess is he's trying to keep everyone focused on you and give her time to escape. And he is trying to scare you, Natalie. Don't let him do it. I give you my word, I'll find another way to clear your name."

She turned to him, her brown eyes dark and murky, filled with fear and a glimmer of hope. "Do you think you can? Even without Jimmy White's help?"

"Hey, I'm Superman in the court room. Just wait until you see me in my cape." A slight smile tugged at her lips. "Now sit tight. I need to run back inside, but I'll be back before you have time to miss me."

"Promise, you'll come back?"

Grady held up three fingers. "Scout's honor." He longed to lean in and kiss her forehead. He didn't. No doubt Jimmy White watched and he refused to give the man any excuse to have him removed from representing Natalie in this case.

He shut the car door, resisting the urge to slam it, and marched back inside the Benedict Arnold. Fitting place for a man like White to stay. Benedict Arnold had been a traitor in the Revolutionary War. Jimmy White was a traitor to all that was decent and good in men. The thought of him setting Natalie up to take the fall for a crime she hadn't committed fueled him across the verandah. He pulled a chair out across from Jimmy and eased his six-foot three-inch frame into the seat.

"Thought you had left."

Grady ignored him and stared straight ahead. A young couple chased their little boy across the grounds. "You and I both know Natalie is innocent." He held up a hand when Jimmy started to speak. "The way I see this, you have two options. You can come clean and clear her name now or I can gather the evidence that will clear her. One way or another, she will go free and you'll pay for your crimes. If you come clean, I'll ask the judge to take that into account. You'll receive a lighter sentence. If you refuse and drag this case out, let's just say I'll make sure additional charges are filed."

"Better men than you have tried to bluff me." Jimmy sounded bored. "It's never worked before and it won't work now."

Grady stood, slid the chair under the table, and leaned down. "One difference between me and those men…I'm not bluffing." He strode out of the Benedict Arnold without looking back.

Chapter Five

GRADY DROVE NATALIE back to where they'd left his car. When he pulled into the lot, he turned the engine off and shifted in the sardine can she called a car until he faced her seat. She hadn't uttered a word since they'd driven away from the Benedict Arnold.

The afternoon sun glinted off her red hair reminding him of the sweetness of summer strawberries. But he knew this wasn't a typical Saturday for her. The dullness in her brown eyes and pallor of her skin beneath the smattering of freckles worried him. Earlier she'd seemed like such a spitfire—now she seemed defeated. Almost in shock.

He reached over and took her hand in his. "Natalie."

No response.

"Natalie." He jiggled her hand until she looked at him. "This isn't over."

"I'm beginning to think it will never be over."

The hopelessness in her voice tugged at his protective instincts—as a man not an attorney. Natalie Bishop was the kind of woman he could fall for. Hard. Whoa! Where had that thought come from? He had seen her five-year plan and there was nothing in his lifestyle that fit with her plans. He needed to defend his heart from the woman in front of him before it was too late.

"This hasn't been a normal weekend. Go home, get some rest and we can discuss your case again Monday." He forced himself to release her hand. "I promise you, nothing is going to change dramatically between now and then."

"Monday!"

Grady had to fight the urge to cover his ears at her shriek.

"I have to be at work. There's no way I can meet with you."

Her brown eyes snapped wide open. They resembled double shots of espresso. Right now, Natalie Bishop looked wired enough to fly through the roof. One of the first things he'd learned as an attorney was how to calm his clients.

"Gotcha, then how about tomorrow afternoon I'll meet you at your house at two o'clock?"

Tension flowed from her body and she visibly relaxed. "That would be perfect. Let me write my address down for you."

"No need." Grady pushed the car door open and stretched his long legs. "It is in your file and I'm familiar with Sheffield. A buddy of mine from college lives there. See you at two tomorrow." He hurried over to his car, climbed in, and left before she had a chance to change her mind.

*

NORMALLY, GRADY REFUSED to work on Sunday. It was the one day of the week he allowed himself for rest. But truth be told, this didn't seem like work, he looked forward to sparring with Natalie again. The drive from Pittsfield to Sheffield passed quickly. Grady turned the car's radio up loud and sang along to the music.

When he took the turn onto Depot Square that would take him through the small town, he turned the volume down and doubts began to niggle at his consciousness. What if Natalie didn't like the plan he had devised? How would she react when he told her Jimmy White had jumped bail without clearing her name? *Father, help me to find the right words to tell her. The right way to tell her without crushing her spirit.*

He should have been praying all the way here. Not waiting until he was practically standing on her doorstep. Grady made the turn onto the Berkshire School Road, and slowed to a crawl until he reached Daphne Drive.

Nice neighborhood for a struggling law student. He topped

the hill and stared at 14804. Although the house was smaller than the other homes on the street, it was well maintained and had a huge lot brimming with flowers. Home prices in Sheffield weren't cheap. Suspicion worked its way into his mind. How could she afford a historic house on Daphne Drive?

Natalie claimed to be a struggling law student. She also claimed to be alone in the world. Her claims and her lifestyle weren't adding up. Grady pulled the car to the side of the road and whipped out his cell.

"Hey buddy, I need a favor," he said when Jack answered.

"Name it and it's yours, with the exception of Libby. Then you're out of luck."

He took a deep breath and spit it out in a single question. "Is Natalie Benton legit or does the family worry about her relationship with Ellie?"

"Ellie told us what happened to Natalie." Jack's tone turned serious. "I'm glad you're representing her. If it were anyone else but you, the family would be hiring a lawyer regardless of how much Natalie protested. To answer your question, she's on the up and up. Gran, as she calls Ellie, means everything to her. Nat would never take advantage of her. Anything else you need to know?"

"That covers it. Catch you later, bro." Grady disconnected the call and stared at his phone. He didn't know how Natalie managed to afford the house, but that really wasn't any of his business. What he had learned was more important. Natalie Benton could be trusted and inspired loyalty from some pretty impressive people.

*

NATALIE PULLED HER tiny compact car under the carport next to her cottage. The trip to the market had taken longer than expected, but since Grady had volunteered to work on Sunday to help her out, she intended to feed him well. Still, rushed or not, she never came home without taking a moment to thank God for blessing her with a home. After ten years in foster care, owning her own home never failed to thrill her heart. She loved her old house. To save money she had even painted a great deal of the two-story, white frame house with its colonial blue shutters and front door herself.

She hauled her two small bags of groceries inside the house and hurried into the kitchen. Once she had the fresh rainbow trout safely in the refrigerator, she gravitated toward the blue and white chintz-covered window seat. It was her favorite spot in the house. She kicked off her turquoise blue flip flops, propped her back against one of the thick pillows, and looked out the massive window to her front garden. Pink coneflowers and yellow coreopsis danced in the afternoon breeze. Her aunt had spent a fortune on landscaping, but never maintained any of it. When Natalie moved into the house, she'd spent countless backbreaking hours restoring the gardens. It had been worth it, even if she did sport a few hundred new freckles.

Grady certainly didn't have any freckles. Whoops! She'd better check that line of thought. She fanned her face with her hand, trying to tamp down the heat flooding her face. Still, he appeared to be an outdoorsy kind of guy, maybe they would eat al fresco.

A few minutes later he pulled into the drive. Natalie debated between running to the door and staying put. She may have been watching for him out the window, but she didn't want him to know that. So she forced herself to stay planted in the window seat until he knocked on the door. Then she very slowly stood and walked to the front door.

"Hey, Grady, any news?"

"Jimmy White jumped bail last night. The police have an APB out but haven't found him."

The news threatened to shatter Natalie's confidence until she remembered a verse from this morning's sermon. *Now faith is the substance of things hoped for, the evidence of things not seen.* The news sounded bad, but her faith rested with God, not Jimmy White.

"So what's your next move, Counselor?" She cocked an eyebrow and waved him inside.

"I like the way you're thinking ahead instead of letting the news bother you," he said.

Even in the midst of the severity of the situation, Natalie had to chuckle. Grady looked ridiculous. The black leather briefcase looked like a visual oxymoron with his navy shorts and green and navy striped polo shirt. Obviously he worked out on a regular basis. His arms and legs were muscular and tanned.

"What?"

"Sorry, the briefcase just doesn't go with the shorts."

Merriment twinkled in his blue eyes. "Drat. I planned to try it the next time I went to court."

"Yeah, let me know how that works for you." She waved him into the living room. "Pick whatever spot works best for you."

Grady sat on the sofa and placed his briefcase on the coffee table. He flipped it open and withdrew two folders.

Natalie settled into the armchair next to the sofa and waited. After what seemed an eternity, Grady handed her one of the folders. She opened the notebook and scanned the list of names.

"I don't understand." Confused she looked from the paper to Grady. "Who are all these people? I don't recognize a single name on this page."

A self-satisfied smile spread across his face. "That is precisely what I had hoped you would say. Those people," he pointed to the list, "are all individuals that Natasha Benton scammed. My plan, if you agree, is for us to talk to the clients. We need to find someone willing to swear you are not the woman who swindled them out of their hard-earned money." Grady ran a hand through his hair. "The problem is, you're running a risk. Someone could look at you and swear you are Natasha. You're dancing on a two-edged sword. My recommendation is for you to talk to Mr. Montgomery and get a notarized statement of employment from him."

A part of Natalie wanted to take the easy road and talk to her boss. She knew he would provide her with proof of employment during the months the Chicago scam had taken place. But if she did, she would never land one of the coveted internships with the firm. If Jimmy and one of the people on the listed identified her as Natasha Brent, she wouldn't stand a chance. On the other hand, she knew she was innocent so she went with her gut.

"It's a risk I'm willing to take."

Chapter Six

GRADY PULLED HIS Mustang to a stop in front of a huge, three-story sprawling colonial. He turned to glance at Natalie. Her hands gripped the strap of her purse so tight he feared she might snap it off. When he had told her to dress demure he never expected her to end up looking so young. With her red hair left straight and loose, minimal makeup, a cotton fit and flare dress in pale blue, and matching shoes, she looked like a sixteen-year-old.

"You ready?"

She took a deep breath and exhaled. "I'm ready."

Grady walked to her side of the car and opened the door. He took her soft hand in his and helped her from the car. The scent of vanilla and strawberries wafted from her hair and he forced himself to turn his head rather than bury his face in her gorgeous hair and inhale the fragrance he had come to associate with her.

"Tim and Jessica Lockhart, like everyone we'll be meeting today, have agreed to talk to us." He shut the car door behind her. "Try not to look so scared. And whatever you do, don't answer to the name Natasha."

Her brown eyes snapped upward in surprise. They resembled those of a hunted doe. For the hundredth time, he questioned the wisdom of what they were doing. Still, just one sworn statement would be enough to cause reasonable doubt in the eyes of a jury or judge. It might even be enough to get the charges dropped. Once he had such a statement he planned to visit the district attorney's office and reason with the prosecutor on this case.

"Takes them forever to answer the door."

"It might help if we actually rang the doorbell." Natalie leaned forward and pushed the button.

Before he could come up with a retort, the door opened.

"Mr. Lockhart, I'm Grady Hunter." He shook hands with the older gentleman.

"Come in. My wife's in the Florida room." The octogenarian hobbled down the hall. "She'll need to take a look at the girl. My eyesight isn't what it used to be."

Grady felt Natalie grip his hand. He gave her fingers a reassuring squeeze before guiding her into the Florida room.

"Jessica, can you tell if this is the lady?" Mr. Lockhart asked.

"Oh, dear, let me get a closer look." She walked around Natalie, holding a magnifying glass. Stopping from time to time to peer at a different feature. Finally she stepped back and looked at Grady, totally dismissing Natalie "I simply don't know. There's something not quite right. I don't think it is the same woman, yet the resemblance is remarkable. I simply can't be certain either way."

Natalie's head dropped and Grady longed to take her in his arms and comfort her. Instead he said, "Thank you both for meeting with us. We won't take up anymore of your time. However, if you remember anything else, don't hesitate to call me." He handed them each one of his business cards.

"Okay, that was a bust," Natalie said the instant he slid into the car and shut the door.

"True, but we knew it was a possibility." He shot her a smile. "Just be thankful they didn't see you and scream *that's her, that's the little tart that stole our money.*"

"Now I feel so much better." Natalie couldn't contain her laughter. "Oh, I hope that doesn't happen."

"Nah, stick with me, kid." Grady stretched out his hand and smiled when Natalie took it. "I'll keep you safe."

*

NATALIE FELT SAFE with her hand resting in Grady's. More

secure than she did with a full bank account. Gran told her time and again not to put her trust in money. That it could be taken from you in a second. But then Gran had a family who loved her. She didn't understand the devastation of being eight and discovering you were such a horrible daughter that your mother wanted to get rid of you. Or of being eighteen and learning that you had an aunt who knew you existed, knew what had happened to you, but you were such a burdensome child she chose to leave you in foster care and die alone rather than have you beside her. These life lessons had taught her to take care of herself and not to trust others. Thankfully, she had met Jesus and realized she could trust Him.

Gran had been brought into her life by God. Of that Natalie had no doubt. Thanks to God's blessing, she now had a Gran and two women who treated her as a cousin. Still, to be on the safe side, she made sure to never ask them for anything. She refused to ever be in a position where someone could claim she had used them. That's what made this entire Natasha business so surreal. She was being accused of being the one thing she vowed, strived, and swore to never be.

"Earth to Natalie."

"What? Sorry, I was thinking."

"They must have been sad thoughts. Care to tell me about them?" Grady asked.

She pulled her hand from his and reached for her purse. "Nothing important. Are we almost to house number two?"

Tempted to squirm under Grady's stare, she forced herself to sit still until the light turned green. Grady made a right turn into a well-established neighborhood.

"About two minutes away."

Thank You, Lord. The man was far too intuitive for her peace of mind. Any longer than two minutes and she would be blabbing her entire life story to him. The second the car pulled to a stop, she exited the sports car and strode up the walkway. When he reached her side, she pushed the doorbell. Five minutes later, they left the house empty-handed. The Smiths also claimed they couldn't be certain she wasn't Natasha Brent.

By the time she left the sixth house, her shoulders slumped in defeat, her head ached, and her stomach let out a loud growl.

"Sorry." Too exhausted to even be embarrassed, she continued. "This morning I was too nervous to eat breakfast." Natalie leaned her head back against the headrest. "How many more of these appointments do we have today?"

"None."

Startled, her eyes popped open and she turned to faced Grady. "What? That's it? I know there were more than six names on that list. Did all the others refuse to meet with us?" She spit the questions out in rapid succession without giving him time to answer.

He held his hands up and made a T. "Timeout."

"Sorry." Natalie could feel heat creeping up her neck and leaned forward in the hopes her red hair would hide her red face.

"I hoped today would take longer than it did, so I only scheduled six appointments. There are plenty more names on the list to try."

Relief flooded Natalie and washed away the flaming heat from her skin. "I'm exhausted and ravenous. If you don't mind dropping me off at my car, I'll grab a bite to eat and we can talk later."

"I've got a better idea," Grady said. "There's a deli on the corner. We can stop there for lunch, pick some more names off the list, and I'll start making calls."

"Considering there's actually an empty parking spot in front of the deli, I'd say it sounds like a perfect plan." Natalie unhooked her seatbelt the second he turned the engine off. "My treat."

"No. My idea, my treat." He hit the lock button on the key. "I may be a lowly public defender who would never make the cut for your five-year plan, but I can afford a meal out now and then."

"I never meant to infer you couldn't." Even as she made the denial, Natalie realized she had treated him as a poor man. She stopped dead in her tracks. "What's your obsession with my five-year plan anyway?"

"Two years ago, I was engaged. Audrey saw my time as a public defender as a means to an end. I would put in my time, build a good win-rate, and then move on to private practice."

"What happened?" Natalie didn't want to ask. Had a feeling she knew. But the words came out anyway.

"When she discovered I intended to make a career as a public defender, she ditched me. Something about me made her a little nervous, so even though Audrey claimed to love me, it seems she had another man on the side. Jeffrey had more ambition and a healthy family bank account. Six months after we broke up, she married him in the society wedding of the year.

Words escaped her. The woman had been a fool, but how could she tell him that when she had exhibited the very same behavior? Gran had told her more than once that her five-year plan was a waste of paper and displeasing to God. Could she be right? She pushed the disturbing thought to the back of her mind and walked into the deli.

The deli boasted a black and white checkerboard floor, white beadboard halfway up the wall, with the top half painted red. The tables sported chrome legs with black tops and the chairs were chrome and red. The ambiance reminded her of a fifties diner.

Once in line, she turned to face him and blurted out the words on the tip of her tongue. "Please, tell me I didn't come off sounding like a social-climbing moneygrubber."

"My momma always told me if I couldn't say something nice, then not to say anything at all." Grady sent her a saucy wink.

Since he seemed determined to lighten the mood, she followed his lead. "Just for that, I'm ordering the most expensive thing on the menu and letting you pay for it." She shot him a smile and scanned the menu.

Grady read over her shoulder for a few minutes and then leaned down to whisper in her ear. His warm breath sent a shiver down her spine.

"Looks like my wallet is safe here. Too bad White didn't take you to a place like this, then you wouldn't have been out so much money."

Natalie turned to face him, their faces scant inches apart. "Oh, you are so wicked. You'll definitely pay for that barb, Counselor."

"May I take your order?" The man behind the counter asked.

"Yes, I'll have the barbequed grilled salmon sandwich with a side salad, iced tea, and the fresh fruit plate."

"Anything else, miss?" The man asked. "Would you like a slice of cheesecake perhaps?"

"Ah, no, I think I'll pass on the cheesecake."

"I'll have the same," Grady paid their tab and they selected a corner table.

"How many people refused to see me?" She held her hand out. "Come on, hand over the list."

"Only one person and he refused to file charges. Neither he nor his family want their name made public." Grady handed her a folded sheet of paper. "They claim the hundred thousand they lost is inconsequential."

"Who thinks a hundred grand is nothing?" She slumped back against her seat.

Before Grady could answer, the server stopped at their table. They waited while he placed their food before them.

"Can I get you anything else?"

They both shook their heads and the waiter left.

She stared at the table full of food and didn't know if she could choke down a single bite. Five minutes ago she had been joking with Grady—now tears burned the back of her eyes. If this case wasn't settled soon, she wouldn't have a single steady nerve left. "Should we just work our way down the page?" She reached for her flatware and it clattered to the floor.

Chapter Seven

THE WAITER HURRIED over with another set of flatware. As soon as he left, Grady reached across the table for her hand. Her delicate fingers trembled beneath his.

"Why don't I ask God's blessing on our meal?"

He waited until she bowed her head. "Father God, we ask your blessing on this food and thank you for our abundance. And we pray for wisdom to settle this case swiftly and for justice to prevail. In Jesus name, amen."

Grady tucked into his food with gusto, hoping Natalie would follow suit. The barbequed salmon melted in his mouth. In five minutes, he'd downed half the sandwich. He looked up to find her staring at him with a slight smile on her face.

"This thing," he tilted the other half of his sandwich her way, "is amazing. Try yours." He noticed she hadn't touched her sandwich. Instead she played with her side salad. Now and then she forced herself to swallow a bite of lettuce or a cucumber.

Natalie picked up her sandwich and bit into it. The delight on her face kicked his heart rate into overdrive.

"It's incredible."

They finished their sandwiches in companionable silence. While they ate their fruit, Grady was happy to see Natalie looked more like her normal self. He needed to get this case cleared up fast. The stress it was putting her under disturbed him.

"I have a plan."

The bite of cantaloupe halfway to her mouth hit the plate. "Spill it."

"Do you remember the man I mentioned that lives in Chicago?" he asked.

"I already told you I'm not involving the law firm in this mess. My employers wouldn't appreciate it." She crossed her arms in front of her chest defensively.

"It would make things much easier if you would. But this doesn't involve your employer. I want you to call your office and ask for the rest of the week off—vacation time."

"Vacation time? Why? I can't afford a vacation!"

"I'm not suggesting you take a vacation." Her cheeks flamed as bright as her hair and he bit back a grin. "But I do want you to fly to Chicago with me. We're going to pay a visit to Mr. Samuel Hutchinson and have him sign an affidavit that you are not the young woman who scammed him."

"What's the point?" She blinked back the tears threatening to overflow. "We tried all morning to get someone to say I wasn't Natasha. The woman must be my doppelganger. No one seems to be able to tell us apart. Going to Chicago is just a waste of money that neither of us has."

"Natalie, two things are really starting to bug me. One—I'm well and truly sick of you talking like I don't have a dime to my name. I'm not a pauper. Two—your lack of faith in me. After this morning, I can make an allowance for that. But I've already spoken to Samuel and he remembers exactly what Natasha looks like. He even managed to snag a picture of her. He told me she reminded him of his late wife when they first met."

"Then why didn't we start with him?"

"I assumed if he was so positive one of the people in Pittsfield would be as well. My mistake." He ran his hand through his close-cropped hair. "I was trying to be economical."

"Whatever your reasons, I'm just jazzed this thing is about over. Can we leave tonight?"

"Whoa." He held up a hand. "Slow down. Not tonight. I need to call Mr. Hutchinson and see when he can meet with us and you need to see if you can take time off work. Also, I need to clear it with the district attorney. The last thing we want is for you to be accused of jumping bail."

"Time off work shouldn't be a problem. Just last week, Mrs. Lindstrom, my immediate supervisor, mentioned my vacation days were piling up." She looked straight at him. "You call Mr. Hutchinson, then I'll call my office."

Grady whipped out his cell phone and placed the call. "Sir, this is Grady Hunter from Pittsfield, Massachusetts. We spoke the other day." He listened to the older gentleman talk. "Yes, it does look like we are going to need your assistance. If I bring my client to meet you, will you be able to determine whether or not she is Natasha Brent?"

He couldn't hold back the smile spreading over his face. "Yes, a copy of the photo would be excellent to have as evidence. What day would be convenient for you?"

He gave Natalie a thumbs-up. "That's perfect. We'll be there in time for dinner Wednesday evening. Thank you for your help, sir." Grady disconnected the call.

"I think you'd better call your office and ask for that time off work." Grady downed the last of his iced tea before continuing. "Mr. Hutchinson has volunteered to help us any way he can."

She stood and gathered their trash. "I'll go make the call now. I want my name cleared."

"I'll drive you back to your car. Once your time off work is approved, I'll contact the district attorney and then make the travel arrangements. Later tonight I'll email you our travel plans and itinerary."

*

THEY ARRIVED IN Chicago late Wednesday afternoon. Natalie wished they could drive straight from the airport to his house. As irrational as it was, she wanted to storm into his home and demand he confirm then and there that she wasn't Natasha Bishop. Good grief, how did the woman work these scams nonstop? Just trying to find one person who could clear her name had turned Natalie into a bowl of Jell-O."

They pulled into the hotel parking lot. "You stay here while I get us checked into our rooms. We have reservations so I should be back in a minute," Grady said. "Oh, and leave the car running. I had no idea it was so humid in Chicago."

"Tell me about it." She fanned her face with a brochure she'd picked up at the airport. "Even with the air going full blast, I feel like I'm melting."

She could hear Grady's laughter as he slammed the car door shut. He returned to the car in five minutes and unloaded their small bags. "Go on inside and I'll park the car. Trust me, you'll love it. The place is freezing."

Natalie practically ran from the car to the hotel. The second the cold air hit her, a smile of joy lit her face. She walked to one of the chairs in the lobby and sank down in relief. A few minutes later Grady waltzed in, rolling their suitcases behind him. He stopped beside her.

"Come on lazybones. You can rest in your room while I call Samuel Hutchinson and confirm our dinner meeting."

She pushed herself out of the chair and followed Grady to the elevator. "What time are we meeting him? And where?"

"Six for dinner at an Italian place on the Magnificent Mile." He glanced at his watch. "That should give us about two hours to rest before we need to leave."

They stepped off the elevator and walked the short distance to their rooms. Grady slid the keycard into the lock and pushed the door open. Natalie grabbed her suitcase and rolled it inside. She shifted from foot to foot. "Well, uh, I think I'll take a nap until it's time to get ready for dinner."

The door closed and she leaned back against it. She couldn't believe she'd travelled from Massachusetts to Chicago with Grady Hunter. The line between her gratitude for his work as her attorney and her growing feelings for him as a man were starting to blur.

The thought scared her and she pushed away from the door. The small suitcase fit on the luggage rack easily, and she started unpacking. Grady was a Harvard graduate who worked as a public defender and had no desire to venture into private practice. And she needed a man with enough motivation to comfortably support a family. Her children would never endure the kind of childhood she had.

*

GRADY PARKED HIS suitcase inside his room and loosened his tie before removing his suit jacket. He looked at the bed and decided to take a short nap before calling Mr. Hutchinson. He'd enjoyed the plane ride. Truth be told, what he had enjoyed was Natalie's company.

Her five-year plan flashed through his mind. He didn't fit anywhere in that plan and more importantly, he didn't want to. Yet every time he prayed about Natalie he felt as if God was leading him to spend more time with her. He rolled to his side, "God, I don't get it but I'm trusting you. Because even after telling her about Audrey, she doesn't seem willing to let go of that ridiculous plan."

An hour later his alarm went off. He grabbed his cell phone and called Samuel Hutchinson. The phone rang and rang, but no one answered. He disconnected and tried again. Same response.

He tossed the phone down and decided to freshen up before making a third call. He hoped the old guy hadn't developed cold feet. A lot of men his age were embarrassed to admit they'd been scammed by a younger woman. He grabbed his key and left the room. Natalie's room was down the hall. He rapped his knuckles against the door.

A couple of seconds later, she opened the door. He sucked in a sharp breath and almost forgot to exhale. He would never think of brown as drab again. The soft looking fabric matched her eyes and served as the perfect foil for her red hair. His gaze travelled over her until he reached her feet—impossibly high heels in a leopard print. The shoes made him smile.

"You look phenomenal." His voice sounded husky and he cleared his throat. "Do you mind if I come in and try Mr. Hutchinson. I haven't been able to reach him by phone."

"Oh, I hope everything is okay."

Grady wanted to ease the worried look on her face. Rub his finger over the worry line between her brows, but he didn't have that right. "He probably didn't have his phone handy or he could have left it on silent. I'll try again."

The phone rang three times before it was answered.

"Mr. Hunter," a woman said. "This is Sylvia Thompson. I believe you were supposed to meet with my father tonight."

"Yes, Ms. Thompson. Is everything okay?" Grady glanced towards Natalie. She looked as worried as he felt. He shrugged and waited for a reply.

"My father had a heart attack today. He's in the Cardiac Care Unit recovering from bypass surgery." She took a deep breath. "I'm sorry, but he isn't up to proceeding with this matter right now."

"Are you sure? I can guarantee you I'll be mindful of his health." He waited while she answered. "No, I understand. Please have him contact me when he feels better," Grady said.

He turned to face Natalie. The disappointment etched on her face left him feeling as if he'd failed her. She'd been counting on this—counting on him—to clear her name.

"I'm sorry, Natalie, but Mr. Hutchinson had a heart attack and bypass surgery. He is in CCU and his daughter thinks talking about the scam right now could jeopardize his health."

Chapter Eight

THURSDAY AFTERNOON NATALIE sat on her patio overlooking the garden and for the first time since she had moved into the house, could find no peace in the beauty of the flowers or the graceful swimming of the koi in the pond. There were four days until she had to return to work—four long days in which she should be enjoying her freedom.

Instead she felt antsy. She needed something, anything, to occupy her mind. She could putter in her garden, paint her utility room, or start that legal thriller she'd always wanted to write. Write! Without giving herself a chance to reason it away, she jumped up, ran into the house, grabbed her laptop, and raced back to the patio. She took a deep breath and began typing.

Buzz. Buzz. Buzz. Her phone danced on the bistro table where she set working. She grabbed it off the table, disgruntled by the interruption. A quick look at her watch showed that three hours had passed. She had been dreaming of this book so long that the words had flowed effortlessly. The caller ID displayed Grady's name.

"Grady, any news from Mr. Hutchinson?" She reread the last sentence she had typed.

"Is it okay if I drop by? I need to go over some details with you."

"Sure, just tell me what time." Drat, she didn't want to quit writing, but if she confessed that to her attorney, he might decide to let her have plenty of writing time—in jail.

"Well, I'd banked on your agreement, so I'm already on my way. I should be there in fifteen minutes," he said.

"Sounds serious. I'll see you then." After she disconnected the call, she forced herself to shut down her computer. She carried it inside, ran a brush through her hair and arranged it in a messy bun, then freshened her lipstick. Why had Grady wanted to meet today and why had he waited until he had almost reached Sheffield to call her? The questions racing through her mind worried her. Whatever it was, it couldn't be good news. She dropped her head and prayed.

Five minutes later, the doorbell rang and Natalie yanked it open. The look on his face didn't reassure her. His brow was wrinkled and his hair disheveled from where he'd ran his hand through it. His blue eyes looked as stormy as the ocean before a gale.

She led him outside to the bistro table where she'd been happily working earlier. "So, spill it. What's going on with my case that made you want to meet this fast?" she asked.

"They picked Jimmy White up this morning in New Hampshire. He waved extradition. The district attorney set a trial date for two weeks out. Since they set a date for his trial, I'm expecting word on yours." He cleared his throat and continued. "I'll try and delay for as long as possible. I should be able to get a postponement until Mr. Hutchinson recovers, but there's no way Mr. Montgomery and the other partners at the law firm won't find out."

He reached across the table and covered her hand with his. "Also, I don't think Jimmy's case will go to trial. A friend of mine in the district attorney's office expects him to cop a plea bargain.

She snatched her hand out from under the comfort of his. "You aren't suggesting I do the same, are you?" Without giving him a chance to answer, she plowed forward. "I'm not guilty. Why would I admit to anything?"

"Whoa, Natalie, I'm not suggesting any such thing." He looked straight into her eyes. "I know you're innocent. But at this point, I really think you have no choice except to get a statement from Mr. Montgomery."

The words were like a pin hole in her balloon of righteous

anger. Grady believed her. No proof. Her word. And it was enough.

Tears clogged her throat and she fought hard to keep them at bay. "I need some time to process everything." She stood and turned away from him. "Can you please go, and I'll call you later?"

He walked around the table and placed his strong hands on her shoulders. "You don't have to do this alone."

The soft words waltzed over her wounded soul. And she leaned back against him. The beat of his strong heart echoed in her ears. The fear she'd been carrying since this whole crazy mess started lifted. So this is what it felt like to have someone else help you bear your burdens. Immediately on the heels of that thought came a terrifying one. How bad would she be wounded when Grady walked away from her?

She forced herself to pull free from his embrace. Better a little pain of her own choosing now than the devastation of being abandoned. She'd coped with that once in her life. She didn't think she could live through it a second time. The sound of her flip-flops hitting the flagstone path filled the silence. Grady's muffled steps followed her through the house to the front door where she finally worked up the courage to continue her story.

"I've been handling life alone since I turned eight." She laughed, but there was no merriment in the sound. "My mother gave me a belated birthday present I've never forgotten. She abandoned me."

Grady sucked in a startled breath. "I didn't know. What about your dad?"

"My dad was never in the picture."

"Is this how you meet Ellie?"

"From the ages of eight to eighteen, I lived in nine different foster homes." She turned to face him. "At sixteen, I went to live with Gran and never left. She won me over with her love."

She straightened her back, her heart filled with resolve. "Grady, please leave. I need time by myself to think this through."

"Natalie, don't do this. Don't send me away." The screen

door squeaked when he opened it. "We've got something special. I'm willing to put my heart on the line and I'm asking you to do the same. Forget your five-year plan. Forget the past. Don't push me out of your life."

She didn't have the courage to let go of the past—to trust another human with her future or her heart. "Don't make me ask again, Grady. I told you I need time alone. I'll call you as soon as I've reached a decision." She forced the words to sound harsh. If he didn't leave the house soon, she was going to break down and beg him to stay forever.

His only answer was the slamming of the screen door as it shut behind him.

*

NATALIE COLLAPSED ONTO the sofa and cried harder than she had in her entire life. When Grady's car reversed out of her driveway, it felt like he'd driven over her heart. She cried for the little girl whose mother had never loved her, who had been abandoned at eight, who'd bounced from home to home, the same little girl whose aunt had chosen her career over raising a niece. If it hadn't been for Gran, she would have never known love. Never known what being part of a family felt like. Never have been introduced to her Savior.

Gran. She pushed herself off the sofa, grabbed her cell phone, and called the one human being who had never let her down.

"I hope you're calling to invite me to dinner. Blake has a men's meeting at the church and I'm on my own tonight."

"Oh, Gran…" Sobs overtook her, and Natalie couldn't go on.

"Natalie, what's wrong? Are you home? I'm coming right over." She could hear her Grandmother's key fob beep as she opened the door to her car.

"Wait. I'm okay." Natalie swiped the tears from her face. "I, uh, I just need to talk and you know that's something I do better over the phone than in person."

"Okay, I'm going back in the house and I'm sitting on the floor beside your old bedroom. Now you pretend like you're on the other side of the door and we'll have one of our heart-to-heart talks. Just like when you first came to live with me."

"I drove Grady away tonight." Natalie slid onto the floor and rested her back against her bedroom door. "The game's up. I need to prove my innocence and fast."

"Is Mr. Hutchinson still unable able to talk to you?"

"His daughter says he's too weak. And honestly Gran, I don't want to take a chance on hurting his health."

"I'm proud of you, Nat. I know how scared you are, but you're putting Mr. Hutchinson before yourself. So tell me why you pushed Grady away. Because I think that's the real issue here."

A laugh escaped from Natalie. "You always know how to get right to the heart of an issue. Grady told me I didn't have to do this alone, that he would help." She allowed herself to remember what it felt like, resting in his strength for that short minute. "And it felt so good and I felt safe and cherished."

"You mean you got scared."

"Terrified. What if I give him my heart and he stomps all over it, just like everyone else in my life has done?" A sob escaped her throat. "I don't think I can go there again."

"So instead you're going to spend the rest of your life alone. Sounds like a coward to me."

"Gran!" Stunned Natalie sat straight up. "I can't believe you said that. You, more than anyone, know my story."

"And you know mine. I loved my husband and lost him. Yet I'm willing to try for a second chance at happiness with Blake. We're old, Natalie, Blake or I one are going to go through a lot of pain one day, but I wouldn't trade my time with him to escape being hurt." She could hear her Gran take a deep breath. "And what about me? Tell me when I've ever let you down? Or when Libby, Stephanie, or even Stacey, for that matter, let you down? From the day you landed on my doorstep, I invited you to call me NeNe, just like my other granddaughters. You're the one who refused and made a distinction."

Hot shame coursed through Natalie's blood stream. *God forgive me for my selfishness.* "Never, none of you have ever let me down." She had been given a wonderful family on a silver platter and had been too blind or too stupid to grab it with both hands.

"And we never will. Love doesn't come without risks. I can't promise that Grady won't break your heart. But if you don't take a chance, you'll never know what a glorious life you could have."

"My five-year plan..." Natalie started.

"Please, tell me that man doesn't know anything about that ridiculous plan. And don't even begin to defend it to me one more time. That plan is what will ruin your life," Gran said.

"Not only does he know about it, he has seen it, and," Natalie took a deep breath and rushed on, "I told him he didn't fit anywhere in the plan and he lacked ambition."

The silence on the other end of the line lasted so long she feared Gran had hung up on her. "Gran?"

"Was this before or after he told you that you didn't have to go through this alone?"

Natalie wasn't sure she had ever heard Gran sound so weary. "Before."

"Honey, if that man knows all about your five-year plan and loves you anyway, then you are crazy to turn your back on him. I want you to promise me you'll read Luke 12:18-31. Then pray about it."

"I promise." Natalie swiped away a fresh onslaught of tears. "I love you Gran and I'm sorry for being so stubborn."

"All my granddaughters are stubborn, but I've never given up on any of you. I'm not about to start now."

The call disconnected in her ear and Natalie pulled herself to her feet. She reached for her Bible on the nightstand and flipped to the passage in Luke that Gran had told her to read. Fresh tears fell onto her Bible as she read the passage.

When she finished, Natalie fell to her knees. "Oh, God, forgive me for being like that man and thinking I'll store up enough wealth that I'll be safe. I want to be rich in You, not in possessions."

She stood to her feet with a much lighter heart and knew what she needed to do. In the bathroom, she rinsed her face, applied a quick touch of lipstick, and hurried downstairs to her car. Before this night was over, before her courage failed her, she intended to talk to Grady Hunter.

Chapter Nine

Natalie stood in front of Grady's townhouse door with her hand poised over the doorbell. Her index finger shook as she uttered a final prayer for courage and a plea for a second chance. When she said *amen,* she jabbed the button twice.

"What?" Grady yanked the door open. His beautiful blue eyes were red rimmed. "Natalie, what are you doing here? I thought you didn't want or need my help."

He looked straight at her. Grady wasn't a man to hide his emotions or back away from a challenge. "Grady, I was a fool. I need you and I can't do this without you."

"I'm your lawyer. No matter how things stand between us, I won't step away from your case. I'll make sure your name is cleared. I promised you that and I won't go back on my word."

"Please, I'd rather not have this conversation on your doorstep. Can I come in?" For a moment, she feared he might refuse. His arm blocked the doorway and he looked like he wanted to slam the door in her face.

Finally, he swung the door open wide. "Come in?" He walked across the living room and leaned against the stacked stone fireplace. "Have a seat."

Natalie glanced around the room. It looked like Grady. The townhome was obviously new construction, but had been built in a historic style and he seemed so at home in the space. Family photos lined the mantle, and she saw an older couple who must be his parents, another photo that had to be his sister's family, and one of him with his other sister. She looked maybe a couple of years older than Grady. The last photograph was a group shot of all of them. Their love for each other shone from the prints.

"I thought you had something to say." His words interrupted her musings.

Natalie cleared her throat and plowed forward. "I know you think I never listen to anything you try and tell me. You're wrong, I do. And I know I shouldn't have sent you away tonight. I needed you. I needed your strength and your support." She couldn't bring herself to say love. Not yet. Not when he might still send her away.

"I told you"—his head dipped forward—"I'll make sure your name is cleared."

"The thing is, Grady, that's not what I need you for." Her legs felt like overcooked noodles. Without waiting for an invitation, she sat down on the brown leather sofa. "After you left, I called Gran and we had a talk. Before I came here, I went by the office. Mr. Montgomery hadn't left yet. I explained everything to him, and I do mean everything, that has happened since I met Jimmy White."

Grady strode across the room and dropped down on the sofa beside her and took her hands in his. "You told him about your arrest and the charges. I thought you were afraid you would be fired." The concern in his voice coupled with the warmth of his touch gave her the strength to continue.

"I'm innocent. I decided if I could work for Montgomery, Haynes, and Preston for this long and they would fire me over something that wasn't my fault, well then I didn't want to work for them."

A smile spread across his face and she felt the first glimmer of hope. "I'm proud of you. What did Mr. Montgomery say?"

She held on tight to his hands. "Exactly what you said he would. He told me none of this was my fault and of course they would supply me with an affidavit stating I'd been at work during the timeframe Mr. Hutchinson was scammed in Chicago. In fact, he told me I should have come to him first thing. The firm would have represented me pro bono."

"They'll do an excellent job. I'll send them my files tomorrow," Grady said.

"Oh, no you won't. I told him thank you, but I had a wonderful attorney and he agreed. Mr. Montgomery will have the affidavit delivered to your office tomorrow." She smiled at him. "I'll probably be the one who delivers it. You know I volunteer to run all the errands."

"Once I have the affidavit, I'll petition the district attorney to drop all charges against you. I think he will agree."

"Great, I'll be glad to have this mess behind me." She sent him a megawatt smile. "Will you listen while I tell you another story?"

"Is it relevant?"

"Very."

"Then fire away." He leaned back against the thick sofa cushion.

Her hands felt empty without his wrapped around them. "I'm sure you've had to wonder how I managed to afford my house. Unlike so many people, you've never pried or asked." She tilted her head up and looked him in the eye. "Unless you've checked through legal channels."

"I've been tempted, but no, I never checked." Grady's gaze never wavered. "I decided when you wanted me to know, you would tell me."

"Thank you for that." Her lip trembled and she swallowed before continuing. "I inherited the house from my maternal aunt."

"Wait, I thought you were a foster child for eight years before going to live with Ellie."

"I was. My aunt's name was Kate Gentry. She worked as an executive assistant to the president of a Fortune 500 Company. Apparently, her career dominated her life and left no room for an abandoned eight-year-old girl. DHS contacted her and I'll quote, 'Her mother and I parted ways long ago. I don't have the time nor the inclination to care for the child.'"

"How could she do that? I would never allow one of my

nieces or nephews to end up in foster care instead of living with me." Grady wrapped his arm around her and pulled her close. "She missed out on a wonderful gift by not taking the time to know you."

Natalie rested her head against his strong, broad shoulder. "Maybe out of guilt or maybe she just didn't know what else to do with it, but my aunt left me her house in Sheffield and enough money to pay for my bachelor's degree in her will. If I didn't use the money for education, then I forfeited it. My aunt left me a sense of security but I can tell you, I would much rather have had her love."

She looked up at Grady with all the honesty and love she could muster from within. "I don't want to be like my aunt. Yet I nearly went and did the same thing by creating that insane five-year plan. Gran told me from day one that I was crazy to make such a list. Tonight, she told me to read a passage from Luke 12. It reminded me that my security comes from God, not in how many treasures I can store up on this earth."

"My parents have been married for thirty-eight years and I can tell you their security has always come from God and their family." Grady kissed her temple. "I wish you could have had an extended family like mine. Experienced a childhood playing with sisters and cousins the way I did."

"My family came late in life, but Gran, Libby, Stephanie, and even Stacey became my family, a grandmother and cousins. But Grady, what I really wanted to tell you is I love you."

She held up her hand when he would have spoken. "I love you just the way you are. I admire your public defender work and the fact that you value helping others over money. That you spend your Thursday evenings coaching basketball for underprivileged youth. That you would give anything, do anything, to help your family. To try and change any one of those components would change you." She reached up and traced his brow. "And that's the last thing I'd ever want to do. I fell in love with you the way you are."

Grady leaned forward and kissed her on the forehead.

Warmth spread downward from her forehead to the tips of her fingers. For the first time in her life, she felt cherished.

"Now I have something to tell you." He gave her another kiss on the forehead then leaned back. "Eighteen months ago, my great uncle passed away. My mother had always been his favorite niece and for some reason instead of leaving his money to her, he left it to me. Her only son. Uncle Frank had always been very chauvinistic. It seemed unfair to me that I received such an inheritance while my two sisters received nothing."

"I understand. You could always split the money with them." The solution seemed logical to her and if she had sibling, she would have wanted to do the same.

"Neither of them would take the money. Not because they were angry, but they said the money had been Uncle Frank's to do with what he wanted and he wanted me to have it. So far I haven't done anything with it." Grady shrugged his shoulders. "So you see, I'm really a very wealthy man."

Natalie rested her head against his chest. "But what do you want to do with the money? I can tell you have something in mind."

"You know me too well." Grady laughed. "The place where I volunteer on Thursday evenings is run by a minister friend of mine. Derrick and I went to high school and college together. He's a good man and the work he does makes a huge difference in the lives of dozens of kids. His center's basketball facilities need to be redone. I'd like to renovate the outdoor courts and then I'd like to build a gym with indoor courts, locker rooms, and buy new equipment."

"Then go for it," she said.

"I love you for saying that." He kissed the top of her head. "When my ex-fiancée found out I had inherited money, she tried to win me back. I may have been fooled once, but I wasn't falling for her lies a second time. That's why I had such a bad reaction to your five-year plan."

Grady disentangled himself from Natalie. She felt cold the moment he left her side. Was that stupid five-year plan going to ruin everything? Grady walked out of the room and returned a moment later. He stopped in front of her and bowed down on bended knee. Natalie's heart jumped and landed in her throat.

"I've known since the first day I met you that you were the only woman I wanted to share my life with." He pulled an aqua blue ring box out of his pocket. "When we were in Chicago, I saw this ring in the window at Tiffany's and knew it belonged on your finger." He took a quick breath and rushed on. "Natalie Benton, I love you more than life. Will you marry me? I can provide a secure future for you and our children. And I will always take care of you."

Natalie looked at the beautiful square-cut diamond solitaire surrounded by a row of pink diamonds and then another row of regular diamonds. She had never expected such a beautiful ring, but nothing was as beautiful as the love shining from his eyes.

"Grady Hunter, I love you more than I ever dreamed it would be possible to love another person. I would be honored to be your wife. But my security doesn't rest in your money. My security comes from God's provision first and then your love. I want us to have a marriage like your parents. A marriage like Gran and Blake will have." She held out her trembling hand.

Grady slid the ring onto her finger. It fit perfectly and Natalie knew that their lives were going to fit together just as perfectly.

She reached down and pulled out a frayed slip of paper from her purse. "This is my gift to you. My five-year plan." The sound of paper ripping filled the room. Natalie tossed the pieces in the air like confetti. "Now go build that gym," she said seconds before his lips captured hers in a kiss that promised forever.

A Match Made in Freedom

by

Lisa Belcastro

LISA BELCASTRO LIVES with her family on Martha's Vineyard. She loves time with her family and friends, running, gardening, outdoor activities, cooking, chocolate, reading, traveling, a healthy dose of adventure, and her cat, Ben, who keeps her company while she creates fictional lives for the numerous characters living inside her head.

Lisa runs as an ambassador for TEAM 413 (www.team413.org), and has completed a marathon (26.2 miles) in all fifty states.

Lisa is a member of the Wednesday Writers, and can't thank them enough for all their support, critiques, suggestions, and friendships. Writing is better with: Catherine Finch, Connie Berry, Cynthia Riggs, Janet Messineo-Israel, Linda Guilford, Matthew Fielder, Nancy Woods, and Stephen Caliri.

When she's not at her desk, Lisa is living in paradise, volunteering for Community Services, serving in her church community, planting and weeding her numerous gardens, walking the beach looking for sea glass, or enjoying a great meal while she pens the cuisine column for Vineyard Style Magazine. You can visit Lisa on: **LisaBelcastro.com** and **Facebook**.

Books by Lisa Belcastro

Winds of Change

Shenandoah Nights
Shenandoah Crossings
A Shenandoah Christmas
Shenandoah Dreams
A Shenandoah Family Christmas,
Shenandoah Song (coming Christmas 2017)

Possible Dreams

A Dream for Love
Audition for Love (coming September 2017)

Chapter One

"This Island is too small." Stephanie Gould slammed the door and stormed across the floor of her store and escaped into her private design studio.

A minute later, her shop manager Zoey Pierce peeked in the studio door. "Everything okay, Steph?"

Okay? No, definitely not.

Her emotions swinging from hurt to anger, Stephanie drew in a deep breath. "I stopped in the bakery to pick us up some croissants, and who do I see? Tim and Kay, that's who."

"Oh, wow. I didn't know they were back."

Stephanie, fit and lean in faded jeans and a lavender blouse, paced behind her drying table, eying the four necklaces waiting to be polished before they'd be moved to a showcase in the store. Kay had been wearing a beige dress accented by a stunning sea glass necklace of greens and blues. At least the necklace wasn't one of hers.

"Oh, they're back, all tan and happy from their honeymoon. I was next to order when I heard Tim talking from the back of the line. Two years of dating him, and I'd recognize his voice if I was blindfolded." She'd recognize a lot about him, but she hadn't expected to feel so angry. Or hurt.

"Did he speak to you?"

Stephanie flinched. "Of course. 'Hey, Steph. How you been?' As if he were my friend, as if I wanted to speak with him. Kay just stood there looking smiley and happy, not a visible sign of remorse or a fraction of guilt."

"What can I get you? Tea? Chocolate? A gun and an alibi?" Zoey drew an imaginary gun from her hip and pretended to fire.

Her manager had read one too many crime novels, but the action gave Stephanie a brief chuckle. "I'll leave the guns and revenge to you and your murder mysteries. I had all I could do to walk out without tossing a few choice words at them. I love living on Martha's Vineyard. I wouldn't want to live anywhere else. But sometimes the hundred square miles are not enough."

"I hope you thanked Kay for cheating with your fiancé before you married him. Let Tim cheat on her now that they're living in wedded bliss." Zoey snapped her fingers.

Stephanie knew Zoey was right. Better to find out that Tim was a two-timer before they had a home and children. But the searing pain in her chest wasn't lessened by that knowledge.

Had it really been five months since she'd walked into the crafting studio to find Tim and Kay locked in what was nothing short of a passionate embrace? She hadn't seen that one coming. Kay Salazar had been her partner in From the Sea Designs, and she'd thought they were friends. She'd thought wrong.

In one day, she'd lost her fiancé and her business partner. She didn't want him back, not as her husband or even as a friend, but this morning's meeting revealed there was still pain residing in her heart. Why wasn't healing as easy as the pop songs made it sound?

"Steph?"

"Huh?"

"I said you should get away. Take a vacation. Go to a spa and relax. Get pampered."

"That sounds miserable. What would I do all day?" Frowning at the thought of being subjected to hours of manicures, pedicures, and hair appointments, Stephanie shuddered. She picked up a large piece of green sea glass from the workbench and ran her finger around the smooth edges.

Zoey, blond hair perfectly coiffed and a French manicure on her fingernails, laughed. "Right, I forgot who I was talking to. How about a visit to the Berkshires? You haven't seen JoJo in two months and your family would be overjoyed to have you visit for more than forty-eight hours."

The Berkshires. Childhood memories brought a smile to her face. Western Massachusetts was beautiful in October. Joanne Homlish, or JoJo, her best friend since first grade and her college roommate throughout their years at the Rhode Island School of Design, had been raving about the great fall colors this year. She could help JoJo in the gardens at her bed and breakfast, spend an afternoon or two at the Norman Rockwell Museum, and go running in the mornings around Stockbridge Bowl and the Lily Pond. Stephanie also wanted to spend a little quality time with her grandmother NeNe and cousin Libby, if those two world travelers weren't off jet setting.

Stephanie wasn't one to leave the Island during the perfect fall weather, but a little time away might clear her head and give her a bit of inspiration for the Christmas line she wanted to create.

"Excellent idea, Zoey." Stephanie put the sea glass on the table and walked over to her appointment book. "Can you handle things here? I'll only go for a couple of days, maybe a long weekend."

Her manager waved her off. "Forget a couple of days. Go for a week or two. I've got you covered."

*

TWENTY-FOUR HOURS LATER, Stephanie drove off the *Island Home* ferry, and began the three-hour drive to Stockbridge. She turned up the radio and tuned out her thoughts.

The traffic was light for a Sunday, and hours passed easily. Her cell phone rang while she was belting out TobyMac's "Move (Keep Walkin')," and the hands-free system in her SUV turned off the music and switched to her phone.

"Where are you?" JoJo asked.

"I just passed Exit 3."

"Great. You'll be here for lunch. Want to meet in town at the Red Lion Inn and eat in the Tavern?"

Stephanie's mouth watered as she thought about the Tavern's

Eggs Benedict served on the best buttermilk biscuits north of the Mason-Dixon Line. "You know my weakness. I'll be there in forty-five minutes."

Driving along Route 102, the leaves on the trees defined fall in New England—brilliant reds, burnt oranges, and deep yellows interspersed with forest green pines. They were beautiful. Stephanie rolled down the window and breathed in the crisp fall air. She couldn't wait to go for a run tomorrow morning, which she would undoubtedly need after a hearty lunch and whatever gourmet meal JoJo would serve for dinner.

The parking along Main Street in Stockbridge was bumper to bumper. Stephanie made a left onto Route 7, another left onto Laurel Lane, and then left again onto Elm Street to circle back toward the restaurant. Finally, she saw someone walking toward a truck.

She slowed to a stop and waited for his parking spot. The guy didn't start his engine. She glanced at the clock. A car passed her. What was he doing? Forty-five seconds passed. Couldn't he see her? She pulled up alongside the black pickup, two minutes and counting.

Rolling down the passenger-side window, Stephanie leaned over and waved to get his attention. He was talking on his cell phone. Annoying, but safer than holding the phone, talking, and driving. He glanced over and held up one finger.

A safe driver and good looking. He flashed her a smile. Definitely good looking. With short black hair, kind eyes, full lips, and wearing a jean jacket and flannel shirt, this man had "country boy" written all over him. Except, his posture was formal and there was an air of authority to him as he spoke into the phone. Stephanie couldn't hear a word he said, but he appeared to be in charge of the conversation.

About a minute went by, and Country Boy rolled down his window. "Sorry 'bout that. What can I do for you, ma'am?"

Did he just call her ma'am? She was only twenty-nine years old. Why was a guy who couldn't be much older than she calling her ma'am? She didn't know whether to laugh or be offended.

"I'm looking for a parking spot." Stephanie said, stating the obvious, or so one would think.

"Oh, right. Been a while." His expression was more confused than apologetic.

"No problem. I saw you were on the phone. Are you leaving now?"

"That all depends."

"On?"

He stared at her. "If you'll agree to have dinner with me."

"What?" The word came out harsher than she'd intended. "I don't know who you are. For all I know, you're a serial killer."

He threw his head back and laughed. "My mother would be insulted."

"I doubt your mother would be as upset as mine would be if I turned up dead." Why was she having this conversation?

He opened the door to his truck, stepped out, and reached a hand into her open window. My, oh my, he was one fine looking man. She really should hit the gas pedal, but she'd probably run him over.

"Captain Henry Lewis. Pleased to make your acquaintance."

A police officer. That explained the "ma'am," and his formal tone and stance. Stephanie reached over and shook his hand. "Stephanie Gould. Nice to meet you officer."

"About that dinner. I lost a bet—"

"Ah, not the best pick up line, Captain Lewis."

"Probably not. Let me start again. If I don't have a date by tomorrow night, I have to attend some singles speed dating event this Saturday."

It was Stephanie's turn to laugh. "I've heard a few come-ons in my life, but that one is a first. So tell me, Captain Lewis, how could anyone force you to go to a speed dating thing?"

"As I said, I lost a bet." His matter-of-fact response was devoid of humor and not the least bit amused.

Steph was entertained nonetheless. "You bet someone that you could, or couldn't, get a stranger to go out with you?"

"No. I bet a buddy that I would beat him in last week's 5K

road race. He failed to mention that he'd been training in sprints."

Now she was truly interested. Betting on running, or pretty much anything to do with running, grabbed her attention. "What was his time?"

"20:47"

"And yours?"

"20:53"

"Dang." Steph smacked the steering wheel. "Nice pace. Running less than seven-minute miles. I do my speed workouts on Wednesdays, but I'm not that fast."

"You run?" he asked, appreciation gleaming in his dark brown eyes.

"Five days a week, maybe six or seven." Truth was, she ran outside or worked out on the elliptical seven days a week. It was the best stress reliever on the planet.

"Have dinner with me. Please. If you have a miserable time, you can run home."

Funny, too. But there was no way she was going out with him. "As tempting as that sounds, I'm not interested in dating. I'd still like to have your parking spot though." Stephanie batted her eyelashes for effect.

His smile faltered for a second. "Can't blame a guy for trying. Let me get out of your way."

"Thanks, and good luck with your speed dating. Don't get a ticket." Stephanie chuckled at her joke.

He saluted her. "You're all heart, beautiful."

Stephanie hustled to the restaurant, mulling over the "beautiful" comment. JoJo was waiting for her outside and wrapped her in a long hug. "Where have you been? I saw you drive by ten minutes ago."

"There must be something in the water here. I asked a guy for his parking spot, thinking he was getting ready to leave, and he asked me for a date."

"That's priceless." JoJo looped her arm through Stephanie's and led her toward the stairs. "Who was it?"

"Are you kidding me? You want to know who it was? Shouldn't we be thinking the guy might have a screw loose?"

"Maybe, but not until I find out if I know him."

"He said his name was Captain Lewis."

JoJo's eyes widened. "As in Henry Lewis?"

"Great! You know him?"

"Everybody knows Henry. Please tell me you said yes."

Stephanie rolled her eyes. "Wasn't happening. He said he lost a bet, and it was date me or attend a speed-dating event. I wished him luck with the speed dating."

A strange look, mischievous or perhaps devious, crossed JoJo's face. "Funny you should mention that."

Chapter Two

THE HOSTESS SEATED Stephanie and JoJo at a corner table. Stephanie glanced at the menu to confirm the Eggs Benedict were still there. They were. Now it was time to get to the bottom of JoJo's odd remark.

"Funny I should mention what?" she asked. "Henry Lewis? His truck? Parking difficulties?"

JoJo lowered her menu. "I think I'm going to try something new. Maybe the chickpea and quinoa patty. You going with your favorite?"

"I am." Stephanie bumped her menu against the one in JoJo's hands. "Now start talking. You're avoiding the question, which makes me nervous. What is funny? And why is it funny?"

The waitress arrived to take their orders. When she left, JoJo reached into her purse and drew out a section of a newspaper. "I was reading the paper last night, and I noticed an ad. We'd just gotten off the phone, you'd told me about Tim being back, wanting to get away, and I know you're over Tim, and you're better off without him, and you're here for a week or more, and you are incredible, and I thought you could do with some fun."

The run-on sentence built up a wall of dread inside Stephanie. "What have you done, Joanne Homlish?"

"I haven't done much. Consider it a slight nudge or a helping hand."

With those words, her best friend placed a folded section of newspaper on the table. An ad for Berkshire Speed Dating covered the bottom half of the page.

Stephanie scowled. "No. You. Didn't!"

JoJo pointed to a line on the ad, tapping her nail on the words a few times. "See this? It's painless. You go in, have a seat, chitchat, and see if there's any sparks. If you connect with someone, you can talk more. If not, it's over in six minutes."

"Six minutes? Six minutes times how many men? You have no idea who could show up and pretend to be someone he's not." Stephanie didn't want to fight with JoJo, but she had to get her friend to think clearly.

JoJo shook her head. "They're legit. Valerie Jenkins met Travis O'Connell through them, and they're head over heels for each other, even looking at dream honeymoon trips at your grandmother's travel agency. The service isn't like most online dating sites. That's why I signed you up."

"You posed as me?" Stephanie glanced around her. She hoped her voice wasn't as loud as the pounding in her head.

"Be serious. I would never do that."

"Thank God." Stephanie began to relax, then keyed in on the apprehensive look on her friend's face.

"JoJo?"

"I filled out the forms and hit send. There wasn't anyplace where I had to forge your signature or anything. Don't be mad, Steph. I'm your best friend. I want you to be happy and to open your heart to love again." JoJo passed her a registration confirmation slip with the event time and address.

"Tell me this is a bad joke. Does your husband know you're on a dating site?"

"Derek told me not to meddle, but he's a guy and doesn't have a clue."

"Derek is right. You'll have to call and cancel. I'm not going." Stephanie pushed the offending newspaper and registration form to JoJo's side of the table.

"I'll go with you. It'll be fun."

"Fun is going for a run at six in the morning along State Beach as the sun is rising over the ocean. Fun is walking the beach looking for sea glass and finding large pieces of greens and blues. Fun is going to the movies, eating a large tub of popcorn, and watching a great romantic comedy."

"Exactly!" JoJo flashed her a smug smile.

"What am I missing here?"

"You said romance is fun."

"No I didn't say romance was fun. I said watching a movie was fun." Stephanie wished their food would arrive so JoJo would stop talking about men, dating, and romance.

"Sitting close in the theatre is a great way to spend two hours with a boyfriend," JoJo said.

Shaking her head, wanting to shake her friend, Stephanie drew in a deep breath and exhaled her frustration, loudly. "I don't have a boyfriend. And, what is the point of dating someone who lives on the mainland, and three hours away? I'm only here for ten days. Have you lost your mind?"

Sliding the ad back into her purse, JoJo stared hard at Stephanie. "I have not lost my mind. I'm doing you a favor. The whole point is to go on a date or two without the threat of anything long term. You need to get back out there. This will be problem-free. A confidence booster."

"I don't want to get back out there."

Stephanie was about to elaborate on the many reasons she had no interest in dating, but the server arrived with their lunch. The Eggs Benedict smelled as good as she knew it would taste. The conversation had to change, or she wouldn't enjoy her food.

"Let's talk about something else. How's the bed and breakfast doing?"

JoJo talked between bites, sharing amusing and touching stories about guests, their exploits, and the renovations they wanted to do during the slower winter season.

"Do you want to pop into any stores before we head to the house?" JoJo asked as they left the restaurant.

"I'm eager to see your gardens, and I'd love a quick walk on the trails if you have time."

"A trail walk would be perfect. I'm parked straight ahead on the right," JoJo said. "I'll wait for you to come around."

Don't hold your breath. I'll drive around, but I won't come around to your idea of speed dating. Not today. Not ever!

Stephanie kept her comments to herself, walked to her car, and followed JoJo out of town and up Prospect Hill Road to her Maple Ridge Bed and Breakfast. The quarter-mile driveway was lined with maple trees, alive with color. Their beauty was a true gift from God. Stephanie would carve out time to take pictures tomorrow night at sunset.

They parked to the right of the stately home passed down to JoJo and Derek from her parents, who now lived in the guesthouse beyond the vegetable garden.

"I've put you in the Silver room. I've got to check the message board and the answering machine. Do you want to unpack, or roam the grounds?" JoJo asked.

"Unpacking can wait. I've been sitting for most of the day. I think I'll walk around. Do you need anything from the garden?"

"We're all set for dinner. Go check out my new topiary. I'll catch up with you in a bit."

Between their walk, preparing dinner, and then enjoying shrimp fettuccine, garden salad, and hilarious conversation, thanks to Derek, Stephanie had yet to unpack her suitcase. She hung her black slacks in the closet, refolded her sweaters and stacked them on the closet shelf, and placed everything else in the large mahogany dresser.

The artist in Stephanie appreciated the special touches JoJo had designed in each room named after a species of maple trees. Her Silver room had pale silver walls, white trim, a shimmering silver duvet, and touches of yellow, red, and orange in the pillows, flowers, carpet runner, and afghan throw to signify the fall leaf colors of the silver maple. Tasteful, simple, yet luxurious. JoJo, an interior designer, had created another masterpiece.

Teeth brushed, hair combed, Stephanie stared at her reflection in the bathroom mirror. Captain Lewis had called her beautiful. It'd been a while since she felt beautiful. Did men cheat on beautiful women? Yeah, they did. The tabloids in the grocery store had dozens of articles about such sad stories.

Her long auburn hair had been down today instead of up in her usual ponytail. No makeup, ever if she could help it, but her hazel eyes were large and she had naturally long lashes. She wasn't unattractive. Yet Tim had cheated and left her. Two years thrown into the garbage, as if the relationship was nothing more than a disposable razor.

Enough bad memories. Stephanie turned off the bathroom lights, walked across the room, and crawled into bed. Setting her alarm for 5:30, she picked up a *Berkshire* magazine off the nightstand. She turned to an article on the area's fall festivals. There, jumping off the page, was an ad for Berkshire Speed Dating.

Stephanie tossed the magazine to the floor. "I'll drive down there tomorrow and ask to speak with the organizer, which will last for as long as it takes me to tell them that I'm not interested."

Chapter Three

STEPHANIE DROVE INTO town and parked two blocks down from Berkshire Speed Dating. JoJo had practically begged to go with her, but Steph didn't need moral support for a meeting that would last less than five minutes, maybe less than two.

A simple: "Hello. Nice to meet you. My well-intending friend signed me up for your service, but I'm not interested. Thanks so much. Have a great day."

Walking up the street, Stephanie saw him before he saw her. She stopped, and then eased between two parked cars, hoping to go unnoticed. Captain Lewis wasn't kidding when he said he'd be signing up for a whirl around the speed-dating track. He'd just walked out of the building she was about to walk into.

He was smiling, so it couldn't have been too painful. Perhaps his friend had done him a favor, unlike JoJo with her meddling. He glanced her way. Too late to move. He began walking toward her.

"Well hello, beautiful. Have you come to gloat?"

The man filled out a pair of jeans as if the denim had been made for his body. He had to be six-foot-two if he was an inch. Nice height to her five-eight. *Wait! Why am I thinking along those lines? I'm not interested. Zero interest. Not for coffee, not for tea, and definitely not for dinner.*

"Hello, Captain Lewis. I didn't expect to see you this morning." If she didn't acknowledge that she knew why he'd mentioned gloating, then she wouldn't have to admit where she was going.

He pointed behind him to the dating service front door. "I just conceded the loss."

Stephanie hadn't lost a race, but she guessed how painful going into that office was. "You don't sound the least bit excited, Captain."

"I'm honoring a bet, not making a planned and strategized life decision."

Stephanie made an exaggerated smile before speaking. "Cheer up, Captain. There are worse things in life." Okay, she was really trying to convince herself. Maybe if he believed it then she would believe it and not want to strangle JoJo for forcing her into this activity.

"Yes. There are," he said, far too serious for the conversation. Seeming to catch himself, he shook his head quickly. "And please, call me Henry."

Calling him Henry might be fatal or invite more than she wanted. A formal salutation kept him and his too-appealing smile a safe distance from her heart and mind.

"Nice to see you again, Captain Lewis, but I don't want to keep you." Stephanie needed to hurry their chat along. She wanted to get her name off that dating list as soon as possible or she'd be as miserable as the man before her looked, and, well, from the irregular heartbeats she was experiencing in his presence, she was beginning to like Henry and that wasn't a good thing.

"You're not keeping me," he said with a grin. "I'm free all afternoon. Have you had lunch? No date, as you made it clear yesterday you don't date. We'll merely be two soon-to-be friends getting to know each other better."

Great. Now she had to lie, or fess up. Lying wasn't an option. "Sorry, I have to go speak with someone."

He surveyed the street. "Can I walk you to wherever you're headed?"

Oh bother! Why was this man so persistent? "I'm less than two hundred meters from my destination."

Henry, Captain Lewis, turned around full circle. When he

faced her again, he looked as if he was about to choke or burst out laughing. "Should I guess where you're going?"

"No, please don't. My annoying friend, whom I love dearly, decided to enroll me in your dating service. I won't be but five minutes in there. I'm only here to tell them that I won't be joining."

He was laughing. Okay, he was chuckling, but it was grating.

"Good luck with that. The woman at the front desk has more enthusiasm than a puppy with a new toy. You'll be lucky to be out in half an hour."

Stephanie accepted the captain's words as a challenge. "Watch me."

She could hear his deep laugh all the way to the front door. She was actually relieved to step inside the office and close the door on Captain Henry Lewis's wise-guy chortling.

A woman dressed in an attractive pantsuit, probably in her mid-thirties, crossed the foyer, and extended her hand. "Hello. Welcome. This is a great day to be in the romance business. You're my second potential lovebird in less than hour."

Prospective lovebird? No way!

"Um, I'm not here to sign up for your services. I came in to cancel." She couldn't resist looking out the window to see if Captain Lewis was still there. He was. If he was timing her, and as a runner he probably was, she had four minutes left.

"Cancel? Now why would you want to do that? Have you met someone?" The woman also looked out the window. "I see," she said in that drawn-out way people use when they think they see something secret.

Stephanie felt as she had when her mom caught her waiting for a boy to call but she'd fibbed and said she was waiting for JoJo to ring her.

"Do you know that man?" Stephanie asked.

"I met him today. You don't know him?"

Stephanie shook her head. "No. I mean, I met him for a minute when I asked him for his parking space."

"I thought by the way you were looking out the window that

you two were acquainted. My vibes aren't usually wrong." The woman extended her hand, "I'm Cass Reinholdt. Come on back to the hospitality room, and let's talk about you."

"Cass, I don't want to waste your time. When I say I want to cancel, I mean it. I have no interest in dating."

Turning slightly to encourage Stephanie to follow her, Cass asked, "If you don't want to date, why did you sign up for speed dating?"

"That's it exactly. You see, I didn't sign up. A friend filled out your forms online and sent them in. She meant well, but I'm not interested." Even as she said the words, Stephanie was following Cass down the short hallway.

"Maybe your friend did you a favor? What have you got to lose by one night of speed dating?"

Stephanie shuddered. Was Cass serious? What did she have to lose? How about her heart? "I'm sure your company is great. It's me. I'm really not interested in dating. I'm only here for ten days. JoJo, that friend I mentioned, she can be a little bossy sometimes."

Stephanie glanced back toward the front door and wished she could run through it. Captain Lewis was most likely taking his turn to gloat. Her five minutes were about to expire.

They stepped into a comfy room with three oversized chairs, a large walnut coffee table, a love seat, and open books that displayed couples on each page.

Cass reached down, picked up one of the books, and held it out to Stephanie. "Before you withdraw, why don't you read some of these stories?"

Stephanie shoved her hands in her pockets. Those books were like mousetraps. The images on the pages appeared as inviting as a wedge of cheese, but one bite and the spring would snap and she'd be crushed again. Not going to happen. "That won't be necessary."

"Are you nervous? Scared?" Cassandra gave her a sympathetic look. "Honestly, speed dating is painless. Sure there are some odd folks, but a few minutes with Mr. Wrong is nothing when you finally spend six minutes with Mr. Right."

Stephanie tried to laugh, but it came out as a gagging sound. "I'm sure you're right. I keep trying to tell you that I'm not ready to date again."

"Oh, recent break-up?"

"Yes. And the last thing I need—"

"Is to sit at home and spend another day mourning a bad relationship." Cassandra pointed to the chair. "Tell me what happened."

For reasons Stephanie couldn't fathom, she sat down and poured out her story to a complete stranger. Cassandra nodded and sighed and tsked in all the right places. She never once interrupted to ask a question, give an opinion, or emit an emotional response as all her family and friends had.

"Seeing the two of them at the bakery was too much, at least it felt that way then. Now," Stephanie paused. She hadn't shed one tear while telling Cass her story. Her heart wasn't clenched or throbbing. "Now, I'm glad I saw them and I'm glad I'm visiting my family and friends."

"You're better off without him," Cassandra declared, standing up and walking to the mini-fridge. She returned with a bottle of water for Stephanie. "I can see why you're gun shy, but I can also see why your girlfriend wants you to get out and meet people. You're here. You're glad you're here. And you just happen to be here while our event is taking place. If you want to cancel, I'll take you off the list but I think a fun, un-entangled night out might be just what the doctor ordered."

Could it be what she needed? Everyone else seemed to think so. Stephanie slumped deeper into the chair. "How long does it take?"

Cassandra's eyes lit up. "The evening is four hours, which—

"Four hours?" Stephanie exclaimed. "How many men will I have to talk to? Four hours, at six minutes each, could be forty men. That's a nightmare, not a fun night out."

Laughter eased Stephanie's tension. "The event is four hours, that includes an optional cocktail hour beforehand, an hour for the dating, and time to mingle and enjoy appetizers after the speed dating. You'll probably talk with ten men, including that hunk Captain Lewis."

At the mention of Henry's name, Stephanie felt her pulse quicken. What would one night of speed dating hurt? She didn't have to accept a date with anyone. And everyone from JoJo to Zoey to NeNe to Libby would then have to give her a break about dating. Surely ten "dates" would be enough to get them off her back for a few months.

Walking toward her car, Stephanie kept replaying the meeting in her mind. How on earth had Cassandra talked her into going to the event this Saturday? During the drive home, she'd figure out how to explain the meeting to JoJo so she didn't spend the next five days speculating on whom Stephanie might meet.

Under her windshield wiper, a flyer waved in the afternoon breeze. Stephanie lifted the wiper and turned over the paper.

I waited for ten minutes. Let's hope we both avoid speeding tickets. Henry.

Chapter Four

THE NOTE SAT on her dresser staring smugly at her. Okay, a piece of paper couldn't stare or be smug or have any feelings or reactions to her, but Henry Lewis's note created more thoughts and feelings in Stephanie than it ought to.

Closing the top drawer a little too firmly, Stephanie watched as the paper slid a few inches toward the back of the dresser. If the note fell to the ground, she wouldn't see it if she didn't pick it up. Then again, she'd removed it from her car windshield, carried it into the house and up to her room. Why had she saved it? Why hadn't she thrown the silly note away?

Three days of glancing at it, re-reading it, and staring at it, and the words were still the same. She'd driven through town yesterday and hadn't seen Henry, in uniform or in those sweet-fitting jeans, so he wouldn't be giving her a speeding ticket. He might not even work for the Stockbridge police department. She hadn't asked JoJo where he worked, and she wouldn't be opening that can of worms by asking.

Stephanie picked up the note and read it yet again. ". . . let's hope we both avoid speeding tickets." Did he mean he wanted to avoid her? Other women at the event? Or getting his heart run over, crushed, mutilated, and left bleeding on the highway of lost love?

"Still oogling your love letter from Henry?" JoJo teased.

Stephanie spun around, clutching the note in her fist. "JoJo! Now look what you made me do. Don't you knock?" Stephanie placed the note on the dresser and smoothed out the creases.

"I knocked. You were oblivious, under the influence of Henry I'd guess."

"I'm not under the influence of anyone. This note reminds me that I might have to murder my friend for setting me up on ten blind dates."

JoJo walked across the room and tapped her finger on Henry's note. "Or you'll be buying me chocolates and a spa gift certificate to thank me for introducing you to the love of your life."

"For the umpteenth time: I am not interested in Henry. Or any guy for that matter." As the words left her mouth, Stephanie swiped the letter off the dresser intending to throw it out. Her hand hovered over the silver wastebasket to her right.

"For someone who's not interested in a guy, you sure are hanging onto his every word."

Cringing at the truth and her desire for it not to be true, Stephanie folded the note and slipped it into her back pocket. "It's just funny. A souvenir from a wild night on the town just like we did back in college when we'd save matchbooks from dance clubs even though we didn't smoke."

"At least you admit it's a keepsake. Be sure to show the souvenir to your grandmother and Libby at lunch." JoJo was grinning, and she was absolutely smug.

"Go weed a garden!" Stephanie grabbed her sweater from the chair and started toward the door.

"And miss lunch with your family? No way! Let's go." JoJo hurried past Stephanie, chuckling as she went by.

The thirty-mile drive to Williamstown took fifty minutes, and Stephanie was thankful that not one minute was spent talking about Captain Henry Lewis or the upcoming speed dating event. They pulled up to the curb in front of NeNe's house just as Libby was getting out of her car.

"Steph!" Libby ran to the passenger door before Stephanie exited. Her cousin wrapped her in a hug as warm as sliced apple pie, fresh from the oven. "How are you? I was so sorry to hear about the run-in with the pair-who-shall-not-be-mentioned."

"Huh?" Stephanie drew back. "Oh, Tim. Yeah, that was miserable."

Tim. She hadn't thought about him in days. She didn't have time now to think about why she hadn't thought about him. "Enough about me. I want to hear all about you and Jack. But before we go inside, anything you want to tell me about NeNe and Blake?"

Libby shook her head and smiled. "He's perfect for our grandmother. I love him more as time goes on. He grounds her without stifling her, and his love for her is as obvious as chocolate in a chocolate chip cookie."

"That's what I want to hear."

As if on cue, Ellie Schuyler opened the front door. "Hurry along, you three. I don't want to miss anything you're talking about."

After a serious round of hugging, Ellie led them into the kitchen. The scent was better than Stephanie remembered. "What are you cooking, NeNe?"

"Winter Squash and Apple soup, buttermilk biscuits, and a surprise for dessert." NeNe stirred the soup, lifted a spoon to her lips for a quick taste test, nodded, and turned the heat to simmer under the large pot. "Let me put the biscuits in the oven, and then you can tell me everything happening in your lives. JoJo, I heard you're planning a few renovations this winter."

JoJo nodded. "We are doing some minor repairs and a major painting overall. It's been ten years since my parents last had work done, so the walls need a fresh look and I can stop scrubbing at scuffmarks that don't come off. Those clients you send us will be even happier with our new look next year."

"Everyone raves about your bed and breakfast. I'm trying to convince Blake that we need to visit and treat ourselves to a weekend away now that Honeymoon Travel is in the black." Ellie turned the knob on the timer and pushed start.

"You two have a pair of rooms waiting for you any night you want to come down for a stay. We'd love to have you," JoJo said. "And perhaps you'll share your biscuit recipe?"

Stephanie could almost taste the biscuits. NeNe was a fabulous cook, a trait Stephanie had not inherited. She loved to eat, but struggled with anything beyond basic recipes.

"I'll write you a copy before you leave. Now let's have a seat. I want to hear about Stephanie's visit. What have you been doing? Any exciting plans for the coming weekend?"

Why had NeNe asked about the weekend? Stephanie glanced between JoJo and her grandmother and cousin. "Did JoJo tell you?"

"Tell us what?" Libby and NeNe asked at the same time, leaning forward in their chairs.

Earnest faces eagerly awaited her answer. Stephanie still might have to murder JoJo, at least in her mind. She glared at her best friend.

JoJo shook her head. "Don't give me the death glare. I didn't say a thing."

"Say what about what?" Libby asked, and then smiled. "Hey, do you have a date or something?"

"No!" Stephanie snapped. She winced at her tone and the half-truth. "Technically, I don't have a date."

"More like ten or twelve dates," JoJo said, chuckling.

"Alright you two, what is going on? My granddaughter is certainly not dating a dozen men."

Massaging her temples, Stephanie drew in a depth breath and exhaled. The next words out of her mouth were going to sound ridiculous. She should've cancelled and spared herself the humiliation now and on Saturday night.

"JoJo, my darling best friend, signed me up for a speed dating event this weekend."

Libby burst out laughing. "Please let me come and watch."

Stephanie couldn't decide whether to laugh or cry. If Libby were the one going, she'd be laughing, too.

"Would one of you please explain what speed dating is, and why Libby finds this so amusing?" NeNe asked, a slight frown appearing on her gentle face.

"Don't worry, NeNe, it's a harmless event, and I'm not really going to date anyone. Single men and women will meet at the event. The women will take seats at the specified tables. The guys then move around the room, stopping at tables to chat for six minutes, and then go on to the next table."

"Someone considers that a date?" NeNe asked, frowning and shaking her head.

"No," JoJo chimed in. "Steph will have a scorecard that she fills out either between chats or at the end of the hour. The guys also have a scorecard. Everyone turns their scorecard in, and if there are matches, then the company contacts the people and provides either email addresses or phone numbers."

NeNe reached for Stephanie's hand. "Please tell me you will not give a strange man your phone number."

"No, I gave them JoJo's." Stephanie felt a moment of pure delight. Libby started laughing again.

"You what?" JoJo practically choked on the words.

Stephanie finally had a moment of smugness. "Yes, I gave them the number of the bed and breakfast. I am fully confident that I am not going to meet anyone that I want to go on a date with so you don't have to worry about the phone ringing off the hook."

Patting her hand, NeNe said, "I think that was a wise decision."

"Steph, you could always give Joanne's cell phone number out just for fun," Libby said, clearly enjoying the conversation more than anyone else. Of course, she had recently fallen in love again with Jack, her college sweetheart, and every day appeared happier than the previous day.

"My phone might ring. There is a certain someone who might be calling," JoJo said, zapping Stephanie's momentary smugness.

The timer buzzed from the kitchen. NeNe rose. "Let's take this conversation into the kitchen."

Stephanie draped an arm across JoJo's shoulders as they walked, and bumped her hip with hers. "You're lucky you drove, JoJo, or you'd be walking home."

"Yea, yea. Talk to me after the event, after you see you-know-who again."

"I want to know who you're talking about? Someone on the Island or up here?" Libby asked.

"Stop. Let's get the food on the table before Stephanie shares her news," NeNe said.

News? She didn't have news. Henry wasn't news.

He was . . .

He . . .

He was merely a fellow speed dater trying not to get run over.

With that thought clarified, Stephanie carried two soup bowls that NeNe passed her and placed them on the set table. As always, their grandmother had used the good silver and china. Time together was always a special occasion to Ellie.

Placing her napkin in her lap, Ellie reached for Stephanie's hand and then Libby's while they held hands with JoJo. "Father, thank You for this meal and our time of fellowship. We ask Your blessings upon our family and friends, and pray that we may each serve You in accordance with Your will for our lives. Amen."

Stephanie dipped her spoon into the thick creamy soup and took that first delicious mouthful. It seemed that JoJo and Libby where both waiting for NeNe to ask her additional questions. After her fifth spoonful, Stephanie was grateful her grandmother had taught them all years ago not to talk and eat at the same time.

She reached for a biscuit, and split it open. "Libs, can you pass me the butter please?"

"So dear, who is the man that JoJo has referenced?"

Done in by a biscuit. Stephanie wished she'd kept spooning soup into her mouth. Too late now.

"JoJo is exaggerating. I talked to a guy on Sunday when I met JoJo at the Red Lion for lunch. He was in his truck getting ready to leave and I asked for his parking space. On Monday I had to go back into town to visit Berkshire Speed Dating, so I could remove my name from the event this weekend that my supposed best friend had signed me up for. I saw him leaving the dating service office and we said hello. No big deal."

"Show them the note." JoJo interjected.

JoJo's four words ended any chance of the conversation about Henry Lewis being over.

"He wrote you a note?" NeNe asked. "And you have it with you?"

"No. Yes. Sort of a note," Stephanie stumbled over the words. She cleared her throat and started again. "It's a joke, not a note."

"If it's a joke, you should share it with us," Libby said, extending her hand toward Stephanie.

There was no point objecting. Her family was not easily deterred. Stephanie lowered her butter knife and extracted the note from her back pocket. She passed it to NeNe, who would handle it with care.

"I waited for ten minutes. Let's hope we both avoid speeding tickets. Henry," NeNe read aloud.

"Why did he wait ten minutes? Were you supposed to be meeting him? I thought you only ran into him twice." Libby waited with expectant eyes for Stephanie to answer.

"Don't read into it, Libs. I had told Captain Lewis that I would only need five minutes to cancel. He bet that I wouldn't make it. He was right."

"Well, he has a wonderful sense of humor. Speeding tickets. I understand that now," NeNe said with a soft chuckle.

"And your captain will be one of your dates on Saturday night?" Libby pried.

"No, he will not be my date. He might be one of the men who sits at my table, or maybe he won't. He already knows me." Stephanie caught the slight catch in her voice when she considered Henry not speaking with her. She hoped no one else noticed.

NeNe dipped her biscuit into her soup, but paused before putting the bite into her mouth. "I suspect your Henry will be stopping at your table."

"He's not 'my' Henry," Stephanie protested, stabbing her spoon into her bowl.

"We'll see," JoJo sing-songed.

*

ELLIE CLOSED THE door after her company left and picked up the phone. She dialed Blake's number, hoping he wasn't with a customer at their travel agency. A smile wider than the miles from Williamstown to Martha's Vineyard stretched across her face.

"Hello dear. How was lunch?" Blake asked.

"God has heard our prayers." Ellie said, her cheeks tingling.

"What has the good Lord done for us now?"

Ellie chuckled. "Do you remember that kind fellow who helped us with the flat tire?"

"Henry Lewis?" Blake asked.

"Yes. And do you remember my comment after we drove away?"

Now it was Blake's turn to chuckle. "Of course I do, my sweet matchmaker. You told me that you thought Henry would be perfect for Stephanie. Am I to guess that you have arranged for Stephanie and Henry to meet?"

"Better, Blake, so much better. God already took care of it. They met the day Stephanie arrived, and she's smitten. She's denying it, but I can see it." Ellie knew she was right. She'd always been able to read Stephanie, from the time her granddaughter was toddling around the old house through her crazy teenage years.

"Did he ask her out?"

"Yes, but she turned him down. God has other plans though, and they will date each other on Saturday. I'll tell you all about it at dinner." Ellie grinned as she hung up the phone. God never ceased to amaze her.

Chapter Five

"YOU LOOK GREAT," JoJo declared as Stephanie walked out of the bathroom.

Great wasn't exactly what Stephanie had in mind. Casual or disinterested was more of what she wanted to project to any man who might sit at her table tonight.

JoJo had other ideas and had suggested Stephanie change outfits from her original selection of jeans and an angora turtleneck sweater. Now on the third option, her black slacks, JoJo's cream silk blouse, and JoJo's low-heeled pumps, her best friend finally appeared satisfied. Thank God!

Stephanie opened her jewelry pouch and withdrew a silver necklace with a single medallion of dark green sea glass encased in thin silver ribbons.

"Lipstick?" JoJo practically begged.

"No. This is me, or as close to me as you'll let me be." Stephanie's stomach tightened. How many times had Tim said that he loved her natural look? Then he chose Kay, who wore makeup and dresses. Maybe she should put on a little lipstick and mascara?

Stephanie turned toward the mirror. Her hair was loose and long, falling softly beyond her shoulders. Henry, Captain Lewis, had even called her beautiful. She wasn't unattractive, and foundation or eyeliner or blush would make her self-conscious. "No makeup, JoJo. I look good, though I'd be more comfortable in jeans and hiking boots."

"You look stunning. The green in the necklace sets off your

hazel eyes." JoJo pointed to the clock. "Now you'd better get going so you don't miss your first date."

"You do know, don't you, that there is something fundamentally wrong with the phrase, 'miss your first date.'" They both laughed.

Stephanie was trying to laugh as she drove to the Country Inn and Conference Center just outside of Stockbridge. She parked and scanned the lot. A couple of guys were walking toward the entrance. She had to get out of the car and go inside or start the car and go home. Option B would be her choice if she didn't have to face JoJo, NeNe, Libby, and Zoey.

Resigned, Stephanie strode into the hotel and followed the signs to the conference rooms for Berkshire Speed Dating. The large ballroom was pleasantly decorated, not garish or tacky as she'd feared. Flowers were centered on each tablecloth and two chairs were set around a few dozen tables. A bar and buffet occupied the back of the room, where a large number of men and women were talking.

Stephanie crossed the floor to the check-in station and said hello to Cassandra. "I'm so glad you're here, Stephanie. It's going to be a great night."

Accepting her welcome package, Stephanie pinned her nametag on, found her assigned table, and walked to the bar to get a bottle of water. Her throat was suddenly dry. Very, very dry. She eased her way past and through twenty to thirty people and asked the bartender for water.

She took a few sips while surveying the crowd. She guessed most people were in their late twenties or thirties. Surprisingly, there was, at first count, an even number of men to women. Made sense. Cassandra probably accepted equal numbers.

"I wondered if you were going to be a no-show."

She recognized the voice and smiled. The night instantly became better. She turned. "Hello, Captain Lewis."

"Hello, Stephanie. Your presence here tells me that you were unsuccessful in your attempt to cancel the evening." Henry grinned, that slow, not-quite-a-smile grin she'd seen the previous two times they'd met.

He was witty, and he looked darn good in khakis and a blue button-down shirt. Stephanie liked him more and more. Good thing she was leaving town in a few days. No dates. No broken heart.

"Now tell me, Captain, since you have made an appearance at this event, does your bet require you to stay?"

"Regrettably, yes." He leaned closer. "If I could escape, I would. Honor requires I remain."

"Pressure keeps me here." Now why had she said that? Stephanie gave him a cute grimace hoping he wouldn't ask questions.

"Pressure?" He raised an eyebrow.

"Well intentioned friends and family. It's a burden I have to bear." And that's all the detail she would give tonight. No insight into broken engagements, recent sightings of the happy backstabbing couple, or her family's desire to fix her up with a 'nice' guy.

"Ladies and gentlemen," Cassandra's voice came over a loudspeaker, "it's time for our date night to begin. Ladies, please take your seats at your designated table. Gentlemen please come to the front of the room. You have six minutes max per date, which will be counted down by the clock on the back wall. Make the most of your time. Don't forget to fill out your date cards so we can connect you with your matches."

"I guess it's time to start." Stephanie refrained from asking Henry to sneak out the back door with her. He seemed to be taking the honor thing rather seriously.

"Marching orders," Henry said, sounding as enthusiastic as she felt.

"We'll survive," Stephanie offered as she walked by him.

"Don't get a ticket," Henry quipped.

Stephanie didn't reply. She kept her mouth closed so she wouldn't divulge to Captain Henry Lewis that she wanted him to give her a ticket, or at least stop by her table for six minutes and perhaps keep coming back through the entire event.

Taking her seat at Table 13, a knot twisted in Stephanie's stomach. Thirteen. Her table number was thirteen? Geez Louise! She wasn't superstitious, but did she have to be at thirteen? *Lord, please help the next hour to go by quickly. And, painlessly, or as painlessly as possible.*

The buzzer sounded to begin the first round. An attractive man approached. He wasn't as good looking as Henry, who was sitting across the room with a blonde. Did he like blondes?

"Do you mind?"

"Huh?" Stephanie looked up at the stranger talking to her.

"I asked if you'd mind if I sat down."

"Oh, no, please do." Stephanie extended her hand. "My name is Stephanie."

"Chris. Nice to meet you." He shook her hand, pulled his chair in, and slid the flowers to the far left although they were not blocking their view of each other. "I'm allergic to flowers."

"Really? All flowers?"

"Pretty much. Haven't found one I don't react to."

"Wow, that's horrible." Cross him off the list. She loved flowers, and had them around her all the time. "I'm allergic to cats."

"Cats, dogs, horses, anything with fur." Chris extracted a tissue from his jacket pocket and blew his nose. "Dust, pollen, pine, and don't get me started on my food allergies."

Though he said not to get him started, and Stephanie didn't ask, Chris then listed every food, spice, and liquid that he had a known allergy to or had tested positive to on a skin test and therefore avoided. He finally paused to once again blow his nose.

"Would you like me to put the flowers on the floor?" Stephanie asked, grateful for any interruption of his allergy litany.

"No, it won't help. It's probably more the numerous perfumes in the room. I should have known you ladies would be wearing your signature scents to entice us gents."

Was that a joke? Or was Chris serious? Stephanie winced. She wasn't trying to entice anyone. Far from it. "I prefer not to wear perfume, or makeup for that matter. Anyone I date will be attracted to my brain or I won't be attracted to him."

"Spoken like a true feminist. Good for you."

God help her. Now. Did he think that was funny? She hoped he wasn't sincere. Either way, Stephanie didn't care. She didn't need another minute to know that Chris, however nice he may or may not be, was not the man for her. "Oh, the buzzer just went off. Guess our time is up. Good luck tonight."

Zero. An easy score for Chris.

With not quite a minute to relax, a young, sort of pudgy Kurt Russell lookalike sat down across from her. "How ya doing? Blane. Work in plastics. What do you do?"

Blane spoke so fast Stephanie wanted to lace up her running sneakers to keep up with him. Not having that option, or the option to run outside and go home, Stephanie slowed everything down.

"Hi, Blane." She paused. Smiled. "Nice to meet you." Another pause. Was he sweating? "I'm a designer." She didn't mention jewelry so Blane wouldn't be able to Google "Stephanie, Jewelry Designer."

Cassandra had mentioned that she could keep her info as private as she wanted to. And she wanted the extremely private option.

Blane was definitely sweating. She felt sorry for him. She was only slightly more comfortable then he appeared to be. "I hate these things, don't you?" she asked.

"I'm getting more comfortable at them. This is my fifth one. I'm sure this time will work out better than the last one," he spewed out in less than four seconds.

Stephanie wanted to tell him to relax, but that would probably make him more nervous. "This is my first, and my last. Too nerve racking for me."

Wiping his upper lip with a cocktail napkin from the table, Blane nodded. "You're doing great. I need another drink. How about you?"

"No, thank you. But why don't you go get one now so you don't miss your next date," Stephanie offered, praying he would take her up on it.

"You don't mind?" he said, rising from the chair.

"Not at all. I could use a few minutes to relax. My nerves. Relax my nerves." Technically she was slightly nervous. Not an outright lie.

"I hear you. Good luck tonight. Nice to meet you."

And date number two was gone. Thank you, Lord.

A quick surveillance of the room and Stephanie spotted Henry. Another blonde. Guess that ruled her out.

Chapter Six

AFTER THE FIRST two dates Stephanie was sure the next two, or eight, would be somewhat better. She was wrong. Not only did Captain Henry Lewis continue to circulate the room and avoid her table, but the men who had chosen to sit at her table she wished had walked past.

Bruce was so painfully shy Stephanie feared asking a second question after he muttered and stuttered through his line of work. Kane thought so highly of himself and his muscles, there wasn't room at the table for her. He asked Stephanie three times if she wanted to touch his flexed biceps. He was serious. She was repulsed.

The next four included a chef, who wanted to cook for her and serve her breakfast in bed—on their first date; a wanna-be cowboy who owned a horse but talked as if he owned a ranch in Montana and smelled like a pine forest; a banker who wanted to share the latest certificate of deposit rates and why long-term investments were better than day trading; and a teacher who was a really nice guy, just not the guy for her.

Fifty-three minutes had ticked by and her date card had eight zeros next to eight names of men she'd rather forget. Not necessarily their fault that there wasn't a single spark with one of them. She would have given the teacher a six, because he was a six, but she didn't want to take a chance on being matched to him.

With only two dates left, she was all too aware that Captain Henry Lewis had yet to date her. She'd seen him chat with a few women, and he was laughing a couple of minutes ago with a super-fit strawberry blond in a sparse dress who was seated two tables over.

"Hi."

"Hi." Stephanie looked up at a man in faded jeans, relaxed, well-worn t-shirt, light brown dreadlocks, tan skin, and an engaging smile. "Have a seat if you'd like. Name's Stephanie."

"Abe. How long have you lived in the Berkshires?"

Fourth time she'd been asked that question tonight. "I grew up here. How about you? I know we didn't go to school together."

Abe scooted his chair around the table closer to Stephanie. "Two weeks."

"Wow, and here you are. What brought you to the area?" Something about his uninvited closeness told her Abe's answer would be interesting.

"I'm an artist. I'm here for a month, maybe six weeks, to paint the fall foliage."

"And you're looking for a relationship?" Stephanie tried to contain her incredulousness.

"No. I'm not looking for a girlfriend. I'm looking for some fun while I'm here. A warm body to cozy up to at night."

A bubble of laughter escaped her lips. "Well, that's honest."

"Honest, direct, unentangled, carefree, and fun. You interested?"

Whoa! Stephanie stared at the handsome man before her. Was he a true reflection of the men in her age group? Was he, and the previous eight men, the best she could hope for. She was doomed. Absolutely doomed.

"Uh, no. But thank you for asking." If she was being polite, did that make Stephanie a liar? She wasn't thankful he'd asked. She would be grateful if he stood and moved on.

"No problem. Can't hurt to ask," Abe said, totally unfazed by her refusal.

"I'm curious, have you had any takers on your offer?" Asking the question was like opening Pandora's box. Stephanie knew that, but she couldn't stop herself.

"Sure. At least two women are potential dinner dates and then we'll go from there."

He sounded pleased. Stephanie held her amazement in check. "You'd date two women at the same time?"

Abe sat back and crossed his right leg over his left. "For dinner? Absolutely. For companionship? No. I'm a one-woman guy."

"As long as you're in town."

"Exactly."

The pride in Abe's voice was unmistakable. Was she missing something? Or was he? A question formed in her mind. She had to ask. "How much traveling do you do? How many states or cities do you visit each year?"

"I move with the seasons. At least four locales a year, but more often than not it's seven or eight. From here I'll head south for the winter. Hit the tourist towns, paint and sell my work. Depending on whether I island hop in the Caribbean or stay in Florida, I'll have been in at least eight fantastic locations this year. It's a great life. You only live once, and I'm not wasting a second."

Abe's enthusiasm for his lifestyle was genuine. He was a zero for Stephanie, but she had no doubt he'd rate his life a ten. JoJo would be amused. NeNe would be aghast. Her grandmother had loved two men, her grandfather and Blake. And that's what Stephanie wanted. Maybe she was born too late to have that dream.

Sighing, she spoke to Abe. "I hope you paint beautiful pictures during your visit here." She extended her hand, formally ending their conversation. Abe rose, moved his chair back to the other side of the table, and cheerfully looked for his next candidate.

Thank God she only had one more "date" to go. The evening had been proof positive why one should never, as in NEV-ER, participate in any event of this kind. It also confirmed that she had no interest in dating for the rest of this year, maybe ever.

Resting her head in her hands, Stephanie massaged the pressure point above her ears. She deserved a real massage after this evening, though she was going to settle for a shower as soon as she got home. JoJo's interrogation would have to wait until after she felt clean.

"Headache?"

She recognized that deep voice. Had he struck out with all the blondes and now needed to score at least one "follow-up date" to fulfill his bet obligations?

Lifting her head, she ran her fingers through her long hair and settled back into her seat, unexpectedly alert and ready for a bit of snappy repartee with Captain Henry Lewis.

"No headache. How about you? Enjoying your evening?"

"I am now." He stood, smiling but more stiff and formal looking than relaxed and comfortable. If he were the picture of enjoyment, she wouldn't want to see him tense.

"May I?" he asked, pulling out the empty chair across from her.

"Am I your last resort again?" The annoyance in her voice was louder than her actual words.

Taking the seat, sitting very upright, Captain Lewis looked her directly in the eyes and held her gaze. "I saved the best for last. Intentionally."

Flustered, but pleased, Stephanie recovered her wit and replied, "How could you know since you hadn't met the other women before tonight?"

"I knew because I'd already met you." Henry maintained eye contact.

"Oh," passed through her lips as the air left her lungs.

Her brain wasn't working. She couldn't hold onto one clear thought. She lost her voice.

"This surprises you?"

All she managed was a nod. They were approaching dangerous ground, territory she wasn't prepared to walk in.

Time to run.

No, he was faster than her.

Hmmm, time to divert the conversation. "Who was the uber-fit woman you were talking with?"

"I have no idea," Henry answered.

"What? You just spent five or six minutes in conversation with someone and you don't remember her name?" That felt better. Safer ground. Much safer. Plus, his answer sort of ticked her off.

"I know her name, but I don't know who she is. I asked superficial questions to pass the time of day. I knew where I wanted to be and when I was going to get there," Henry stated.

His tone was factual. Henry wasn't smooth-talking her, which was worse for Stephanie. They had three minutes left. She had to steer them in another direction.

"When's your next race?"

"End of the month. You should enter. It's a 10K."

Finally, an out. Stephanie shook her head. "I won't be here."

"Going on vacation?"

"No, going home from this vacation." The relief she first felt vanished when Henry's full lips drooped into a frown.

"You don't live here?"

"No. I grew up here, but I live on Martha's Vineyard. I came up for ten days to visit my family and friends."

The buzzer signaled the end of their date and the end of the speed dating rounds. Stephanie eased her chair back. "Looks like we survived. I don't want to be rude, but I'm planning to make a break for the exit before the start of the after-party."

Henry stood. "If you don't mind, I'll escape with you?"

"Let's go then," Stephanie said as she rose.

"Hey, don't you want to fill in your last date and turn your card in?" Henry grinned and waved his dating card.

"If I make a confession, can I skip turning my card in?" Stephanie asked.

"What's your secret?"

"I gave everyone a zero, so they wouldn't match me with anyone. There's no point turning my scores in." Stephanie passed him her card.

Henry turned it over. "You left one blank."

"Uh," Stephanie nibbled on her bottom lip.

"I don't get a score? Or were you planning to give me a zero, too?" If he wasn't smiling at her, Stephanie might have felt guilty.

"Captain Lewis—"

"Henry," he insisted.

"Henry, if you insist on a score I'll be happy to make you number one on my card."

He gave her a curt nod, grinned, and passed her the scorecard.

Stephanie smiled, picked up the pencil on the table, glanced up at Henry to be certain he was watching her, and then she wrote "Henry," peeked up at him again, and in the score column wrote 1.

He groaned. She chuckled.

"May I borrow your pencil?" He asked.

Placing his card on the table next to hers, she noticed that he, too, had rated his previous nine dates a zero. She watched him write her name, and then almost laughed out loud as he wrote a 1. Her mouth went dry as his pencil then made a 0 next to the one.

"The best for last," he said without looking at her.

He straightened and offered her his arm. "Shall we hightail it? No need to turn these in. I think I'll keep my scorecard as a souvenir. Did you want yours?"

Words stuck in her throat. If she'd had a voice, she would have said that she wanted his. Instead, she stood there mute.

"Well, if you don't want yours, do you mind if I keep it?" Henry reached in front of her.

"No," the word eeked out. Stephanie cleared her throat, then opened her water bottle and took a sip. "I want mine."

Snatching the card up, Stephanie all but sprinted to the door. Henry caught up to her and held the door for her. She said nothing, just kept walking as quickly as she could toward the main lobby.

Once outside, Stephanie breathed in the chilly night air. The cold cooled her cheeks. She was grateful she hadn't worn a jacket. Striding toward her car, Henry matched her step for step.

"I'd love to see your sprint workouts," Henry joked.

Stephanie liked the man. He was funny, kind, appeared to be honest, and God knew he was attractive in that rugged, down-home way. She sighed.

"I'm just not ready." The words escaped her lips in a whisper.

"Ready for what?"

"What?" Stephanie hadn't meant to speak her thoughts. How could she answer?

"You said you weren't ready. I'm guessing you're not talking about your speed workouts." Henry didn't step closer to her, but he felt closer.

Stephanie said nothing until they got to her car. She pressed the key fob to open the lock, and then turned to face Henry, staring at a man she could not deny her attraction to. "I was engaged. He cheated. Now they're married. I just saw them last week when they returned from their honeymoon. I ran away from home and came here. I can't . . . You're nice, but I can't—"

"I'm sorry. I understand. Timing is everything." Henry spoke softly, interrupting her. He leaned over and opened her car door. "Thank you for the best date of the year. Please drive home safely. And take good care of yourself, beautiful. You are a ten, and he was a fool."

Stephanie eased into her seat, buckled her belt, and mouthed goodbye to Henry after he'd closed her door. She started the engine and shifted into drive. Henry was watching her and waved as she drove past him.

She wanted to stop. She knew, in her heart she knew, that Henry was a good man. Never mind that JoJo knew him and that he was respected and liked by others in the community, though Stephanie had insisted she didn't want any details. She wanted to go out with him, but she couldn't.

Fingering the cross hanging from her rearview mirror, Stephanie felt the first tear roll down her cheek. "Father, I can't get my heart broken again."

She let the tears freefall down her cheeks, fairly certain that her heart might already be breaking.

*

HENRY STARTED HIS truck. The engine turned over immediately.

Timing.

Life was all about timing. One second too slow, and your best friend dies. One minute too soon, and you take a bullet in the thigh. One relationship too late, and the most intriguing woman you've ever met is still in love with her ex-boyfriend.

Henry shifted into drive and pulled out about half a mile behind Stephanie. He followed her down Route 102. His heart lurched as she signaled left, and then turned onto Pine Street and drove out of sight. Out of his life.

"Lord, Your will. I'm done dodging grenades."

Chapter Seven

SUNDAY DAWNED BRIGHT and a tad warmer than the previous days Stephanie had gone running. She laced up her sneakers, pulled on her ear band and gloves, and slipped quietly out the kitchen door, hoping not to wake anyone, especially JoJo.

After she got home last night, they'd stayed up talking until the wee hours of the morning. With a house full of guests who would be wanting breakfast starting at eight, JoJo needed to sleep as long as possible.

Stephanie walked for two minutes then picked up an easy pace, her legs surprisingly light after so little sleep.

Turning left out of the driveway, she could clock in six miles and be home, showered, and ready to help in the kitchen before the guests came down.

Running in the early morning, the sky not quite light but no longer dark, Stephanie mulled over JoJo's comments during their talk. Her best friend had been right when she'd said that Henry wasn't Stephanie's problem, nor were the miles between the Island and the Berkshires. She was afraid, afraid of getting hurt, afraid of choosing the wrong guy, afraid of being deficient in some way that would cause any man to cheat and leave.

Stephanie felt more than saw the road take on an uphill slant. She dug into her reserve energy and ran through the gray of pre-dawn and the gray areas of her heart.

The slight incline became a hill and Stephanie pumped her arms as she ran up the mile-plus stretch. With every exhale into the cold air, her warm breath created a surreal fog that dissipated as she ran through it.

Wasn't that how love could be? Magical one minute and gone the next?

Yup, that was her problem. Cynical. Or Doubtful. Or just plain terrified. Fear that if she let Henry in, the relationship might be great, and then it would disappear. Then the pain would come again. The pain stayed much longer than the love.

Pushing harder, through the physical and emotional aches, forcing her lungs to expand, Stephanie crested the hill and sucked in a deep breath. The view was stunning. She slowed to a walk, stopped, and took another breath. A low morning mist clung to a farmer's field, while colors bursts to life in all directions as the sun rose behind the hill on the other side of the valley.

The long climb had been worth it. The downhill would be gentle and easy. Taking one last slow appreciative look, Stephanie kicked back into her run. She found her rhythm in a matter of seconds.

If only love were as easy as running. Push up a hill, strain and groan, pause for a minute to survey the efforts of your climb, start running again, and move as if you'd never struggled or stopped. Maybe she should only go on running dates.

Chuckling, she couldn't stop an image of Henry forming in her mind. He ran, and he'd probably go on a running date, but then he'd want another date, perhaps not in sneakers, gloves, and reflective jackets.

The gradual descent was soft on her knees and great for her pace. And, great thinking time. Maybe one of the benefits of coming to JoJo's wasn't to date Henry, but to uncover her fear of dating Henry or any man. Facing the fear, acknowledging it, could help her move beyond it just as facing a mountain and huffing and puffing her way up allowed her to enjoy a great view and then coast on the downhill.

Mulling over that thought, the run back to JoJo's was peaceful. JoJo was in the kitchen baking when Stephanie returned. Stephanie ran up the back stairs, showered, and was ready to pitch in before the tables needed to be set in the breakfast room.

Half an hour later, the guests were enjoying eggs, pancakes, bacon, fresh-squeezed orange juice, local maple syrup, and JoJo's famous sticky buns.

"Another basket of buns for the nice couple at the corner table," Stephanie said as she walked into the kitchen. JoJo drizzled fresh glaze on two buns, and passed them to Steph.

"O women who are greatly loved," Sarah Hyde said, making a grand entrance. "Fear not! Peace be with you; be strong and of good courage."

The older woman laughed as she hung up her coat. JoJo had said Sarah was going to the eight o'clock church service before coming into work, and by her welcome announcement, she'd clearly been.

Stephanie chuckled at Sarah, who had been working at the inn for as long as she could remember.

"You all hustle on out of here," Sarah said as she tied on her apron. "You don't want to miss the worship music this morning. They were praising the roof off. And the pastor's sermon is going to inspire you to conquer all your fears."

Fears? Stephanie drew in a sharp breath as she pushed the swinging door open into the breakfast room. Wasn't it just like God to arrange for her to hear a sermon on the exact subject matter she was contemplating on her run? She walked across the room and set the basket of cinnamon buns on the Broderick's table.

A sermon on fear might be just what she needed. A hill climb in church could do for her soul what a hill climb on a run did for her body. After all, didn't she tell everyone that working out is what kept her sane? Time to apply that motto elsewhere.

Singing with the band got Stephanie's blood pumping again. Sarah wasn't kidding about the worship music; it was definitely uplifting. No sign of Henry though, and she wasn't about to ask JoJo if he attended her church. Probably for the better, just looking for him drew her attention away from the lead singer as she prayed between songs.

"Fear," said Pastor Neil as he took the microphone. "Fear can paralyze you at work, in relationships, in school, in competition. There is no end to the ways the enemy will use fear to distract you, derail you, or even degrade you."

She knew that all too well. Stephanie leaned forward and waited to hear what the pastor would offer for a solution.

"Let me be honest," he continued, "there are no easy answers. I'm not going to sugarcoat this message and tell you to 'fear not' because God is with you. Fear is a natural emotion. So often we're afraid of what we do know and afraid of what we don't know."

Stephanie sighed, and slouched back against the pew. She wanted an answer, preferably an easy answer. JoJo glanced over and offered her a reassuring smile.

"What we are going to talk about today is how we can battle our fears with the weapons God gave us. Turn in your Bibles to 2 Timothy 1:7. Here we find three keys to counter fear: "For God hath not given us the spirit of fear; but of power, and of love, and of a sound mind.""

Stephanie underlined the verse in her Bible, and then flipped her missalette over so she could write on the back. For the next twenty minutes Stephanie took copious notes as Pastor Neil gave insightful ideas. She wanted to clap when he was done, or at least high-five someone.

As folks filed out of the pews, JoJo walked past the refreshment table and headed for the exit.

"Hey," Stephanie called to her friend. "Slow down so I can grab a cookie or two."

Derek paused at the snack table with Stephanie. "She's worried about juggling guests and their afternoon schedules. We'd better grab and go," Derek said after selecting a brownie and one peanut butter cookie.

"Did she miss the part about a sound mind?" Stephanie joked while picking out two pumpkin spice cookies. She snatched a chocolate chip cookie for JoJo, and then the two of them hightailed it to the parking lot.

JoJo was on the phone, sitting in the passenger seat when they got into the car. Stephanie passed her the chocolate chip cookie when the call ended. "Something sweet to sweeten your day."

Breaking the cookie in half, JoJo then took one large bite. "Perfection. I bet Myrna made these. Now I'm going to sweeten your day."

Stephanie wondered if the phone call had been about Henry, or from Henry. *What?* Why did her brain go there? The call was not about Henry. Geez Louise, she needed to get a grip.

"Do tell. What great news do you have for me?" Stephanie asked.

"I've got two couples that have asked for rides into town this afternoon," JoJo said as Derek pulled out of the parking lot onto the main road. "The Nelsons inquired about the Norman Rockwell Museum at breakfast. Any chance you'd be interested in taking them? You could do your thing and arrange a time to meet up to bring them back,"

"No need to ask me twice." Stephanie loved the museum, and hadn't been yet during this visit.

"I thought you'd say yes."

Two hours later Stephanie was parking her car at the museum. She gave Irene and Josh Nelson her cell phone number. "There's so much to see. Why don't we plan to meet back here in three hours? If you need more time, just call me."

Stephanie meandered through the main gallery and the sports gallery, taking her time to appreciate each piece. Saving the best for last, she finally stood before the four "Freedom" paintings. She could easily spend an hour here.

The Thanksgiving feast in *Freedom from Want* always filled her with fond memories. She could taste the turkey at her grandmother's table, smell the gravy as she poured NeNe's liquid gold over everything on her plate, and anticipate her mom's pumpkin pie for dessert just by viewing the painting.

As she absorbed the full impact of the painting, it was clear the family had all they needed: love, food, shelter, clothing, warmth . . . and, definitely love. She had all of that, too. Like the people in the painting, she was, in all areas that mattered, free from want.

Turning to her left, she wished she'd thought to call her grandmother and invite her and Blake to meet her at the museum. *Freedom of Speech,* the first of the paintings published in the *Saturday Evening Post,* inspired Stephanie to stand up for what she believed in. Her grandmother had always taught her to speak out for those who didn't have a voice. NeNe dedicated her life to serving, and worked for decades in the mission field, always a voice for those less fortunate. Every time Stephanie looked at the depiction of the man standing at a town meeting to object to the topic of discussion, she could reimagine the artwork with NeNe as the person fighting for a cause.

Turning slightly, Stephanie let her gaze settle on *Freedom of Worship,* NeNe's favorite of the four "Freedoms." She liked the painting, but the one next to it called to her as if she could hear her father's voice saying prayers before bedtime. She stepped closer to *Freedom from Fear,* wanting to reach for the dad's hand and tell him not to go.

"It's my favorite."

Stephanie didn't have to turn around to know who was speaking. She'd grown accustomed to his voice, the deep timbre somehow soothing while at the same time triggering a bounce house of nerves in her stomach.

"Hello, Captain Lewis," she said without facing him. "Are you stalking me?"

"Hardly." He laughed. "I work here. I came over to make sure you didn't touch the artwork."

She spun around and all but had to smack her jaw shut.

"You're a security guard? I thought you were a police officer." Stephanie hoped she wasn't staring too hard at his blue uniform with the museum insignia on the left shirt pocket.

"A cop? Why did you think I was a police officer?" He asked, an amused twinkle in his eyes.

"Captain? As in police captain," Stephanie stated. "I had no idea security guards had officer positions." Goodness, did she sound stuck up? Or stupid? The man had caught her off guard.

"I was a captain. United States Marines Corp." He saluted her. "At your service ma'am."

Now it all made sense. The formality, the sometimes-rigid posture, the crease in his pants as if he'd ironed them this morning, and the "ma'am," he'd called her the first day they met. "So, you were one of the few, the proud?" She said repeating a motto she'd heard years ago.

"Yes, ma'am," he said, snapping his heels together and coming to attention. "Semper Fi."

"What?"

"Semper Fidelis."

"I know I should know, but what does that mean in Marine terms?" Stephanie asked.

"Always faithful."

He had spoken the words with such reverence Stephanie allowed herself to ponder their meaning. "Always faithful" was not what she had expected him to say. Yet, always faithful was exactly what she wanted. Longing and defensiveness battled within her, fear gaining slight ground.

"Are you?" Was there a sharp edge to her voice? Why did she ask him that?

"Yes, I believe I am." Though he was no longer standing at attention, in jest or for real, Captain Henry Lewis looked as serious as one could look answering a question.

A few hundred questions raced through her mind, each one focused on faithfulness and what that meant, how he meant it, with whom he meant it, when he meant it, was he talking about the Marines, God, country, or every area of his life? She kept the questions to herself. "It's a good quality to have."

"Thank you. I'll take that as the first compliment you've given me." He half bowed and then grinned as he straightened.

He was even more attractive when he grinned. His eyes twinkled ever so slightly, as if he was enjoying the moment on a private level, too. It would be so easy to flirt with him, to open her mind to the idea of dating him. But he lived here, and even if he was always faithful, it was impossible to truly date someone when an ocean and a couple of hundred miles separated you.

"So tell me," he interrupted her thoughts, "what draws you to my painting?"

Chapter Eight

"YOUR PAINTING?" STEPHANIE laughed. "Did you buy this Norman Rockwell original or are you trying to tell me that you own the museum or you're a descendant of Rockwell's?"

Captain Lewis's grin widened. Flecks of gold sparkled like explosions of laughter in his brown eyes. She surely could grow fond of this man.

"Perhaps the legal ownership is questionable, the sentiment is not," he answered.

She'd only known him for a week, and had barely spent any time with him, yet Stephanie could not deny the intense attraction she felt. His sense of humor alone was reason enough to tackle her fear of dating. Pastor Neil had said that she had a choice to step out in faith, trusting that God was in full control, or she could spend her life waiting for everything to get perfect.

Stephanie took a small physical step toward Henry. "We might have to share custody." He would have no idea the hugeness of the emotional step she just took.

"Do I get a date first before you break up with me and we're hashing out custody issues?" He joked, though his serious eyes told her he wanted the date as much as she did.

You can do this. Don't chicken out. Everything that comes into your life must first pass through God's permissive, loving hands.

"Yes." There, she did it. If there were a chair, she'd take the opportunity to sit before her Jell-O legs gave out.

Henry stared at her, opened his mouth, then closed it, then stared a moment longer. A smile creased his face. "May I take you to dinner tonight?"

A pack of runners rushed across a marathon start line in her stomach, or it felt like they did. Butterflies would be gentler, but whether runners or butterflies were messing with her insides, Stephanie wanted to take a chance with Captain Lewis. "Tonight would be great."

"I'm off at five. Can I pick you up at six thirty?" Henry asked.

Stephanie nodded, her brain flashing an immediate warning: she hadn't brought any fancy clothes. Her available wardrobe, or lack thereof, was barely acceptable for the speed-dating event. She hadn't wanted to impress anyone there. Dating Henry was different. She wanted to look good. Thank God JoJo loved clothes and was willing to share.

Stephanie exhaled an audible sigh of relief. From worry to gratitude in less than two minutes. First fear conquered.

"Or later if six thirty doesn't work?"

Oh no! Had Henry heard her sigh and thought she didn't want to go? "Six thirty works," Stephanie said.

Henry leaned slightly closer to her. "Annndddd, you're now going to tell me where you're staying?"

"Oh, that might be helpful," Stephanie giggled, actually giggled, and then gave him JoJo's address. Her cell phone beeped almost simultaneously. The Nelsons were ready to leave.

"Problem?" Henry asked.

"I've got to leave. I drove some other guests here from the inn and they're ready. I thought I'd have another hour or so, but I guess not." She was disappointed, but at least she'd have more time to get ready for her date.

"You can come back tomorrow," Henry said.

And see you, Stephanie thought but did not say. "That's a great idea. I think I'll do that. So you'll be seeing me tomorrow too, Captain Lewis."

"Three times in twenty-four hours. Better than winning the lottery."

Warmth rose in Stephanie's chest and inched up her neck. She could feel the blush spreading over her cheeks. Her phone beeped again. This time she was grateful. "I've got to run."

Henry nodded. "And I should get back to work. I'll see you in a few hours. Drive home safely."

Stephanie rushed down the hall hoping Henry hadn't seen her face turning multiple shades of red. She put her hand to her cheek and felt the heat. The Nelsons would probably assume she'd run to meet them and was flushed from exertion. That was fine with her. She wanted to hold her thoughts of Henry close.

*

"HELP!" STEPHANIE CALLED as she ran out back to the garden where she'd spotted JoJo when she'd pulled into the B & B's parking area.

JoJo looked up and came to her feet. She walked to the fence, a bunch of carrots in her left hand. "What's wrong? Did you lose the Nelsons?"

"No. They're inside," Stephanie answered, stopping next to the fence. She put both hands on the top rail. "Are you ready for this?"

"What?" JoJo placed a hand on one of Stephanie's.

"I have a date. Tonight. With Henry. He's picking me up. I have nothing to wear. You've got to help me," Stephanie gulped some air into her lungs. Somehow she'd spoken a string of words without taking a breath.

'Yes!" JoJo's left hand shot into the air, waving the carrots like a flag.

JoJo picked up her basket, shovel, and carried them along with her carrots to the back door. Stephanie opened the door, took the carrots from her friend and put them in the sink. "Let me get these dirty clothes off and wash my hands."

Stephanie yanked a towel off the rack, and held it out to JoJo.

JoJo dried her hands. "Okay, let's go find something stunning. I have the perfect dress in mind."

*

HENRY PARKED HIS TRUCK and absorbed the beauty and grandeur of Maple Ridge Bed and Breakfast. He had no doubt they garnered a hefty fee for a night's stay. If Stephanie was here for two weeks, she lived on a budget that was beyond his reach. He had no care for money, except that necessary to live and enjoy the simple pleasures in life. If war had taught him anything, it was that life mattered and a big bank account didn't stop a bullet from killing a man.

As he thought about his date, he couldn't remember a single time when he'd seen Stephanie that she was overdressed, walking around in designer labels, or dropping names as too many people did. And hadn't she said she was visiting family? Maybe her parents owned the inn, though he couldn't recall her mentioning her parents.

Ending the one-sided debate in his mind, Henry exited the truck and walked toward the front door. He rang the bell, and waited. Eagerly. Expectantly. He hadn't mentioned to Stephanie that this was his first real date in four years. Two tours in Afghanistan had left little time and, after watching his best friend take a bullet, no interest in dating. Friends had invited him to dinner often since his return last year and he would arrive to discover a single woman also had been invited. Despite his friends' attempts, he'd never connected with anyone.

Until now.

The door opened and Derek Willard stood before him. "You're Stephanie's date?"

Henry laughed. "And this is your 'little bed and breakfast?'"

The two men shook hands.

"Come on in," Derek said, stepping to the side. "Steph and Joanne are upstairs. I was instructed to tell 'Stephanie's date' that they'd be right down. You might as well have a seat. JoJo is never 'right down' when we're going out."

Henry followed Derek into a well-appointed living room, or maybe they would call it a library. Numerous shelves filled with books lined the longest wall. "How long have you owned this place?"

"We took over four years ago. It's been in JoJo's family for over thirty years."

Henry sat in an oversized chair. Derek sat opposite him.

"You going to the renovation meeting on Wednesday?" Henry asked. He and Derek served on the building and maintenance committee for their church. "I liked John's proposal last week."

"Me, too. We have the funds, and I think it's doable without too much inconvenience to the parishioners during the construction process."

"The side walkway can be—" Henry swallowed his words as he caught sight of Stephanie standing in the archway. All he could do was stare at her. She quite literally took his breath away.

Derek stood first. Henry rose without taking his eyes off of her. He was certain the smile on his face was that of a dopey high school freshman drooling over his first major crush. Dear God the woman was striking.

How did a plain black dress make her look like a goddess? He didn't know. Didn't care. She was smart, funny, loved art, loved running, and she was gorgeous. He was already grateful they'd met.

"Really, Steph, you should give a guy a break," Derek said.

Henry stepped forward, kicking himself for not complimenting her first. "You're stunning."

She smiled, a slight blush accenting her cheeks. "Thank you. I wasn't sure where we were going. I can change if I'm overdressed."

"No!" Henry and JoJo said at the same time.

Everyone laughed.

"Okay then," Stephanie said, "the black dress it is."

JoJo passed Henry a long coat. He held it out for Stephanie to put on. He looked forward to arriving at the restaurant and helping her out of the coat. He would be mute if he had to explain what about the dress undid him. It fell just above her knees, revealing shapely runner's legs. The scoop neckline was modest, yet the way the fabric folded or rippled or whatever women called the effect, was soft and sexy on Stephanie. The longer he stared, the more mystifying the dress became.

"Where are you going?" JoJo asked, interrupting his thoughts.

"La Tomat."

"Nice," JoJo replied.

"Her curfew is midnight. Don't be late," Derek joked.

"I shall do nothing to tarnish the lady's honor," Henry replied. And he meant it. Semper Fi. God, country, Marines, but always God first. He would treat Stephanie as the daughter of a king, because she was a daughter of **the** King.

Chapter Nine

"WHAT CHANGED YOUR mind?" Henry asked her as they drove down Route 7.

"About what?" Stephanie suspected he meant about going on a date, but she wasn't about to dive into that sea of turmoil without a shove.

He glanced in the rearview mirror, then gave her a brief smile before focusing his eyes on the road in front of them. "Tonight. Dating. Dating me. What changed your mind?"

How much should she tell him? Could tonight's date really lead to anything? Regardless of how attractive Henry was or how compelling his smile was or how much she already liked him, they lived hundreds of miles from each other. Stephanie drew in a deep breath and exhaled. If they were going to have any hope of a chance, honesty mattered.

"Running and church."

"Care to elaborate?" Henry asked, a gentle hint of amusement in his voice.

"Do you think when you run?"

He nodded. "All the time. Best way to process my thoughts."

"Exactly." Another reason to like the man. "When I was running this morning I was thinking about fear. My fears are a bit like long, hard hills. I can avoid them or I can face them and make the difficult climb. The run up is often painful and exhausting, but I always feel great when I crest the peak. Know what I mean?"

"I do," Henry said. He signaled left and changed lanes,

preparing to head into Great Barrington. "Hills are torture but necessary. You don't want to know the hill repeats we did in-country for conditioning. Plenty a man went down, losing his lunch. But when we were done, I always felt great, invincible."

Stephanie turned in her seat to face him as much as the seatbelt would allow. "That's what hit me this morning. I felt better after the hill than before."

"So a date with me compares to a dreaded hill workout?" Henry laughed as he spoke.

"Ha, I guess it does."

"Ouch."

"You asked for that."

Henry pulled into a parallel parking spot and turned off the truck's ignition. "I'll give you that one. So are we at the bottom of the torturous hill or moving up?"

His question gave her pause. As nervous as she'd been about dating, she didn't feel a single ounce of tension. Amazing. "I, ah, think we might be at the top or close to it."

"How's the view?" His eyes held hers as he waited for her answer.

Staring into his eyes, Stephanie enjoyed the view more than she'd thought she would. There was warmth, and humor, and kindness reflecting back at her. "It's good. Very good."

She heard an exhale. Had he been holding his breath? Or was that her own breathing, which was slightly elevated.

"Very good is a very good place to start. Let's see if dinner and more conversation will enhance your view." Henry exited the driver's door, walked around his truck, and opened her door.

Stephanie placed her hand into his outstretched palm. The view became great.

*

THE WAITRESS SEATED them at a table near the fireplace. After they placed their drink orders, Henry allowed himself a moment to appreciate the room, the evening, and the woman he was with. He was a long way from IEDs, sandstorms, and screams in the midst of explosions. Gratitude was an understatement that a year didn't diminish.

"I've heard about the running portion. How did church effect your decision to date?" he asked, watching her eyes widen as if confused or surprised that he'd remembered what she said during their drive.

"I went with JoJo to church this morning. It was as if the pastor had read my mind or been invisible and running beside me earlier. He preached on facing our fears."

"Second Timothy, by any chance?" he asked.

"Yes. How did you know?"

"I attended the eight o'clock service. Pastor Neil hit a home run."

"He did. I ran out of paper to take notes on."

The waitress returned, placed their drinks on the table, and asked if they were ready to order. She left and Henry returned to the conversation.

"I used to pay Suzy Jackson to take notes for me in high school. Any chance you'll share your notes?" Henry watched a faint blush tinge her cheeks. The woman was stunning.

Stephanie smiled. His heartbeat quickened.

"I left them at home, but they're yours."

"I bet you don't need your notes. What hit you most about the sermon?"

She leaned in and Henry did the same. "When the pastor started talking about God being omnipresent—in the past, present, and future—and how He was in every moment of my life and that nothing happening was a surprise to God or out of His control, that opened my eyes. Fear of the unknown is not unknown to God.

"My broken engagement hurt, but my fear of another relationship and potential break-up was hurting me more. Realizing that God is in every moment, that His loving hand is holding me through every high and low, that was like crossing the finish line with a new personal record."

"I'm sorry. I'm sorry you were hurt, sorry your ex didn't value you." Henry felt that familiar pull of anger twist in his gut, and in the next second he felt gratitude that God had saved her from an unfaithful spouse. "I don't understand why our Father allows some things to happen, but I'm learning to trust that there is a reason."

"I sense that you get it," Stephanie said, her comment more of a question than a statement.

"I do. I watched a bullet take down my best friend during a standard search-and-recovery mission. A sniper, and the next thing I knew, my best friend was dying in my arms. My will and God's will didn't line up perfectly, and my trust in Him waivered in the months after Keith's funeral.

Henry pushed the silverware and bread plate away, recalling that need to push everyone away. "I suddenly knew a fear I'd never experienced before: if I couldn't save Keith then who else would I not be able to protect. I never worried about getting shot. I had a healthy respect for war, for combat, for the daily dangers I faced. After Keith, I couldn't shake the 'what ifs.' When my tour was up, I came home and ended up taking a job here. I spent a few months talking with Pastor Neil, finally grasping that God was with me and Keith in every moment. The sermon today reminded me that I can trust any fear I have to God, because He's already there and already taking care of me in the future."

Henry reached for his glass and took a sip of water. The conversation was a little deep for a first date. He wanted to change the subject before Stephanie thought he was boring or depressed.

"I don't know what to say. I'm so sorry about your friend. I can't imagine losing JoJo. I'm glad you've found peace again."

"Me, too. And I know that God opened the doors for me to move here and work at the museum."

"*Freedom from Fear.* That's why you love the painting so much," Stephanie spoke the words with reverence. She understood.

"Yes." Henry stared out the window on the far side of the room. A calm night. No flashes of light. No soldiers with rifles.

No dead or wounded. He looked back at Stephanie. "I'm one of the fortunate ones. My faith, family, and friends pulled me through. I've got buddies who can't shake their post-traumatic stress.

"Freedom from fear is something I wish for everyone. Rockwell's image captures the innocence of childhood, but also the security of family and love. He painted my dream." Henry gave her an awkward smile. The conversation was definitely too heavy for a first date, yet every word felt natural and easy with Stephanie.

"Mine, too." Stephanie fiddled with her spoon, appearing self-conscious for the first time that evening. "My parents divorced when I was young. Whenever my grandmother would take me to the museum, I'd stare at that picture and wish my dad were home, tucking me into bed. I was thirteen or fourteen when I realized it was too late to have the childhood I wanted, the childhood JoJo had."

Henry reached across the table and gently squeezed her hand. Long, graceful fingers relaxed under his touch. "Pastor Neil once said to me, 'you'll have a better today and tomorrow when you give up all hope of having'—"

"A better past," Stephanie said with him, moving her hand from under his as she gestured agreement. "I love that quote. It's the reason I moved to the Vineyard."

Easing back in his chair, Henry spotted the waitress walking their way, carrying a tray bearing two entrees. Before they started eating, he wanted to hear Stephanie's story. "You are going to elaborate, right?"

She laughed, a sweet laugh that made him want to reach across the table and hold her hand. "It's not a great story, no soul-building crescendo or life-changing encounter."

Their server placed their meals before them. "I'll be the judge of that. Do you mind if I interrupt you first to say grace?"

Stephanie placed her napkin in her lap. "Please do."

Henry blessed the meal, then waited to cut into his pork tenderloin until Stephanie resumed her story.

"I majored in jewelry design in college with every intention of returning to the Berkshires. My mom had moved to Florida during my junior year of high school and I lived with my grandmother, NeNe. Secretly, or maybe subconsciously, I'd always hoped my dad would move back."

Henry swallowed a bite of pork and asked, "Where is your father?"

Stephanie focused on her dinner, pushing a couple of pieces of broccoli and cauliflower with her fork. Henry waited, compassion filling him as the beautiful woman before him struggled with what appeared to be painful memories.

"He's in Portland, Oregon not Maine. He remarried and started a new family. For too long my teenage brain held onto the dream of him walking through the front door, telling me he loved me more than his two new kids."

Stephanie speared a broccoli floret with her fork, but held it inches over her plate. "One afternoon during spring semester of my senior year in college, I heard a guy on the radio say that exact quote about our pasts. It was as if a road opened up in front of me. I wasn't even thinking about my dad, but I had been applying at shops in the Berkshires. Suddenly, I wanted a new path, a new opportunity. I searched the internet and found a position at a jewelry store on Martha's Vineyard. I applied, and the rest is history."

Smiling with satisfaction, Stephanie lifted her fork and began eating. He could hear the happiness in her voice whenever she talked about the Vineyard. He'd never been there, and hadn't had any plans to visit. Until now.

"Sounds as if you love it there."

She swallowed. "I do. I'm an Island girl at heart. I want to feel the sand between my toes, smell the marshy tides as I run in the morning, and walk with my feet in the water as I scour the shores for sea glass and wampum."

Happiness radiated on her face as Stephanie spoke about her home. She reached for her water glass and took a few sips.

"I might have to check it out," Henry said, already calculating when he had two or three days he could travel down there.

Stephanie coughed, coughed again, and lowered her glass of water to the table.

"Or, I could visit Nantucket," Henry joked, hoping she didn't agree to his suggestion.

Waving a hand, Stephanie started to laugh. "Not Nantucket. That's the *other* island. No self-respecting Vineyarder, by birth or washashore, would send you there."

"I could go to the Cape. I've heard it's nice, too."

Stephanie scowled, then waved him off again. "The Cape is nice, but nothing beats the Vineyard."

"I thought your gagging when I said I should check out the Vineyard was a sign that I should go elsewhere." Henry smiled at her, enjoying the many facial expressions she exhibited before answering him.

After a nervous giggle, Stephanie took another sip of water and held the glass, swirling the water. She put the glass on the table and met his gaze. "You surprised me, that's all. I promise if you make your way down to the Island, I'll show you around. It's my most favorite place on earth. I think you'll like it."

Henry grinned. That was exactly what he wanted to hear. "I'm going to take you up on that offer.

Chapter Ten

STEPHANIE TURNED OVER and switched her alarm to "off" before the buzzer buzzed. The sun was rising, and she wanted to run. She had so much to think about, to process, and the road would be the best place. Dressing quickly, she laced up her sneakers and headed down the hall.

One sniff of the cinnamon and maple scents drifting up the back staircase told Stephanie that JoJo was awake and in the kitchen. The house had been quiet last night when Henry brought her back. The questions JoJo didn't ask last night were sure to come now.

"I hear you. Stop tiptoeing down the stairs," JoJo called.

Stepping into the kitchen, Stephanie walked to the fruit bowl. "I was trying to be considerate of your guests, who might be sleeping."

JoJo rolled her eyes. "I've been up for an hour waiting to hear every detail. Start talking."

Stephanie peeled a banana and took a bite. Chewing slowly, she enjoyed every second of impatience on JoJo's face. "Dinner was great. Conversation was great."

"And?" JoJo circled her hand to encourage more details. "Derek all but dragged me upstairs so you and Henry would have some privacy when he brought you back. So?"

"I'm going to see him today at the museum." Her answer sounded as flat to her ears as it felt in her heart. She took another bite of the banana before JoJo could ask for more information.

"That's it?" JoJo was undeterred by the banana eating and her consumption of a little fuel before a run.

Stephanie took two more bites of the banana. "That's it," she said, and then tossed the peel into the compost bucket. "I'll be back in an hour."

"But—"

"Run time." Stephanie opened the door and welcomed the first blast of chilly morning air. She walked down the driveway, pulling her headband into place over her ears and then putting on her gloves.

She turned right at the end of the drive and kicked into a run. There was a park about two miles away. The park had a workout trail and a small hill near a pond. She could do a few hill repeats and the workout trail.

Henry hadn't even tried to kiss her goodnight. A quick hug had been the extent of his departing affections.

She exhaled, then drew in a quick breath. Her pace had increased. Always did when she was in conflict. She slowed enough to even her breathing.

She didn't really care that Henry hadn't so much as tried to kiss her. Not really. Lack of physical contact kept their relationship on a friendship level; friends who would probably never see each other again after she left on Wednesday.

She sucked in another shallow breath. *Slow down, or stop thinking and sprint.*

Easing back on her pace, again, Stephanie replayed every word she could remember from the drive back from the restaurant to when Henry walked her to the front door.

She couldn't remember one uncomfortable moment. She'd asked him in, and he'd begged off saying he had to get up early to stop by the church and check on some construction being done before going to work.

She got that. Then he'd said, "I had a great time. I look forward to seeing you tomorrow at the museum."

She'd thanked him for a wonderful dinner, and then stood there waiting.

Neither one of them had moved for the first, and only, awkward moment between them. Henry finally broke the silence with, "Thanks again," and a quick hug.

Stephanie ran through the entrance to the park and headed for the workout trail. Challenge #1—Three sets of ten pushups with a minute rest between sets. No problem. She did all thirty pushups without a break, and ran to the second challenge.

After squats, pull-ups, balance bars, sit ups, and box jumps, Stephanie stood at the bottom of the hill. A few sprints would work out the last of her frustrations. She surged up the hill, pumping her arms and pushing off the balls of her feet. Cresting the top, she wished she'd worn a watch. How many seconds had it taken her? Sixteen? Twenty?

Too bad Henry wasn't here. Racing him would push her harder.

"Argh!" Annoyed at her brain for thinking about him, she jogged down the hill, turned around, bolted up once again. She counted one, one thousand, two, one thousand. Sixteen, one thousand. She could do better, but running faster wasn't all she wanted.

"Lord, clear my head. Please!"

By the sixth sprint, Stephanie had shaved two seconds off her first count. Her tenth and final sprint she gave it her all. Thirteen, one thousand. Excellent.

She jogged down the hill and headed back to the workout trail. She finished the last five challenges and started the run home.

Her body was loose, her mind was at ease, and her heart was pumping. Running and praying was the best therapy, giving her new perspective every time.

Henry had been the perfect gentleman. Their date had been awesome. She wanted to see him later, and she was going to check with JoJo to see if she could invite him to their dinner tonight. Tuesday she was driving up to NeNe's to have dinner with her family.

Stephanie removed her gloves, shoved them into her pockets, and never missed a stride in her run. If Henry accepted her invitation to dinner tonight, because she knew JoJo would agree, then maybe she would invite him to NeNe's.

Punching a fist into the space before her, Stephanie imagined knocking her fears to the ground. "Take that!" she exclaimed, renewed and relieved. She picked up her pace for the final mile home.

*

HENRY CHECKED THE entrance for the third time in fifteen minutes. Stephanie had said she would be at the museum around eleven. It was 11:05. He studied the monitors. The crowds were still light.

Another ten minutes passed. Henry walked to Freedom Hall. Perhaps he'd missed her arrival. A quick scan of the room revealed what he already knew, Stephanie wasn't in the museum.

He observed the guests strolling about, and headed back to the front desk. He could text her, but that might seem pushy. The woman, unbeknownst to her, was trying every ounce of his patience. No, not patience. Fortitude.

He'd barely resisted kissing her last night. He wanted to honor her, and to him that meant nothing physical until they were both committed to a monogamous relationship.

Henry glanced at the wall clock. He wanted to spend every possible minute with Stephanie before she left. He liked her, and he sensed that she was a woman he'd enjoy spending a lot of time with. Maybe . . .

Thinking about a future with Stephanie after ten days seemed slightly crazy, but he'd seen crazier. His college buddy, Marty, had met Karen on New Year's Eve and married her two weeks later. Six years of marriage and two children, and Marty was one of the happiest guys he knew.

His phoned beeped. A text message. He keyed in his password hoping to see Stephanie's name highlighted. His brother. Answering briefly, Henry put his phone back in the holster belt clip.

The second he saw Stephanie approaching the front entrance, Henry's heart quickened. Yup, he was in deep. And he had no interest in swimming to the shallow end. He walked around the front desk and met her at the door.

"Good morning, beautiful."

She smiled at him. His heart raced a little faster.

"I could get used to that greeting," she said.

"Me, too." Henry offered her his arm. "Shall we take a walk to Freedom?"

Stephanie placed her hand on his forearm. Warmth radiated under her fingers.

"Are you on duty or something? Are you sure it's okay?" she asked.

Henry nodded. "Part of my duty is walking the halls. You'll be helping me out with my job."

"In that case," Stephanie squeezed his arm, "let's get you to work."

Henry led her to their favorite room. He walked her to stand before *Freedom from Fear*. She stood there for a few minutes in total silence. Henry settled into the peaceful space beside her.

"The picture looks different today," Stephanie said.

"I was just thinking the same thing," Henry replied. "I'm seeing you as a child, alive in the picture."

"Yes," she said, "and I'm seeing you home from war, tucking in your children, keeping them safe."

Henry swallowed the words in his throat, felt his Adam's apple lodge between the air he needed to breathe and the thoughts formed but held in check. He wanted to take Stephanie's hand and tell her that her vision is exactly what he saw, what he wanted, what he dreamed of every time he looked at the painting.

"That's a lovely thought." A lame response considering all he wanted to say. How had this woman touched his heart in such a short time?

Stephanie turned to face him. "I'm sure you have to get back to work, but before you go I wanted to invite you to dinner tonight at seven if you're free. JoJo and Derek are cooking one of their famous feasts."

"I'd love to," Henry said. "Can I bring something?"

"Hmmm, I don't know. JoJo didn't mention anything. I'll ask her and text you."

"Great. I'll see you later." Henry smiled, wider than he was already smiling. He walked back toward the lobby conscious of one thing: he would be visiting Martha's Vineyard as soon as possible.

Chapter Eleven

"JOJO AND DEREK are a hoot," Henry said as he turned onto Route 20 North.

Stephanie laughed. "Tell me about it. And they didn't let up after you left."

Dinner the night before had been filled with joking, recollections of Steph and JoJo's college life, Derek's arrival on the scene to turn the dynamic duo into a triple threat, and stories of JoJo and Derek's wedding and then their taking over the bed and breakfast. The evening had been fun, and Henry had fit into their circle as if he'd been a close friend for years.

Now they were driving up to NeNe's for dinner. Stephanie's heart ached. Today was Tuesday. Tomorrow was Wednesday. She had to go back to the Vineyard. She wanted to go home. She didn't want to leave Henry.

"Where'd you go?" Henry asked, his voice drawing her back to his side while widening the ache.

"The Island." Could she tell him how torn she was? How she wanted more time? Time to get to know him better? Time to discover all he was? Time to learn his hobbies and habits, likes and dislikes.

"Eager to get back?" He kept his gaze fixed on the road, but Stephanie saw the twitch in his jaw. Maybe he was feeling some of what she was feeling.

She could test the waters. "Yes and no. I miss the ocean. I have to get back to work." She shoved fear to the recesses of her mind and summoned the words on her heart. "But I've loved my time here."

The twitch in Henry's jaw turned upward to a smile. "I, for one, am glad you came to visit." He began tapping his fingers on the steering wheel in time to the music playing on the radio.

So was she. And she knew that NeNe was going to love Henry. And, her family would be planning their wedding while Henry drove her back to JoJo's. "Should I warn you about my family? Or do you like surprises?"

Henry glanced at her for just a moment. "Should I be nervous, or are you nervous that I won't meet their expectations?"

Stephanie laughed. "I'm bringing a date, I've already exceeded their expectations."

Henry's fingers stopped tapping. "That's an awfully low expectation."

"Oh, no, not at all." Stephanie held up both hands to halt Henry's negative thoughts. "My grandmother knows I wouldn't bring just anybody to her home."

"So," Henry shifted, sitting slighter taller, and definitely grinning, "I'm not just anybody, I'm somebody? Somebody special?"

Heat surged through Stephanie's veins. Could she play it cool with her face feeling as if she were blistering from a sunburn? "Three dinners in a row must be special."

His fingers began tapping again. "Agreed. Now tell me who will be there with surveillance equipment."

"They're not that bad," Stephanie jumped to her family's defense.

"I'm sure I've been in worse situations."

"Hey, if you don't want—"

He chuckled, then started laughing.

"Very funny," Stephanie said, relaxation moving from her shoulders to her toes. "Just for that, I'm going to sic my cousin Libby on you. She's never lost a game of Twenty Questions yet."

"I love a good challenge." Henry winked at her.

Libby was going to love Henry, as would NeNe. Maybe . . .

*

"EVER BEEN TO the Vineyard?" Libby asked, cutting into her apple pie.

Henry watched Stephanie glare at her bold cousin. He almost laughed aloud. Libby had been grilling him, however casually, since they'd arrived two hours earlier. "I haven't."

"What a pity. You really should go in October. The weather is still good and the beaches—"

"Libs," Stephanie interrupted her cousin, "when did you start working for the Island tourism bureau?"

Libby waved a dismissive hand. "I'm merely highlighting how fabulous the Vineyard is and that Henry should check it out."

"I plan to."

All eyes instantly focused on him. Jack and Blake were nodding from their chairs across from him; Ellie, sitting between Libby and Stephanie on the sofa, was smiling. Libby put her empty dessert plate on the side table, crossed her arms and flashed Stephanie a smug I-told-you-so look. Stephanie sat perfectly still, eyes wide, mouth open. Henry wanted to kiss the shock off her face.

"It is a beautiful place. I'm sure you'll enjoy your visit," Ellie said, breaking the silence. She then rose, and began collecting their dishes.

Stephanie jumped up to help. "No, dear. I know you and Henry need to get going. You can say your goodbyes, preferably without a fork or knife in your hand when you hug Libby."

Henry stifled a chuckle, then stood. He heard Libby whisper to Stephanie as they hugged goodbye that she'd be calling her daily for updates. He liked Libby. He liked them all.

He opened the car door for Stephanie, aware that she carried a bit of tension in her shoulders. He got in, buckled his seatbelt, and turned to face his beautiful date. "Thank you for a wonderful evening."

"I could strangle Libby," Stephanie said.

"I rather like her."

"Oh." There was that look again, startled, vulnerable,

kissable.

Henry faced the wheel and started the car. He didn't want to drive. He wanted to finish the conversation. "About that fourth date?"

"What fourth date?"

"The one where I'm going to take you out to a restaurant on the Vineyard. Are you free for dinner the Friday after next?"

Chapter Twelve

STEPHANIE HELD THE soldering iron in her right hand and reached for the box of blue sea glass to the left of her magnifying lamp. She needed one last small piece of blue to finalize a special-order necklace.

"How you doing?" Zoey asked as she opened the door to the studio.

Stephanie jumped off her seat, and knocked the box of glass over. Dozens of pieces bounced over the wooden floor.

"Oh gosh! I'm so sorry." Zoey rushed across the room and began picking up the spilled pieces. "Steph, you've got to breathe. You've been a wreck all day."

Lowering the iron to the workbench, Stephanie knelt to the floor and helped Zoey retrieve the fallen sea glass. Her hands were shaking. "I can't relax, can't focus. Henry is on his way here. As in this very minute, he is driving to Woods Hole to catch the ferry."

Zoey stared at her, shaking her head slightly. "Is this a problem? I thought we agreed that you were happy about this? Very happy."

A problem? There was a potential list of problems that Stephanie was doing her best not to think about. Henry could hate the Island. He could arrive and wish he'd stayed home. He could get in a car accident driving. He could fall in love with her and want her to move to the Berkshires. She could fall, correction, admit she was already falling in love with Henry and want him to move to the Vineyard. The whole situation could be impossible before it really began.

"Steph?" Zoey's soft voice drew her back from the fear abyss. "Is there a problem?"

"For starters, what if he gets here and decides he's not interested in me after all?"

Zoey erupted with laughter. "Doubtful. Granted, I've never met Henry, but he talks with you on the phone every day. All day. I can't see a guy spending that much time with someone he's not serious about."

"Not all day," Stephanie replied, a blush spreading across her cheeks. "We both work, you know."

Zoey laughed again. "That's right. I forgot. You text message when you're working."

Stephanie didn't deny it. She couldn't. She and Henry chatted throughout the day at every available minute they had. It was crazy. And wonderful. Maybe Zoey was right. No maybe about it. Zoey was on point. Fear was rearing its ugly head again.

"You're right. Why do I let myself get sucked down these rabbit holes of fear?"

Picking up the last piece, Zoey stood. "Steph, it's hard to trust again after you've been hurt and betrayed a couple of times. Something tells me, though, that Henry is a good guy, a really good guy. I'm just hoping you will enjoy the process of falling, as in falling into Henry's arms."

Now Stephanie laughed. "You mean when I'm so nervous I trip walking up to meet him and he catches me before I faceplant into the dock?"

"Not exactly what I envisioned, but if Henry's holding you, I suspect the end-result will be more what I had in mind." Zoey placed the box on the bench. "Why don't you head home and go for a run? Unwind before he docks."

"I ran this morning," Stephanie said.

"Go again," Zoey said as she headed back into the main shop.

Her office manager had a good idea. A run would take the edge off. Stephanie unplugged the iron, turned off the lamp, and tidied up her work area. She kept a few outfits at the shop, which allowed her to change for a quick trip to the beach or a run. In less than five minutes, she said goodbye to Zoey and was on her way to Bend in the Road Beach for a six-mile run along the water to Oak Bluffs and back.

Three hours later, Stephanie was showered and dressed in a pair of faded jeans, a forest green turtleneck, and a cream cashmere sweater. She brushed her hair and left it long and loose.

She toyed with a pair of earrings, then opted for a new necklace she'd finished earlier in the week. She liked it, but she always wore a new piece a few times to see if people commented. Positive feedback, and the necklace would be in the display case for next weekend. No comments, and she'd take another look at, and maybe replace the green sea glass with white opaque glass. She loved the green glass with purple wampum.

Her phone beeped. A text from Henry. "On the boat, sailing toward you."

Her stomach flipped, flipped again, and then did a triple somersault. She sighed. The nervousness felt good, as if every part of her were alive for the first time. That "alive" feeling must be what Zoey meant by enjoying the fall.

She glanced at the clock: 6:30 p.m. The ferry would be docking by seven. If she left now, she could get there and watch the ferry sailing into Vineyard Haven Harbor. Maybe Henry would be on the deck, looking for her as she would be looking for him. She grabbed her keys off the kitchen counter and strode toward the door. She didn't want to miss a second of Henry's visit, even if those seconds were from afar.

Chapter Thirteen

Henry stood at the bow as the ferry pulled into the dock. He spotted Stephanie as she was walking toward the gangway. She hadn't noticed him yet. His heart beat, stopped, beat, stopped, and then beat with a resounding thump that should have come from shock paddles.

He loved her. He had no doubts. They had spent hours every day talking on the phone over the last two weeks since she'd left the Berkshires. Now she was within sight, soon to be within arms length. The question remained, how could he keep her within arms length?

If he'd learned anything from serving in the war, it was that every second mattered. Like the spilt seconds on a stopwatch as a runner crosses the finish line, every portion of every minute mattered. Life could be over in an instant. Henry didn't want to waste time. He hoped Stephanie would feel the same about him, about life.

Henry bowed his head and prayed silently, "Father, I want your will for my life. If Stephanie is the woman you have for me, please open the doors for us to be together, open our hearts to hear you leading, open our eyes to your blessings. If you have other plans for us, please make it clear to both of us this weekend that we should part friends. In Jesus's name I pray. Amen."

The crackling of the loudspeaker drew Henry back to the moment. He opened his eyes and saw Stephanie waving at him. He waved back. The purser's voice told him to exit through door

4. Henry motioned to Stephanie that he'd be down in a minute and headed for the stairs.

The line of passengers moved excruciatingly slow. Henry shifted his duffle bag to his chest and eased around an elderly couple until he finally stood face to face with Stephanie.

"Hello, beautiful." He passed her the single red rose he'd hidden behind the duffle.

She smiled her gorgeous smile, accepted the flower, and stepped a couple of inches closer to him. "Hi. Welcome to Martha's Vineyard."

Henry leaned over and placed a gentle kiss on her cheek. "Thanks. I love it here already."

She laughed. "You haven't even seen anything yet."

"I've seen you. Everything else is superfluous."

"Oh." A flattering blush spread across her cheeks. She was lovely. And he wanted to be alone with her, away from all the people and cars.

"I'm starving. Are you ready for dinner?" he asked.

"Yes, though I did nosh on some almonds after my run," she said, and began leading him to where she'd parked her car.

Henry couldn't believe it. "You've only had a few almonds since your run this morning?"

Stephanie's blush returned. "Um, not exactly. I went for a run after work."

"Uh oh. Two runs in one day. Bad day at the shop?"

She stopped and turned to face him. "Honestly, I was nervous. The run helped."

"Nervous about me?" Henry wasn't thrilled with that. He never wanted her to be nervous about him, his actions, or his expectations. He hoped she didn't think he was planning on sleeping with her.

"A little." Stephanie began walking again. "Maybe a lot."

Henry reached for her hand. She wrapped her fingers around his without slowing her stride. "I don't want you to worry about where I'm sleeping or that I'd—"

"No, Henry. I didn't think that at all. I was just nervous, you know. I only saw you for a few days, and, yeah, we've talked on the phone, but what if you arrived and—" Her pace had quickened. As a fellow runner, Henry knew his pace sped up when he was frustrated or angry or struggling with a situation.

"Hey," he tugged gently on her hand to bring them to a stop again. "There is no 'and' in this scenario. I've been looking forward to this visit since the moment I left Joanne and Derek's home after saying goodbye to you."

Her eyes welled with tears. "Me, too," she all but whispered.

Henry squeezed her hand in reassurance. "Great. Now let's go eat and you can tell me all about our plans for the weekend."

They walked hand in hand to the car as Stephanie chatted about the restaurant.

*

STEPHANIE DROVE ALONG Beach Road from Oak Bluffs toward Edgartown to drop Henry at his hotel. Dinner had been wonderful. They talked and laughed, and many times Stephanie found herself marveling that she'd only known Henry for a month. Though it was nearing ten o'clock, she didn't want the evening to end.

"The moon's almost full. Want to go for a walk on the beach?" she asked as State Beach came up on their left.

"Love to," Henry replied.

Stephanie parked at Bend in the Road in front of the life guard stand, the same spot she'd run to hours earlier. She left the keys in the center console and exited the car.

"You going to lock the car?" Henry asked.

"No need."

"Really?" Henry sounded perplexed. "I realize there's only one other car in the lot, but plenty of people are driving by."

"It's safe. The Island is a really safe place. People leave their front doors unlocked, too."

Henry reached for her hand as they moved toward the wooden walkway. "You're kidding, right?"

"Nope." Stephanie wanted to sigh as his hand closed over hers. "It's a different way of life here."

They crested the small dune and stood before the calm ocean. "Very different," Henry said.

She could hear the appreciation in his voice. The night sky was filled with stars while the moon lit up the dark waters. It was breathtaking to Stephanie, and she saw the same view all the time. Never tired of it. She turned left at the ocean's edge and headed toward the jetty.

Henry reached down and picked up a small piece of wampum. "Is this where you get the shells and glass for your jewelry?"

"I may occasionally find a piece here that's large enough and usable, but the best pieces are on a few of my favorite beaches I'll be taking you to tomorrow and Sunday."

Stephanie smiled as Henry put the wampum into his pocket. "I know I said this in the restaurant, but your necklace is gorgeous. You're really talented. I can't wait to see your shop and studio tomorrow."

His words once again filled her with warmth and pride. Stephanie was eager to show him her workshop and the store. Zoey was almost as eager as she was, though Zoey wanted to meet Henry, not show him her favorite tools and pieces. "We'll go tomorrow right after breakfast."

"Is breakfast before or after our run?" Henry asked.

Stephanie laughed. "Definitely after. I'm already dreading the image of me sucking wind as you push me to the limit. I don't think I could run with you on a full stomach."

"Hey, I'm a gentleman. I'll let the lady set the pace. All I care about is that I'm running by your side."

This time Stephanie did sigh.

Chapter Fourteen

"THE CLIFFS ARE beautiful," Henry said. "I can see why you love it here. There's no pattern to the colors. The clay goes from white to red to black to gray to brown with no visible indication why the color is changing."

Stephanie wanted to shout for joy. They were on their fourth stop on her grand tour of the Island, and she'd told him the Gay Head Cliffs in Aquinnah was one of her most favorite places on the Vineyard. That he appreciated the majesty of the place thrilled her. She leaned down and picked up another piece of wampum.

"And there's jewelry in the making," she said, examining the thickness of the dark purple wampum before putting it into her pocket. "I marvel all the time that as I walk the beach, I find treasures to craft into rings and bracelets and necklaces."

"I'm looking forward to the day when I can watch you turn a piece of wampum into a necklace or earrings," Henry said, then reached for her hand and they began the mile-plus walk back to her car.

Henry's comment about the future was the third or fourth he'd made since their run this morning. They hadn't talked about when they would see each other again or where. Could she move back to the Berkshires and be happy? She'd miss the Island, but she had a sense that life with Henry would be more beautiful than the scenery of the Island.

Her hand in his felt perfect—cherished, protected, and loved. He hadn't spoken the words, nor had she, but the feeling was alive within her and alive in his touch.

She gathered two additional pieces of wampum before they reached the bottom of the wooden walkway at the Moshup Beach trailhead. They found their sandals in the pile of shoes beachcombers left as they stepped off the wooden boardwalk and onto the sands of Aquinnah's famous beach.

It was three o'clock. The fall sun was dipping lower on the horizon. Stephanie's stomach was rumbling. "Can I entice you into trying our local chocolate?"

"What fool would turn down chocolate? That would be as blasphemous as refusing a cup of coffee in the morning," Henry said. "Lead on."

They climbed the hill to the parking lot, side by side, holding hands, Stephanie describing the mouthwatering selection at Chilmark Chocolates. "We can buy a box. A bag is never enough, as far as I'm concerned."

"Captain Lewis." A young man, who didn't look a day over twenty, called out to Henry just before they reached her car. Though not in uniform, the guy seemed to straighten as if he wanted to salute Henry.

"Private Evans." Henry released her hand, walked over, and shook hands with the soldier.

"What are you doing on Island, Captain? You're not living here now, are you?"

"I'm visiting my girlfriend, Private," Henry said, draping an arm around Stephanie. "Stephanie, this is T.C. Evans. T.C., Stephanie."

"Pleased to meet you, ma'am."

Shaking his hand, Stephanie tried to slow her pounding heart. It was beating faster and harder than during a twelve-sprint speed workout. Had Henry just called her his girlfriend? And was he pulling her tighter against him? She wanted to wrap both her arms around him. She wanted to kiss him. She'd been waiting for that moment all day.

"What about you?" Henry asked, oblivious to her impending heart attack.

"I live here, Captain. Working for the big marina in Edgartown, fishing as much as I can." Private Evans picked up the fishing rod leaning against the back of his truck.

"Sounds like a good life, Private."

"It is, Captain. It surely is." He hoisted a pair of waders from the truck bed. "You interested in doing some fishing while you're here?"

"Not this trip, but maybe next time," Henry said. "Take care, Private. Hope you land a big one."

Next time? He said next time. Stephanie no longer needed chocolate. Life was getting sweeter by the moment.

Henry squeezed her shoulder and began walking them toward her car.

"Hey, Captain," T.C. called out. "If you're thinking about moving to the Island, I know a billionaire in Edgartown who's looking for a fulltime security guy, preferably someone with a police or military background. Sweet house on his estate comes with the job."

Henry stopped walking and turned around. "I might be interested. You want to give him my number?"

Stephanie stood there dumbstruck, watching Henry give T.C. his cell phone number and typing T.C.'s into his phone.

"I'll give Mr. Lauder a call tomorrow," T.C. said. "Bet you'll hear from him Monday or Tuesday."

"I might owe you one, Private."

Henry grinned when he turned in her direction. He grinned, but said nothing. Stephanie wanted to scream. Patience was not her strong point. "Ready?" she asked, pretending the exchange she'd just witnessed was nothing more than two friends planning to meet for a beer.

Henry opened her car door and waited until she was seated. Stephanie counted to ten as he walked around the car. If he didn't start talking as soon as the door was closed she might explode.

"God is so good," he said before the door closed.

"You don't say?" Stephanie stared at him. Was that the best

he could do?

Then he reached for her hand, and the expression on his face went from lighthearted to serious. His eyes narrowed and focused on hers. "I knew the moment I saw you from the deck of the ferry that I wanted to be with you, close to you, near you."

He tucked a stray strand of hair behind her ear, then stroked her cheek. "I love you, Stephanie. I know it's fast. Maybe you think I'm crazy, but I love you. I want to move here so I can to date you and convince you to take a chance on me, to take a chance on loving me."

She wanted to tell him that she loved him, too, but Henry's lips silenced any words she might have spoken. She leaned into him and the kiss deepened. When he eased back, her lips wanted to beg for another.

"Is that a yes?" he asked.

She nodded.

"I can't hear you, beautiful."

"I need another kiss." She couldn't believe the words had come out of her mouth. Fortunately, he obliged her without hesitation.

She met him halfway, and laced her fingers in his hair. This time, she was the one who broke away first. "Henry," she said through ragged breath.

He grinned. "Too much for the car, I know."

Stephanie shook her head. "The car? No." She placed a finger on the lips that had just kissed hers. "Henry, I love you, too."

She only caught a second of his signature grin before his lips once again claimed hers.

Epilogue

by

Jean C. Gordon
Terri Weldon
Lisa Belcastro

The Following Spring

"LET ME SEE it," Ellie demanded when Libby joined her in the side room off the vestibule at their church.

"NeNe, today is *your* day." Libby twisted the ring she was still getting used to wearing. "Wait. How did you know?"

Her grandmother smoothed the skirt of her ivory lace dress before sitting down in a folding wooden chair she must have moved from the rack against the wall. "Blake told me Jack had asked for his grandmother's ring. You and Jack were the first to leave the rehearsal dinner last night. It didn't take a lot of thought to figure it out."

"I couldn't wait to tell him that I got the job as the director of the Developmental Education Office at Berkshire Community College. And I would have showed you my ring at breakfast if you hadn't been up and out before I woke up."

NeNe waved off her excuses. "I had an early hair appointment, and then there was Alice Conway's usual PT appointment. She's given up her car. I always drive her."

Libby laughed. "It's your wedding day. I'm sure she could have gotten someone else."

"She lives right here near the church. I just brought my things with me and got ready at her house. Then, I drove us over. Someone is going to have to drive my car back to the duplex. Blake and I will drop Alice off on our way home after the breakfast."

That was so NeNe.

"Getting your car back won't be a problem. Nor will finding

Alice another ride. Like I said, this is your day."

"The ring." NeNe prompted, reaching for Libby's hand. "Let me see it, and then if you brought a comb, can you fix my hair? I think the wind mussed it."

The older woman's bob didn't look any different than it ever did.

Libby presented her left hand with the classic 1950s square-cut diamond flanked not by the usual smaller diamonds on either side, but by blue sapphires. She loved the ring. It couldn't be more perfect if she'd picked it out herself. And not just because of its beauty, but because it was a family heirloom, a part of Jack.

"It's lovely." NeNe held Libby's hand in hers. "You're lovely."

"And you're beautiful, or will be as soon as I get this out-of-place hair combed in." She ran her comb through the back of NeNe's hair.

"My hat," NeNe said.

Libby helped her grandmother with the wide-brimmed hat, which was covered in the same lace as her dress.

Libby's father poked his head in the doorway. "Are you ladies ready? I have Stephanie and Natalie and your sister all lined up out here."

Although Blake had only Jack as his best man, NeNe had asked all four of her granddaughters to be attendants.

"In a second," NeNe said. She looked Libby straight in the eyes. "Are you happy?"

"Unbelievably so."

"Good, I want that for all you girls." NeNe rose. "Let's get this show on the road. I have a honeymoon appointment this afternoon…"

Libby started. NeNe and Blake were having a simple morning wedding with a reception in the church hall afterwards. But NeNe couldn't possibly be thinking of working this afternoon.

"…with a very attractive gentleman who's waiting for me in the sanctuary."

Libby laughed.

"Got you, didn't I?"

"As always. After you." Libby motioned to the door and followed her grandmother into the vestibule.

Her father signaled the organist who began the Lohengrin wedding march. Libby followed Stacey, Stephanie, and Natalie into the sanctuary, pausing at the backmost pew. Her gaze went to the altar and the two handsome men standing there. She'd never seen Jack in a tuxedo before and couldn't take her eyes off him. He smiled, his secret smile, the one she'd come to know was only for her, and her heart overflowed with love.

September and their wedding couldn't come fast enough.

*

NATALIE LEANED BACK against Grady's chest. His strong arms encircled her waist. She never tired of being close to her husband or the rest of her new family. When she had married Grady last fall, the entire Hunter clan welcomed her with open arms. God had blessed her more than she'd dreamed possible.

Right now she looked at the dance floor and thanked God for her own growing family. NeNe and Blake danced cheek to cheek, Libby and Jack moved as one, and Stephanie and Henry looked as natural together as runners on a relay team.

When the song ended, NeNe fanned her face and she and Blake moved toward the refreshment table. An older gentleman stopped Blake and began talking.

Natalie extracted herself from Grady's embrace and gave him a quick kiss. "I'm going to have a quick chat with NeNe. I haven't had a minute alone with her all day."

She stopped by the tastefully decorated refreshment table and snagged two cups of punch. Then she walked outside and spotted her grandmother. When she reached her side, she handed her one of the cups.

"I thought you might like something to drink after all that dancing." She winked at her grandmother. "You and Blake can really cut a rug."

Ellie laughed out loud, then took a long pull of the peach-colored punch. "Thank you, Natalie, I needed that." She wrapped an arm around her granddaughter's shoulder.

"Oh, NeNe, you look beautiful in your wedding dress. It's a good thing Blake has a strong heart. No doubt you took his breath away when you started down the aisle."

"What did you just call me?"

A blush worked its way up Natalie's neck into her face. "NeNe. I believe you told me that's what all your grandchildren call you."

"Natalie Hunter, if you make me cry and mess up my makeup on my wedding day, well, all I can say is it's a good thing this is waterproof mascara." NeNe took the glass from Natalie's hand and placed both glasses on a table. Then she wrapped her arms around Natalie and hugged her tight.

"I love you, NeNe. The day God saw fit to let me come live with you was a new beginning for me and the first bright spot in my life." Her lips trembled, but she continued. "You were the first person in my life to love me. I don't know why you messed with a sixteen-year-old full of bad attitude.

"Oh, it may have been the first bright spot, but it was far from the last. From the minute I laid eyes on you, I loved you. My heart ached for what you had been through. And as far as your attitude—I learned fast it was all bark and no bite." NeNe stepped back. "Besides, look how far you've come. You just graduated with your juris doctorate."

"And I'll probably never practice a single day of law, but it will look impressive in my author biography," Natalie said.

"My granddaughter is an author." Ellie beamed. "You're a natural at writing legal thrillers. And you're a married woman now. I still can't believe you and Grady beat Blake and me, not to mention Jack and Libby, and Henry and Stephanie to the altar."

"Neither of us wanted a fancy wedding. Our simple church ceremony at the old church in Sheffield suited us both," Natalie said.

"Your wedding was gorgeous, unassuming and elegant...like you."

"Well, my honeymoon was anything but modest. In fact, it

was out of this world! The woman who planned it must be a romantic at heart." She squeezed NeNe's hand.

Ellie waved off the compliment. "I want each of my granddaughters to have a honeymoon they'll remember their entire life."

"I know Grady and I will never forget ours." Natalie looped her arm through NeNe's. "I think we'd better go back inside. No doubt Blake is looking for you."

When they reached the doorway and Blake saw Ellie, a smile lit his face. He met them halfway across the room. Natalie walked up to the older gentleman and gave him a hug.

"You're a blessed man, Blake."

"I know. Ellie is a blessing I'll cherish the rest my life." He took his bride's hand and led her back out on the dance floor.

"Just as I plan to cherish you," Grady whispered in her ear as they watched the older couple glide across the room.

*

HENRY DROVE THEM to the Norman Rockwell Museum. "I know it's a bit corny, but I want today's run in Stockbridge to start at the museum."

The man was a romantic, and Stephanie had come to adore him and his simple ways of making life special and memorable. Since he'd moved to the Vineyard last November after accepting the security job for Mr. Lauder, they'd only been back to the Berkshires three times.

When they left the Vineyard on Thursday, Henry had asked her if they could plan their run at the museum on the morning of NeNe and Blake's wedding. Of course she'd agreed. Yesterday had been a bit of a blur with Libby's long to-do list for the family dinner after the rehearsal, helping Natalie pick flowers from JoJo's garden, and stealing moments alone with Henry.

The wedding day had finally arrived. Everyone was excited for NeNe, Stephanie included. She'd come to love Blake, and knew her grandmother would be happy and cherished. She was also grateful she and Henry were staying at JoJo's and had this special time alone together.

"Gorgeous morning," Henry said as he parked the car.

"It is, and I'm ready to go." Stephanie jumped out of the car and squatted down to double knot her laces.

She stood. Henry lowered one knee to the grass. He reached for her left hand and looked up into her eyes. Stephanie's breath caught in her throat.

"People might say that weddings can inspire someone, but my heart has been set on this day for quite some time." Henry reached into his pocket and pulled out a clenched hand.

Stephanie exhaled and then gasped.

"I spoke with your mom last night at the rehearsal dinner. I have her blessing. Now, all I need is you. Stephanie Gould, I love you more than I ever thought possible. I promise to run beside you every day, every step of our lives. Will you marry me?"

Stephanie had never been more certain of an answer: "Yes!"

Henry slid an emerald and diamond ring onto her finger. The ring, shaped like a flower, was stunning. And perfect. She knew he loved her green eyes, and now he'd gone and picked out a ring to match. The man was amazing.

Stephanie grabbed onto his hand and pulled him up, wrapping her arms around his neck as he straightened. "I love you, Henry. I can't wait to run this marathon of life with you."

He placed a hand behind her head and pressed his lips to hers. The kiss was long and soft and sweet, and filled with promises kept.

When they finally broke for air, they each laughed. "Out of breath and we haven't run a mile. What are you doing to me, Mr. Lewis?"

"It's my secret training plan to build up your wind and endurance," Henry joked.

Stephanie's stomach fluttered in anticipation of all that was yet to be. "I'm going to enjoy that training program. A lot."

"So am I." Henry said, holding her hand and leading her into a comfortable jog. "Our first run as an engaged couple. You ready?"

Stephanie smiled. "Oh, I'm ready. I trust you to set a pace I can follow."

"I'll do my best to do just that every day," he said.

"I believe you." Stephanie knew that Henry knew she meant so much more than a running pace.

"Scared?"

She shook her head. "Nope."

"Sure?"

"I'm sure. I know the truth: perfect love casts out fear. I trust God's love for me, and I trust you." She squeezed his hand. "You're the man in *Freedom from Fear*. You're that husband and dad. Now you've just got to keep up." With those words, Stephanie released his hand and shot forward, laughing, smiling, and thanking God.

Henry caught up to her and the two of them ran side by side for the next six miles, talking about their future every step.

That afternoon, Stephanie stood watching her grandmother and Blake glide across the floor. As Sam Cooke sang "You Send Me," Stephanie rocked side to side in Henry's arms, thanking God for NeNe's happiness and stealing glimpses at the beautiful ring on her own left hand and the strong, loving arms wrapped around her.

When the song ended, the disc jockey called for all the single ladies to make their way to the dance floor. NeNe motioned for her to hurry up. Libby was already garnering what she thought would be the best spot to catch the bouquet. Henry gave her a gentle shove.

"I normally hate this tradition," Stephanie said, kissing Henry on the cheek, "but it might be fun this time."

Stephanie walked toward Libby, a competitive urge creating an itch in her fingers. She grinned at her cousin, letting her know the game was on. Libby grinned back, and they both laughed. No matter who caught the flowers, they were both getting married.

NeNe held a gorgeous bouquet of pink, white, and purple lilacs. She smiled at Libby and Stephanie, and turned around. The DJ began playing The Dixie Cups' *Chapel of Love*. Stephanie held her laughter in check and focused on NeNe. Seconds later, the lilacs sailed through the air. Stephanie jumped and grabbed them. She raised her prize in the air and searched the cheering crowd for Henry.

Her future husband rushed across the floor and scooped her up, twirling her in a circle. Stephanie laughed until tears rolled down her cheeks. Henry eased her to the floor and kissed her soundly on the lips. "Our fate is sealed. If you're the next woman in the room to be married, I'll have to get you to the altar before September."

Everyone around them clapped and whooped their delight.

"I know the perfect beach for a sunset picnic wedding," Stephanie said. "How about July?"

Libby squealed a "Yes!" Natalie hugged her. NeNe had tears in her eyes.

"This is the happiest day of my life," NeNe said. "I married the man I love, Natalie is married, and now you and Libby will be married by fall. God has answered my prayers more abundantly than I ever dreamed," NeNe said.

Blake kissed her hand and nodded. "That He has, my Dear, that He has."

46282953R00137

Made in the USA
Middletown, DE
26 May 2019